Love

MW01603088

Gabby Cosette has ⸺ ⸺ ⸺od Ridge, Oregon, and being permanently put in the friend zone has left her dating life stagnant. With no prospects in sight, she clings to her friends and resolves to not let loneliness drag her under. So when the town Battleaxes set their matchmaking sights on her, she figures it can't hurt. Yet the guy they think is perfect for her just happens to be not only her boss at the veterinarian clinic, but her best friend. Sure, Flynn O'Grady is attractive and the nicest guy around, but going there with him would topple both of their carefully constructed worlds and there would be no going back. Even if he is starting to make her girly parts zing.

Having been born deaf, Flynn has already felt like an outsider most of his life. Aside from his brothers, Gabby is about the only person who's gone out of her way to treat him as more than a handicap. Which is exactly why he's banked his secret attraction for his sweet, beautiful vet tech. Except his meddling family is trying to play Cupid and ruin the best thing to ever happen to him. Without Gabby, his work as a veterinarian, never mind his personal life, wouldn't flow. Determined to ignore the antics, he's secure in the knowledge she's not interested in him romantically. But then a kiss changes everything . . . and he's wondering if taking the ultimate shot at love might be worth the risk.

Books by Kelly Moran

Redwood Ridge
Puppy Love
Tracking You

Published by Kensington Publishing Corporation

Tracking You

Redwood Ridge

Kelly Moran

LYRICAL PRESS
Kensington Publishing Corp.
www.kensingtonbooks.com

Lyrical Press books are published by
Kensington Publishing Corp. 119 West 40th Street New York, NY 10018

Copyright © 2017 by Kelly Moran

All rights reserved. No part of this book may be reproduced in any form or by any means without the prior written consent of the Publisher, excepting brief quotes used in reviews.

All Kensington titles, imprints, and distributed lines are available at special quantity discounts for bulk purchases for sales promotion, premiums, fund-raising, and educational or institutional use.

To the extent that the image or images on the cover of this book depict a person or persons, such person or persons are merely models, and are not intended to portray any character or characters featured in the book.

Special book excerpts or customized printings can also be created to fit specific needs. For details, write or phone the office of the Kensington Special Sales Manager:
Kensington Publishing Corp.
119 West 40th Street
New York, NY 10018
Attn. Special Sales Department. Phone: 1-800-221-2647.

Kensington and the K logo Reg. U.S. Pat. & TM Off.
LYRICAL PRESS Reg. U.S. Pat. & TM Off.
Lyrical Press and the L logo are trademarks of Kensington Publishing Corp.

First Electronic Edition: May 2017
eISBN-13: 978-1-5161-0274-7
eISBN-10: 1-5161-0274-6

First Print Edition: May 2017
ISBN-13: 978-1-5161-0277-8
ISBN-10: 1-5161-0277-0

Printed in the United States of America

This goes out to all the gals who've been overlooked or put in the friend box. Love is possible.

Acknowledgements

A big thank you to the team at Brentwood Animal Hospital, especially Lynn, who made sure I got the veterinarian thing down right. Any errors are my own.

Chapter 1

Gabby Cosette smoothed her hand down the simple baby blue sundress she meticulously picked out for this evening and tried not to look too eager. Or throw up. That wouldn't do either.

From a back booth, she glanced around the only Italian restaurant in Redwood Ridge, comforted by the fact it was still early yet for the dinner rush. The place was a good choice. Right? Not as casual as Shooters—the bar she and her friends frequented—but not as formal as one of the seafood restaurants that dotted their Oregon coastal town. A step above grabbing coffee or a beer, yet it didn't scream desperation.

Was a booth in the back too obvious? Had she overdone it with her makeup? Maybe she should've put her hair up instead of down?

No, no. She went for light and natural on purpose. The patrons of Redwood Ridge had known her all her life. It wasn't far out of the realm of ordinary for her to wear a dress and light cosmetics. She was being a basket case.

It's just… Well, she hadn't had a date in a year. A year!

To calm her nerves, she drew in a deep breath and focused on the red-checkered tablecloth. A votive candle flickered on the windowsill to her right, the flame reflecting off the tinted glass. The parking lot stretched beyond, where her date's car was not in one of the available spots.

It was silly to get this worked up over a first date, especially with Tom. She'd gone to elementary and high school with him. His parents still lived down the street from hers. Strange how he'd never shown any interest in her romantically, yet out of the blue, he'd asked her out this week.

Then again, most everyone in town viewed her as the sweet Cosette girl, everyone's friend. Thus the no date in a year. It was hard to get a guy to think about kissing her, never mind imagining her naked, when she had platonic all but tattooed on her forehead.

The waitress strolled over in her apron, holding a notepad in her hand. "Are you waiting on someone, sweetie pie?"

"Yes." She smiled and grabbed her cell on the table. Tom was five minutes late. "He should be here any minute."

"Ooh. Is it a date?" Mavis planted a hand on her plump waist and grinned, the wrinkles around her eyes growing to crevices. Gabby wasn't sure how old Mavis was, no one really knew, but she never seemed to age past the state from when Gabby was a child.

Gabby opened her mouth to answer, but Tom strode toward her, weaving around tables and plopping in the seat across the booth.

"Couldn't find ya at the bar. I wasn't expecting a table."

It was still early, and Le Italy didn't get that crowded even on a Friday night. How hard could it possibly have been to locate her? "Give us a sec," she told Mavis and waited for her to step away.

Tom had blond hair too short for her preference and a thin mouth. His unremarkable brown eyes darted around the restaurant and back to her. He made no attempt to apologize for being late, and it appeared as if he'd just come from work. His jeans and T-shirt were paint-splattered. The hazard of working for his dad's commercial painting and roofing company.

"Thanks for meeting me." He took off his ball cap and scratched his head.

Why did that sound un-date-like? "Um…sure thing. How's work going?" Her gaze dipped to his hands, no better off than his clothes. Maybe she should've picked Shooters after all.

Something felt very, very off as her belly twisted. Not with nerves this time. Confused, Gabby's mind scrolled through their conversation from earlier in the week when he'd brought his dog into the vet clinic where she worked. As he was checking out, he'd anxiously spun around to face her and asked if she could meet him.

"Good. Work's good." He put his hat back on and glanced outside. "Getting to be warmer out, so the jobs are picking up."

Perhaps he was just nervous, too. Her tension drained a degree.

Mavis returned and asked for a drink order.

Tom lifted his hand to wave her off. "Nothing for me, thanks. I can't stay long. Got a poker game with the guys tonight. I need to shower before they show up."

The forced smile Gabby had plastered on her face began to wilt like her mom's petunias in August. What did he mean he couldn't stay long? And why would he ask her out and schedule a card game on the same night? Plus, he could shower for his friends, but not her?

Mavis divided her gaze between them, a mix of bewilderment and irritation lifting her brows. She tapped her pen to her pad as the silence hung. "Can I get *you* something?" She focused on Gabby, her tone indicating she should order something.

"I'll have a sweet tea. Thank you." When the waitress walked away, Gabby looked at Tom. He'd thrown his arm over the back of the booth and had stretched his legs out. The aroma of Eau de Paint Thinner wafted across the table. "So...?"

"Right, right." Tom leaned forward and crossed his arms. "I appreciate you letting me do this in person."

She stilled. "Do what?" Because she was definitely getting the this-is-not-a-date vibe now.

A warring shift in contradiction took over her body. Everything inside grew rapidly chilly while her skin heated in what she hoped wasn't a blush. Her pale complexion always gave away her emotions and she hated that more than she'd hated freshman algebra. Math was evil.

He let out a tense laugh, which sounded more like a guffaw, and drew several heads from other diners. "Not exactly a conversation you want to have over the phone or somethin', ya know?"

No. She didn't know. "Maybe if you just tell me?"

He played with the parmesan shaker, not meeting her gaze. "Well, the whole town's buzzing about Rachel and Jeff's split."

She frowned, not connecting the dots on his crazy pattern. Her older sister had only dated Jeff for a few weeks which, per Rachel standards, might as well have been marriage. Rachel liked to keep her options—and legs—open.

Guilt immediately consumed her for the crass thought, but it didn't make it any less true. She and Rachel couldn't be any more different. Rachel was aloof and sexy. Gabby was the girl next door. Men desired Rachel. The only thing they desired from Gabby was a shoulder to cry on after her sister shot them down.

She twirled a strand of hair around her finger to keep from fidgeting. "I don't understand what Rachel and Jeff have to do with..." Unable to finish the sentence—because she had no idea anymore what "this" was—she waved her hand between them.

"Well," he said in an aw-shucks kind of way that made her want to grind her teeth, "now that Rachel's available, I thought maybe you could put in a good word for me?" He blinked up at her hopefully.

She stared at him for several stunned beats.

The reality of the situation slowly crept into her head and shoved around her skull. Her stomach dropped somewhere near her ankles. When he'd asked her out at the clinic earlier this week, she supposed he hadn't actually asked her "out." The phrasing he'd used had been something more like, *Can you meet up with me on Friday?*

And stupid, stupid her had taken that to mean he wanted a date.

As if. Like anyone would ever be interested in her when her sister had gotten all the good genes and didn't have the reputation of being everyone's pal. Good ole Gabby.

"This wasn't a date," she muttered to herself, more to ground herself to the situation than for confirmation.

"Huh?"

Closing her eyes, she shook her head to let Tom know her utterance wasn't important. To him, it wasn't. Because she wasn't the one he wanted, and there was no sense in amplifying her mortification. It wasn't his fault she'd brainlessly gotten excited.

God, she was an idiot.

Her heart sank a little as hope withered a painful death. She shouldn't be surprised, really. It wasn't like this was the first time someone had tried to use her as a go-between. If not with her sister, then her friends. Still, she'd been looking forward to tonight, had thought it was a blessed break in her dry spell.

A lump formed in her throat as tears threatened. She looked around the room until she could get the pathetic emotions under control. Many of the tables had filled since she'd arrived. Man, if she started crying now…

"So what do you say?" Tom set the shaker aside. "Could you help a friend out?"

Friend. She nearly choked on the word. Instead, she cleared her throat and forced a smile. Who was she to stand in the way of potential true love? "Of course. I'll talk to her tomorrow."

His nervous grin widened into something more genuine, drawing attention to the slight crookedness of his two front teeth. "You're the best, Gabby."

Yep. That was her. She resisted patting her own back in a sarcastic response.

Did she really want a relationship with him anyway? Probably not. He wasn't classically handsome, but he had his charms. His looks didn't matter to her anyway as long as he had a good heart or sense of humor. It was more the idea of having someone that appealed.

Which was not going to happen. Not tonight.

Tom rose from his seat and tipped his ball cap as if it were a Stetson. "Thanks so much. I gotta go."

Of course. Alone again. Maybe she should become a poet. It had worked for Hemingway.

She nodded. Her gaze followed him to the front door, and then over to the bar where she was thinking of doing a little Cuervo therapy.

Flynn was leaning against the bar, his direct sights on her. Still wearing his dark blue scrubs, his posture telegraphed his typical laid-back demeanor. Now there was an attractive man. Tall enough for the top of her head to reach his chin and ropy muscle on an athletic build. Wide shoulders, narrow waist.

All three of the O'Grady brothers were sexy in their own unique way. But, they'd grown up together and there had never been any chemistry between her and them. Cade, the youngest brother, was engaged to their office manager as of a couple months ago, and Drake, the eldest brother, was a widower. Gabby couldn't envision him dating again, at least not anytime soon. Flynn wasn't seeing anyone.

Not that it mattered. She worked for Flynn and his brothers at their vet clinic, so that was an automatic hand-slap.

From across the room, Flynn's eyes narrowed as he tilted his head in question toward the door. *Where'd your date go?*

Flynn was deaf, and through the years, she'd grown to read him easily. They always had a strong connection, being able to understand one another without words. Part of that was being good friends and part was due to working closely together for many years.

She shrugged in answer, keeping her disappointed expression open for him. Sucked to be her.

His brows lowered and he straightened from the bar, poised to head over until the bartender tapped his shoulder. Flynn signed for his takeout and carried it over to her booth, setting the bag down on the table before sitting.

His hazel eyes, framed by criminally long lashes, swept her face. *"What happened?"* he signed with his hands. *"I thought you had a date?"*

Per their routine, she signed and spoke simultaneously. "Me, too. Turns out he wanted my help getting in with my sister." At his scowl, she shrugged, embarrassed enough without the urge to discuss it. "My own fault. I read too much into the initial conversation."

He stared at her with disbelief and shook his head. His handsome, angular face was dialed to irritated and his full lips were twisted. He ran a hand through dark strawberry blond hair just this side of wavy. Flynn had a tendency to forget routine trims.

Mavis made her way back to the booth. Her gaze zeroed in on Flynn. "Decided to eat in?"

Habit had him turning to Gabby. He could read lips, but sometimes people spoke too quickly or didn't face him fully so he couldn't see what they were saying. Gabby signed Mavis's question.

He grinned, back to his usual glower-free self, and nodded.

Well, it wasn't a date, but Flynn was better company, anyway. Gabby looked at the waitress. "He'll have a beer, whatever's on tap, and can I get the largest piece of tiramisu you can find?"

"You got it, sweetie pie."

Gabby watched her walk away before letting out a sigh, chest deflating. When she looked at Flynn, his expression indicated he was patiently waiting for her attention again.

He leaned forward as if to punctuate a point. *"He's an asshole."*

She laughed. "Aren't they all?"

"Not all." He pulled a styrofoam container of lasagna from the to-go bag, opened it, and grabbed her fork from her place setting. He waited for her to take it from him before signing, *"Dig in."*

He picked up his fork and took a bite, then did a double take when she just poked at his lasagna. *"Hey. You all right?"*

"I'll be okay. Just not today. Today, I mope." He was one of the few people she'd admit that to, and since his gaze had softened and worry wrinkled his brow, she forced herself to take a bite. "Thanks, Flynn."

He nodded, watching her intently. *"Movie night. My house. I'll even let you pick."*

Why the hell wasn't he dating someone? Seriously.

Sad truth was, women tended to overlook Flynn because of his disability, just like they overlooked her for being in the friend zone. People sucked. "Maybe we should make one of those pacts. You know, the one where if neither of us is married by the time we're thirty we marry each other."

One eyebrow quirked in his custom you-done-gone-crazy. *"I'm thirty and you turn thirty in a couple weeks. That ship has sailed."*

Yeah. "Fine. Throw logic into my delusions."

His shoulders bounced in a silent laugh.

She smiled. "Okay, hot date. What if I pick a sappy movie?"

He shrugged. *"I'll hide my man card. Tell no one."*

Covering her face, she laughed until her chest ached. When she sobered, her mood was irrevocably lighter. Praise God for good friends. "Just for that, I'll share my tiramisu."

"Deal." He ate a few more forkfuls before his smile slipped a fraction, the hint of seriousness reflecting in his eyes. *"For the record, I would've taken the pact."*

She dropped her chin in her hand before moving to sign. "We would've had such cute babies, too."

"Word. Now eat or I'll make you watch Die Hard *again."*

She scooped a bite of cheesy carb goodness. Calories didn't count on crappy days. "Which one?"

He whipped her a "duh" look. *"All of them."*

Death by Bruce Willis. Could be worse things.

Chapter 2

Flynn barely resisted an eye roll. Parked on the couch in his living room with Gabby's bare feet in his lap and the cheesiest rom-com playing on his TV, he counted down the last five minutes of ridiculousness. The only saving grace from the movie had been Meg Ryan's fake orgasm. Funny shit.

He didn't even need to glance at Gabby reclined beside him to know her eyes would be red-rimmed with "happy" tears. Women and their romance. At least it got her mind off her non-date tonight. He'd love to pummel Tom's face for putting that dejected look on Gabby's.

She tapped his chest with her foot to get his attention. "Am I unattractive?"

His hand stilled in the process of massaging her arches. No matter how he answered this question, he was screwed. To lie and tell her she was not beautiful would put her deeper in some kind of female depression. To speak honestly would hint at something he'd long buried, even from himself.

Truth was, he always kinda had a little crush on her. Nothing serious or monumental. No pining involved. Just…there. At the edge of consciousness. An awareness of her.

It had started the first day of kindergarten and had gone into hiatus in high school when he'd forced himself to ignore it. What made him first descend had been a five-year-old blond sprite with compassion in her eyes who'd marched home after school to insist her parents take her to the rec center to learn sign language because there was a deaf kid in her class. That was Gabby, forever thinking of others. He'd dug his heels in to quash his crush for the same reason. She'd do anything for him and had slowly stopped noticing other males. Such blips would ruin what they had as friends.

Pulling her feet from his lap, she sat up, her expression telling him she was forming her own conclusions during his lack of response. Hell.

He went for humor. *"You're hideous. I can barely look at you without gagging."*

Her pretty pink mouth twisted. Her baby blues narrowed in unamusement. "I'm serious."

"Me, too. I might need to run to the toilet to retch."

She sighed. He couldn't hear it, of course, but he could feel it like a warm caress on his cheek. What in the hell was wrong with Tom, anyway? Gabby was ten times the woman her sister was. He had perfection right in front of him tonight and he'd walked.

Flynn tugged on the ponytail she'd put in when they'd arrived at his cabin. She'd changed out of her dress and into an old pair of his sweats that she'd had to roll three times at the waist before they stopped falling.

"You're adorable." Safe answer, but she was. Adorable.

"That's the problem." She waved her hands as if trying to conjure a cyclone. "Cute little Gabby. She's so adorable."

He didn't see the negative in that comment, so he kept mum.

"No one wants to get it on with cute. I'm never going to get laid again, am I?"

He wasn't touching that one with an eight-inch…pole. He lifted his hands to sign a placating answer, like she'd find the right guy one day or something, but she wasn't done venting.

"I mean, I want a man to look at me how Cade looks at Avery." Her face relaxed into a whimsical kind of serenity as if picturing Flynn's brother and fiancée in her la-la land. "Like she's his everything." Her gaze drifted back to him, sad and gutting. "I've never been anyone's everything."

First thought? Romance movies were bad for her psyche.

He had to force his hands not to respond with she was *his* everything. A gut-punch reaction, but true nonetheless. She was his best friend, his link to sanity, his vet assistant who kept the business end of his life in order. None of which were romantic, and he knew exactly what she meant, though. Things hadn't been very active in his bedroom either, never mind proclamations of love.

"I'm sorry on behalf of my species."

She smiled, but it didn't reach her eyes. "You're not exactly a bad catch. I'm sorry about my species, too."

Yeah. Thing about Gabby? She understood, even when he never once voiced a complaint. He swore she could read his mind most days. He shrugged like he couldn't give a good goddamn.

"Why don't you have women climbing all over you?"

Her question was rhetorical and not necessarily directed at him. And she knew the answer. He might be as attractive as his two brothers, but no woman wanted a long-term thing with someone who couldn't listen. *"People tend to pay attention to the guy who shouts and ignore the one who whispers."*

Her shoulders rose and fell with an exhalation. The understanding in her eyes had him backtracking for a topic change. He glanced at the TV, noting the movie had ended. It was nearly midnight, but neither of them were working tomorrow. He wondered if he should start another chick flick or if she was feeling better and would head out.

Fletch, his golden retriever, unwound himself from the floor by the fireplace and made his way over to drop his head in Gabby's lap.

Her round cheeks lifted in a grin that split her face. She rubbed the dog's ears, her mouth moving to speak to him, but Flynn couldn't make out the words. Wisps of her caramel hair broke free from her ponytail and brushed her neck.

She wasn't sultry or hot by any stretch of the word, but she had some kind of illumination from within. A warmth most took for granted and overlooked. She was so damn beautiful inside that it mattered not what she looked like outside. But unattractive? Gabby? Not one iota.

He may be deaf, but the men in this town were blind.

"Your dog has agreed to marry me."

As usual, she pulled a laugh from him. *"You bribed him with bacon. Admit it."*

"He agreed based on my merits."

There was no arguing with that. She had merit in spades. *"We've had this discussion. You marry my dog, I'm part of the package."* What a ridiculous conversation, but he sensed she needed a little nonsense tonight.

Her gaze swept over his body as if considering…him. After a moment, she looked away, him being no wiser on her conclusion. "Who are you bringing as a date to Cade's wedding?"

His brother and Avery were set to tie the knot late next month. Because it was Avery's second marriage and she didn't like a ton of attention, they'd wanted a small ceremony out at Mom's cabin just down the road. Drake's and Cade's places were on Flynn's wooded private drive, too. But the Battleaxes—as Cade referred to their mother and two aunts—caught wind of the wedding plans and had turned an intimate gathering into a circus. The venue was now set for the botanical gardens with all of Redwood Ridge in attendance.

He hadn't given much thought to a date. If he and Gabby weren't seeing anyone, they were typically each other's fall-back crutch for such events. Come to think of it, he'd spent more time as her plus one than anyone else. *"If some other Neanderthal hasn't plucked you by then, you want to be my date?"*

"We're paired in the wedding party together, anyway. Why not?"

Which brought up another minor anxiety. Okay, a big one.

"What's wrong?" She stopped petting Fletch, much to the dog's discontent, and focused those blue eyes on him. They tripped him up every time. A cross between cornflower and sapphire, he could never resist spilling his guts when she looked at him like that.

He sighed. *"The wedding party is expected to do a first dance, right?"*

Her brows furrowed. "Yeah." She studied him closely. "We've danced hundreds of times together. Prom, town events."

Emasculated, he stared at her until she caught up. Didn't take her long. She nodded gradually. "But never a slow song with everyone watching us."

Yep. It was one thing to observe the crowd and mimic what they were doing, and another to be expected to perform some complicated steps to a tune he couldn't hear.

Gabby had her phone out and was texting in the next blink. Once her message was sent, she watched the screen for a reply.

"Who are you talking to?"

"Brent. He'll know what song Avery picked for our dance."

Brent being Cade's vet tech at their clinic who'd helped Avery with a lot of the wedding plans. But what difference did it make what song they'd chosen?

Gabby's thumbs flew over the keypad in response, then she swiped the screen to pull up YouTube. She scooted closer to him, bringing her light scent of honey with her. "We're dancing to Ed Shereen's 'Thinking Out Loud.' This video has the lyrics typed."

Because if he understood the lyrics, he would feel the mood of the music. He stared at her and, for the umpteenth time in his life, wondered what in the hell he'd do without her. To avoid doing something stupid, like kiss her in gratitude, he focused on her phone.

As he read the lines of the song, he couldn't help but think how it kinda nailed his feelings toward Gabby. From a friendship standpoint, of course. There was no crossing the line in the sand with her. Everything that made his life run smoothly, everything that made a lick of sense, was because they were a solid unit just like this. He was certain his world would implode if anything jeopardized what they had.

When the video ended, she set her phone aside and stood. The sweats he'd loaned her hung from her hourglass hips and threatened to fall. His old tee hid all her willowy curves. She held out her hand expectantly.

"What?"

"Practice, that's what." She grabbed his wrist and pulled him to his feet, or rather, he let her. He had a good foot and ninety pounds on her. Glancing around the space, she pursed her lips in thought as if trying to calculate the best spot to "practice."

After Flynn and his brothers had graduated from veterinarian school, they each had built a house on unused family land deep in the woods at the edge of town. Flynn's was modest compared to his brothers'. A ranch with only three bedrooms and a kitchen half the size of Cade's. Drake had gone grand scale because he and his wife Heather had wanted a litter of kids. Until she'd died from cancer a few years ago. Even though their tastes were different and the layouts unique, all three cabins had naturalistic and masculine elements. Huge stone fireplaces, bare wood floors, rafter beams cut from birch, floor-to-ceiling windows, and clean edges to the designs.

Gabby grabbed the phone and guided him around the couch to the open area between the living room and kitchen where the rug wouldn't trip them up, he assumed. The hardwood planks beneath his feet were cool, despite the temperatures outside finally warming with spring.

She fiddled with the phone and took his hand. "Do you feel the vibrations?"

Barely. It was easier to feel bass from a speaker. He shook his head.

She did something in the settings and looked at him. "Now?"

It was stronger, yeah. The thready pulse pressed a rhythm against his hand. He nodded.

She put the phone in the breast pocket of his tee where the bass thumped against his chest. Maneuvering his right arm around her waist, she took his left hand in hers. The position thrust them closer than he'd anticipated as her soft, sweet honey scent wrapped around him. The warmth from her body drifted near, inviting.

He stilled as his neck heated. He didn't think it was possible to get embarrassed with Gabby, but being this close to her was awkward and...

Hell. He focused on breathing instead.

"I put the song on repeat, so we have time." She smiled reassuringly and his heart flipped over in his goddamn chest. When he made no motion to start, she tilted her head. "We really don't have to do much more than sway back and forth. If you want to learn a basic box step, use your left foot to go that direction and follow my lead."

He was having a hard time reading her lips with the blood roaring through his veins and his vision hazy. Any second now, he'd break out in a cold sweat.

Christ, it was just Gabby.

She gingerly set them in motion, a slight shift to his left. He caught up and went with it. But instead of moving backward according to her pattern, he went forward at the same time she did and they collided. He stepped on her foot. Hard.

He pinched his eyes closed. This was stupid. No one would be paying attention to them at the wedding with Avery in the room all decked out. It didn't matter if he couldn't dance or not.

Gabby's laugh rumbled his chest. She squeezed his fingers and he dutifully opened his eyes. "Relax."

It wasn't as if he wasn't trying. *Sorry,* he mouthed.

She shook her head as if to say, *poor, poor man,* and set her free hand on the back of his neck. The heat from her fingers slid down his spine to a part that best not awaken. Before he could process he was in danger of thinking with his lower head, she carefully placed her tiny feet on top of his, thrusting her breasts snug against him and aligning their bodies. Like how a little girl might dance with her dad, except…he was definitely not her father.

The room vacuumed of air.

It had been way too long since he'd had sex.

Tilting her head back to look up at him, she grinned in good fun, unaware of where his devious thoughts had plummeted. "Now you can't step on my feet. Where you move, I go."

He'd never noticed the tiny, round scar above her eyebrow before. Most likely from the bout of chicken pox they'd had in second grade. All these years, though, and he'd just detected it. Shades lighter than her milky skin, the spot was barely noticeable.

They were close enough to share air. Her warm breath skimmed his jaw. He'd bet his right nut her skin would taste as good as it smelled. Summer and honey and sweet…

Shit. Double shit.

He was not getting turned-on. The situation had nothing to do with the woman and everything to do with biology. She was molded to him like second skin. It was a natural response to contact. Nothing more.

By sheer will—and thinking about his great aunt in a bikini—he roped in the reaction before Gabby became aware. He set them in motion with no rhyme or reason other than to move.

Weaving them around the room, she stayed rooted to him by keeping her feet on his. He kept his arms around her back lest she lose balance. He spun and tracked the open space until they were both dizzy and he no longer felt like a cad for impure thoughts.

When he stopped, struggling for air, she threw her head back and laughed. Her ponytail dislodged, causing a riot with her hair. He pushed the strands away from her face and resisted rubbing his thumb over her jaw. Right now, with her cheeks flushed and her eyes lit, she wasn't so adorable after all. Other adjectives came to mind, but he shoved them deep in the recesses of his mind. He hoped to hell his expression was as blank as he was trying to force it to be.

Her smile slipped a degree and something close to awareness filled her eyes. The fingers on the back of his neck dug in deep. She froze on impact and, after two heartbeats too long, she eased out of his arms. She took great care adjusting the too large shirt she'd borrowed, looking everywhere but at him.

With a rapid flash, as if he might burn her with contact, she took her phone out of his pocket. "Shooters tomorrow with the gang?"

They'd made those plans earlier today, thus no need to remind him. He nodded, not liking the strange rift. *"I'll be there."*

"I'm going to..." She jerked her thumb at the door. "Thanks for cheering me up."

He almost signed *thanks for the dance lesson*, but thought better of it.

Chapter 3

Shooters was roaring with the typical Saturday night crowd. Rock music blared from the overhead speakers. Several patrons danced on the makeshift platform in back. The clack of cue balls from the pool tables could barely be heard over the noise. Desperation hung as heavy in the air as cheap perfume.

From a table in the corner, Gabby picked at the label on her beer bottle as Avery complained about the Battleaxes interfering in her wedding.

"And now Marie says the best part about the cake cutting is shoving it in each other's face."

Marie was the town mayor and the O'Grady boys' aunt. As the oldest of what Cade referred to as "The Battleaxes," she'd been meddling in the lives of Redwood Ridge's citizens since before Gabby could walk.

She shrugged. "I think it's cute. Cade's a fun guy. Why not?"

Avery pushed her brown waves from her face. "I'm not contesting that. I just feel like a circus performer. I mean, we wanted a small affair, and now everything's choreographed like a musical rendition of the nut farm."

Brent laughed and waved his hand with the dramatic flair of an openly gay man. "Baby doll, this *is* the nut farm. Go with it."

Flynn rose from his seat and pointed to his empty bottle, silently asking if anyone wanted another round. Half the table raised their hands and Flynn headed for the bar.

Cade kissed Avery's cheek. "Everyone's excited you roped me into a proposal. No one thought they'd see the day. It'll be perfect. You'll see."

Avery narrowed her eyes. "Roped you into a proposal? Who chased whom?"

Cade laughed in his easy-peasy way that had the female population swooning. "Semantics."

Drake, the eldest O'Grady brother, set his glass down and eyed Cade. "My warning stands. You make her unhappy for one second of your marriage and I'll rain hell on you."

Gabby grinned. Before Avery moved to Redwood Ridge, Cade was the town's playboy and wouldn't know commitment if it bit him in the ass. Since becoming a widower, Drake had been pretty reclusive until recently, and had formed a bond with Avery. Protective didn't cover it, even if Cade was a good guy and his baby brother.

Avery kicked Drake under the table. "Shush."

One corner of Drake's mouth lifted in the closest thing to a grin Gabby had seen in too long. He tipped his glass at her in mock salute.

Gabby darted her glance to the bar to make sure Flynn didn't need help carrying their drinks. He had his back to the table and was leaning on the counter, unaware of the attractive redhead in a barely there black dress straddling the stool next to him. Gabby didn't recognize the woman, so she must be a tourist.

Well, well. Maybe Flynn would get lucky tonight. Her belly twisted as if disliking the idea. Which was stupid. She wanted him to find someone and be happy. Right?

The moment they'd shared at his house last night floated to mind, and she pulled out her phone to interrupt the memory. She'd simply imagined the sudden flash of desire in his eyes. That's what she'd told herself all night after she'd left his place. And if her belly heated and her face flushed with a pull of longing, she'd mistaken that, too.

Behind you. Hot woman alert.

She watched Flynn down at his phone, read her text, and scan the room for Gabby before noticing the leggy redhead. He flashed a contagious grin and nodded.

Zoe, the groomer at their vet clinic, tossed back a shot and looked at Gabby. "How did your date go last night?" She tucked a strand of shoulder-length green hair behind her ear. A year ago, she'd started dyeing it unnatural colors. No one knew why and no one asked.

Gabby opened her mouth to respond, but found her gaze focused on Flynn. Was he closing the deal? She hadn't seen him go home with someone in quite a while. The redhead was leaning in close to him. He nodded at something she said with one of his trademark smiles.

Things were looking pretty okay at the bar. Which was not the reason her stomach twisted and sank.

He put his hands over his ears to indicate he was deaf. Her pulse paced a quick two-step for him, hoping the woman wasn't as superficial as most.

Not even a heartbeat later, the redhead stiffened, grabbed her drink, and stalked off. Gabby ground her teeth.

"Gabby?"

"What?" She looked at Zoe. "Right. Sorry." She swallowed the last of her beer and set the bottle down, mentally retracting her claws. What had they been talking about? Ah, yes. "Turned out to not be a date after all. I wound up watching a movie instead and ate tiramisu in lieu of therapy." At Flynn's. Where she'd tried to teach him the basics of slow-dancing and got discombobulated instead.

Flynn returned to the table and set their drinks down. To anyone else, he looked exactly as always—observant, carefree, and comfortable. Except she knew his little nuances and tics. Being friends and working together for years trained her to watch his body language. His shoulders were sunk in defeat.

Damn. She had half a mind to storm across the bar and show Little Black Dress what a vapid princess she was.

"Eh hem." Brent lifted his brows. "How can a date not turn out to be a date? Enlighten me, sugarbuns."

Story of her life. Even now, surrounded by half the single population of Redwood Ridge, more of the Y chromosomes were skimming right past her and checking out Zoe. "Just a misunderstanding."

"Uh huh." Brent crossed his arms. "What in the name of Gucci really happened?"

Avery choked on her drink.

Gabby gave up. "He was interested in someone else." She flicked a glance at Flynn and away. She was getting sick of men not seeing her. Seeking refuge in Flynn wouldn't change that. "Maybe I should get plastered and dance on the bar. Think that would get guys to stop seeing me as the good girl?"

Cade rubbed his neck. "Um, you *are* the good girl."

She crossed her arms. "I can be bad." She so couldn't.

Brent laughed. "Sugarbuns, your idea of bad and my idea of bad are entirely different things."

Drake glanced at the ceiling like he wanted to be anywhere else, then wiped his face as if trying to remove an unsightly image.

"I can do it. I can dance on the bar. I've got moves like Jagger." She smiled at her joke, hoping no one called her on it or she wouldn't leave her house for a year due to sheer embarrassment. They'd have to send neighbors over daily just to make sure she was still breathing.

She needed to put her big-girl panties on and pull out of this pity party, table for one. It wasn't as if her lack of sex life was anything new. She'd dealt before, she'd do it again. Feeling sorry for herself wasn't productive.

Brent shook his head with dramatic flair. "You got moves like *Walking Dead*, but we love ya anyway."

She laughed. "Yeah, okay. No bar dancing for me." She took another sip, eying Brent over the rim. "Maybe I should start batting for the other team?"

Cade choked on his beer this time, coughing violently.

Zoe shoulder-checked her. "I'd totally do you."

Because Zoe wasn't any more of a lesbian than Gabby, she grinned. "Aw. Really? You mean it?"

"Heck yeah!" Zoe accepted her high-five.

"Jesus." Drake pinched the bridge of his nose. "Now I have that visual."

"Don't we all," Cade muttered, earning a slap from Avery. "What? Two chicks going at it. I'm just a lowly male after all. Even if I have known these two all my life, that's hot."

"Visual, visual." Drake rubbed his forehead.

Zoe's eyebrows shot so high they nearly hit her hairline. "Statistics say men picture women naked within five minutes of meeting them."

Drake pinned her with a glare of contempt bordering on…contempt. "We met as infants." He jerked a thumb at Gabby. "Met her in first grade."

Zoe shrugged, unaffected. "So you started early."

Avery leaned forward. "You met me just a few months ago."

Drake's you're-not-helping glare merely widened Avery's smile.

Aware he wouldn't win the argument, or that Zoe was goading him, Drake glanced heavenward as if praying to a higher power and wisely shut his mouth.

Gabby laughed until her side ached and met Flynn's amused gaze across the table. "Thoughts?"

One corner of his mouth quirked. *"Just take pictures."*

Cade slapped a hand down on the table. "Now that's what I'm talking about."

* * * *

Flynn drove Brent home, not because his buddy was drunk, but because he'd hitched a ride to Shooters with Avery and was without a car. During the short drive, Flynn did his damnedest to get images of Gabby laughing with their friends out of his head, and how it had turned him on more than the frisky redhead at the bar.

Almost three decades of having Gabby in his life as his best friend, and one bumbled dance lesson shot it all to shit. Yeah, he'd thought about it through the years. A stray what-if in passing. But nothing like recently. Like last night.

This wasn't happening. Flat out, wasn't happening. He had to stop letting his mind go there and envision her as more than what they'd always been. Had to stop thinking with his dick. Hard up didn't give him permission to screw up everything.

He wove through Brent's subdivision, comprised mainly of gingerbread houses and curbside cedar trees, and drove to the end of the street while a thick blanket of fog rolled in. Once in Brent's driveway, he turned to face him and did a double-take. His clinic's vet tech had a wicked gleam in his eye.

Flynn looked at him warily, waiting for the cosmic boom which Brent liked to deliver insight posing as casual chat. Brent turned on the dome light so Flynn could read his lips. Even though Brent could sign, Flynn found that most of Brent's vocabulary didn't have a gesture.

"Why didn't you and Gabby ever hook up?"

His first thought was *oh shit*. Was he that transparent people were noticing? But he swiftly shut that down. On the surface, he acted no different than normal. Maybe Brent was three-sheets after all. To be safe, Flynn didn't respond.

"You two can't function without each other. Just seems to make sense to me."

His breath stalled. *"What are you talking about?"* He functioned just fine without Gabby. And vice versa.

"You don't see it, do you?" Brent turned to face him fully, settling in the seat like they'd be there awhile. "Ever notice when we're in a group, you focus more on her than the others? She signs every word people say so you don't miss a part of the conversation."

She'd been doing that for years, knowing he had trouble keeping up trying to follow lip-reading. The larger the group, the more difficult the task. He'd grown so accustomed to it, he'd just learned to watch her instead. Flynn swiped a hand down his face. Hell, it was second nature.

"You know, she does it sometimes even when you're not around. She'll sign a word here or there when talking to someone else."

Of course, he didn't know that. How could he? Something settled heavy in his gut. Guilt perhaps. The scales weren't balanced. He had to wonder what she was getting out of their friendship.

"I think that's part of the reason men don't notice her. Let's face it. She's a cutie. But the ones who have known her the longest see you two as a unit. Like she's off-limits."

Hell. Was that the case? Had he been cock-blocking other guys into not making a move? The hollow ache in his stomach spread until his entire chest cavity was gutted. The blood drained from his face.

"So you two never…? Not once?"

Flynn studied Brent's face, trying and failing not to be leveled by guilt. And Brent was like a terrier when he latched onto an idea. Flynn needed to sidetrack him. *"Known you a long time and we never hooked up. Same difference."*

"Oh, sexy pants. If your door ever swung my way, I'd be all over that." He snapped his fingers and did some sort of jive. "Must be there's no sexual chemistry with Gabs, huh? That's why you never bumped uglies. I get it."

Flynn lifted his hands and found he had no response. Chemistry wasn't the issue, at least on his end. And why the hell was he talking to Brent about this, anyway?

"No worries." He patted Flynn's chest. "I've got ideas."

Warning pounded in his temples. *"What do you mean, you've got ideas?"*

"You know, to get Gabby a little action. Now that I know you're not interested, I can put my clever skills to use. And I got skills." His eyes widened for emphasis.

Damn it. But Brent was out of the car and up the sidewalk before Flynn could force a swallow.

Pulling back out onto the road, he headed for home. Except when he cut the engine, it was Cade's house he'd parked in front of, not his own. And with no recollection of the drive.

Spruce and redwood sheltered the yard and cast deep shadows over the cabin. The canopy didn't allow much moonlight to filter through. The snow had melted in early spring, but leaves were just starting to bud and the perennials to break ground. He put the window down and drew in a lungful of crisp pine-scented air, but it did nothing to clear the cobwebs.

Unable to make heads or tails of the past twenty-four hours, he climbed out and knocked on Cade's door. A light was burning inside the house, so he'd caught him before his brother had turned in. They teased one another and gave each other hell, but he could always go to both his brothers with anything.

Not that this was anything. Because it wasn't. He was merely making a social call at—he checked his watch—midnight, and less than thirty minutes after he'd just seen Cade at the bar.

But Flynn was fine. Nothing to see here. His heart wasn't tripping behind his ribs in panic and he wasn't gripping the doorframe with enough strength to splinter the wood and he absolutely wasn't two seconds from emptying his stomach.

The door swung inward and Cade's form filled the space. "What's—"

"I have a problem."

Cade jerked. "Is Mom okay?"

"Yes," he signed immediately.

Cade blew out a breath and paused to study his face. Nodding slowly, he pointed to a rocking chair on the porch, which Flynn sank into. "Something's wrong?"

Flynn rubbed his eyes and signed, *"Yes."* He swallowed hard and glanced at the yard as night creatures scurried about. *"I think I might...maybe a little...have..."* Hell squared. *"Feelings for Gabby."*

There. Let the gods of friendship and common sense strike him dead.

Cade's laugh started slowly and built in momentum until he gripped his sides and wiped tears from his eyes.

Flynn pinned him with a DEFCON glare.

Cade stilled, then slowly leaned forward. He opened his mouth, but quickly shut it again. After a stunned beat, he rose and went into the house. A moment later, he returned with a bottle of whiskey—the good kind shipped all the way from distant family in Ireland. He passed the bottle to Flynn.

And that about said it all.

Chapter 4

Gabby strode into the Animal Instincts clinic ten minutes before her shift and stopped dead in her tracks.

The Battleaxes, along with Flynn, Brent, and Avery, were all at the front desk chatting. Damn. If Flynn's mother and aunts were here before opening, something was going on. Not good.

She eyed Flynn in a silent question, but he shrugged one wide shoulder and gave her an I-know-nothing look.

"Gabby, just the girl we wanted to see." Marie slung her arm around Gabby's shoulders, causing strands of Marie's short dark bob to poke Gabby's eye.

Double damn with oh shit on top. Most of the town knew to take off sprinting when the Battleaxes headed their way. The women meddled. A lot. Not only as a hobby, but a life mission. Rarely was Gabby bothered by their appearance, though. It was an infrequent day in hell when they saw fit to screw with her. Good girl and all.

"Um, okay. What can I help you with?"

Rosa's grin resembled something like the cartoon version of the Grinch in plot mode. Flynn's middle aunt used to be their office manager before hiring Avery, so Gabby knew that look and it caused cold sweat to trickle down her back.

Marie stepped away and folded her hands. "As you know, the Spring Fling is coming up."

"Uh huh." Redwood Ridge did several holiday events throughout the year. The Spring Fling took place in the park near the coast and was Easter-oriented. Typically, it was Gabby's favorite since it was close to her birthday.

"And you also know it's the council's policy for the kissing booth to be run by a single member of the community. Avery was going to do it, but she's not single anymore. We picked you to replace her."

Flynn's eyes shot wide as they met hers.

"Uh…" Gabby rubbed her forehead. "I don't think that's a good idea." Who would pay to kiss her when she couldn't get anyone to do it for free? The venue wouldn't earn the town one red cent.

"Nonsense," Gayle quipped. Flynn's mother was typically the quiet, reserved one in the bunch, but her expression illustrated she wasn't messing around. "You're a pretty girl and they'll line up for a chance to lay a smooch on you."

Rosa crossed her arms. "You don't want to disappoint the single men of Redwood Ridge or the event committee, do you?"

Her pulse tripped. "No, of course not. It's just—"

"Good." Rosa nodded as her thumbs ran rampant over her phone she'd conjured from who knew where.

"Wh-what are you doing?"

"Tweeting." She grinned. "There. It's official. You are the kissing queen." Gabby opened her mouth, but Rosa cut off any possible response. "Oh look, we have two responses already."

The Battleaxes had a Twitter and Pinterest account, both of which they used routinely for gossip. Or what passed for news around here. Gabby looked longingly at the back of the clinic. If she fled from the room screaming would they leave her alone?

Flynn straightened. *"Doesn't seem like she wants to do the booth. Why don't you pick someone else?"*

God. She could kiss *him* in gratitude, but that would only encourage them.

"Pah." Marie waved her hand, dismissing him.

Flynn appeared a little disturbed by the idea himself. His gaze darted between her and his aunts, his shoulders tense beneath his dark blue scrubs. He lifted his hands to sign, but Gabby missed what he said when Brent interrupted.

"Told you." His singsong tone made her belly churn in warning. More so when he looked at Marie and raised his brows in confirmation.

What was going on? "Told her what?"

Marie ignored her. "You did tell me, and I think you're right."

"Right about what?" This whole conversation was turning into a twisted version of Abbot & Costello's *Who's on First.*

"Moving along," Marie said. "As in the past, we're having two members from each small business participate in the games during the event. You and Flynn will represent Animal Instincts."

The games consisted of things like relay races and an egg toss. Nothing crazy. But the hair stood up on the back on her neck. This was beginning to look an awful lot like the Battleaxes were trying to play Cupid. They'd "arranged" similar coincidences for Avery and Cade not a few months ago. But…why her and Flynn? And why now?

She looked at Brent. "I thought you and Zoe were representing the clinic."

Avery's tone was wry. "Funny thing. He twisted his ankle." Her expression indicated she believed that as much as she believed the tooth fairy would descend upon them and hand over a winning lottery ticket.

Gabby narrowed her eyes and spoke through clenched teeth. "The Spring Fling is a couple weeks away. You should heal by then. If not, I can participate with Zoe."

Rosa shook her head. "Nope. Gotta be one of each gender."

"Since when?"

"New rule this year." Rosa shrugged like this wasn't part of her master plan.

Panic was this close to cutting off her air. If the Battleaxes had their sights on matchmaking, she and Flynn would never escape. She had no idea what brought this on, but she had to nip it in the bud or almost thirty years of friendship and a solid business unit would go up like kindling.

Flynn shook his head. *"I'm going to make sure our bags are packed. We need to be on the road in ten minutes."*

She and Flynn did house calls three days a week to neighboring farms and disabled residents. Gabby made sure the car and bags were always stocked. And if she didn't, Avery was an organizational Nazi. "You know the car is ready." She mouthed, *coward.*

Flynn grinned and straightened from the counter, throwing her to the wolves. *"Better to be safe than sorry."* He saluted her with two fingers and strode into the back room.

Brent skipped off after him, merrily avoiding her wrath.

Gabby frowned. "Twisted ankle, huh?"

"It comes and goes," Brent shouted from the hallway.

She glanced at Avery for support, who looked no more pleased than Gabby, but the Battleaxes were leaving in a flurry of motion designed to distract and deploy.

Gabby stared at the door after they'd exited and sighed. "When did I get to Oz?"

Avery laughed. "It'll be okay. It's just one day. Whatever they have cooking will be leftovers eventually."

She didn't think so, but she headed to the back room and printed their patient list for the day, figuring she'd think about the problem later.

Flynn was waiting in the passenger seat when she got to the clinic SUV parked behind the building by the kennels. Because a lot of their home visits were up the mountain or along the coast, an all-terrain vehicle was required. The hatch was loaded with two tranquilizer guns, a satellite phone, and extra first-aid supplies, along with their veterinarian bags. Gabby checked the back to ensure they were loaded before climbing in the driver's seat. Flynn liked to do his electronic charting while she drove. Saved time.

She eyed him, not over her mad. "What happened to your balls? Did they disappear with your backbone?"

"Oh, come on. It's not that bad. So what if you have to compete with me at the Fling?"

He was not that dense. "They're trying to set us up."

One pale eyebrow quirked. *"For what?"*

He was that dense. She whipped him a *duh* expression and waved her hand between them.

He reared back, understanding dawning. And if she wasn't mistaken, panic hit his eyes. *"That's...ridiculous."*

She banked down the flare of annoyance that even her BFF thought a relationship with her would be absurd. Or maybe he meant his family trying to shove them together. Either way, neither was wrong. She just had her panties in a wad because of her dry spell. Flynn could no more thwart the Battleaxes than a Band-Aid could help with an amputation.

She reached for the GPS and loaded the patient addresses for the day. Before she could put the car in gear, Flynn's hand landed on her arm.

"Are you really going to do the kissing booth?"

She thought for sure he'd razz her about it or tease her into next week. But his eyebrows were pinched together in concern. "It beats bar dancing or going gay." Not that anyone would show up at her booth. Who wanted to kiss their sister? And that's pretty much how men viewed her.

After checking the settings on the dashboard to make sure the digital display's closed captioning was activated for Flynn, she put the SUV in drive. His hand closed around her forearm again, more firmly this time.

His expression seemed conflicted as he stared at the dashboard like he'd never seen the song lyric readout before.

Flynn obviously couldn't hear, but she'd learned back in high school that he liked music. Often, he'd put his hand over the speaker or, since she'd had the digital satellite radio installed, he'd read the music when not charting. The way he was acting, it was as if he'd never noticed.

She dipped her head to draw his attention. "What's up?"

Tenderness shone in his eyes when his gaze met hers, and something crackled in the small space between them. Awareness. Acceptance. There and gone in a blink, leaving the car suddenly feeling too cramped for comfort.

God. She was losing it.

Rolling her shoulders, she backed out of their space and headed for the main road. "Know what I like most about you?"

"Would you stop signing while you drive?"

She grinned at his age-old argument. "I can drive with my knee. See?"

He growled. It wasn't often she heard him make noises or sounds. On rare occasions, he spoke words here or there, but only with no one else around and only when his hands were too occupied to sign, like when treating an animal.

After a beat, he sighed, conceding. *"What do you like most about me?"*

She glanced at him long enough to catch him signing and reverted her gaze back to the road. "You never mind when I sing." She cranked the volume and sang along to an Aerosmith classic. Poorly. She couldn't carry a tune in a wheelbarrow and knew it.

Flynn stared at her with affection warming his eyes and shook his head.

It figured their first patient of the day was Mrs. Crosby. By Gabby's estimation, the woman was three centuries old and in excellent health. She also owned six cats and lived alone. Blessedly, Avery had blocked enough time—half the day—for the visit as they usually spent a lot of time with the elderly woman.

She rang the bell while Flynn scrolled through the e-chart on his device. The pungent stench of ammonia hit Gabby in the face once Mrs. Crosby opened the door. Flynn took an involuntary step back in response. They shared a mutual *ruh-roh* expression. Someone hadn't been helping the woman empty her litter boxes.

They stepped inside and got pleasantries out of the way.

Mrs. Crosby, with the aid of a cane, waddled over to a brown recliner in the cluttered living room and sat. There were newspapers and knickknacks on every available surface. The aged wall paneling held ancient family photos.

Two cats were on the back of the plaid sofa, three were winding around her legs on the threadbare shag carpet, one jumped onto the elderly woman's lap, and another balefully looked on from the bay window. Gabby did a mental head count and looked at Flynn.

"Did you get another cat, Mrs. Crosby?"

"Oh yes, dear. This one here is Fluffykins." She stroked the gray and white kitten's back in her lap. The gnarled knuckles of rheumatoid arthritis were worse than when they'd made their last house call. Her hair, though combed and tidy, was longer than typical.

She sighed and wondered if this was going to be her in forty years. Alone, collecting felines to fill the void. Townsfolk would call her the crazy cat lady and she'd be too senile to know.

Joking aside, her heart panged for the woman. Setting her bag down, she signed to Flynn that she was going to do the litter boxes before they got started. It wasn't a part of their services to do these things, but it was obvious Mrs. Crosby's son hadn't been by to check on her recently.

Walking through the tiny outdated kitchen, Gabby headed for the mudroom and shook her head. The boxes were so full the cats had begun avoiding them altogether. She pulled gloves from her scrubs pocket and found a garbage bag under the kitchen sink.

After dumping the old litter and cleaning up the droppings around the boxes, she dumped fresh litter in and poured some baking soda over the top to absorb some of the stench.

She checked the cats' food and water supply, noting they were fine there. She opened a kitchen window to air out the place and snatched a bottle of fabric refresher, targeting the furniture and curtains. From there, she poured more baking soda over the carpets and did a quick pass with the vacuum. She tossed out the past-dated food in the fridge and pantry, then finished off by emptying the garbage.

All in all, she had everything done in under thirty minutes. There was no excuse for the son not to have taken care of things for her. It wasn't good for Mrs. Crosby to be living in these conditions.

After washing her hands and donning a fresh pair of gloves, she made her way back into the living room where Flynn was examining one of the cats. "You doing okay?"

He nodded and set the cat on the floor. *"Two down. No health issues to note. All six will need vaccines."*

She carried vials in a hand cooler and always waited until he was finished with exams to not make the animals anxious. While he was doing his thing, Gabby grabbed her stethoscope and listened to heart, bowel, and lung sounds on the cats as he finished with them.

He worked his way through the other four cats until getting to the new addition. Fluffykins's hair stood up on her back as Flynn drew near. He stepped away to give it some space.

Gabby interpreted his questions for Mrs. Crosby and then reached for the furball to hold her while Flynn did an exam.

"Female. Approximately ten weeks old. Declawed in front. Vitals normal. Abdomen soft. Ears clear."

"Everything looks great, Mrs. Crosby. We'll just do their shots and you should be all set."

"Wonderful, dear."

Their routine was down to a science. Flynn held the cats while Gabby drew the syringes, did the pokes one by one, and tossed the used needles in a portable biohazard container. While he had them distracted, she gave each of the cats their heartworm chew and applied the flea and tick solution.

The new kitten was not happy and growled by the time they got to it. Knowing she had to be quick, she waited for Flynn to have a secure hold and quickly doled out the shot.

Flynn motioned to let the cat jump down, but it flew at Gabby with teeth bared and a hiss of pure pissed-off feline. A gray and white flurry of fur whizzed past her peripheral. Before she could react, the thing sank its back claws into her thigh, bit her left hand good, and sauntered off down the hall.

She sucked a breath through her teeth and winced. Pain shot up her arm, hot and sharp and searing. Eyes watering, she glanced at the damage. The bite had broken through the glove to skin and was lightly bleeding. Great. Cat mouths were riddled with bacteria and it didn't take much for an infection to take root.

Flynn reached for her, but she shook her head. They'd clean it up in the car.

More hurried than usual, she scrawled a note for the son and set it on the fridge with a magnet, then washed her hands and said her goodbyes to Mrs. Crosby.

Flynn had the first-aid box open on the back hatch when she stepped outside. A deep groove worried between his brows. *"Let's have a look."*

She set her supplies down. "Mrs. Crosby didn't notice it had happened. I didn't want to worry her."

He nodded his understanding and inspected the bite. There were four punctures along her pinky. And they were deep. Without much tissue on that area of the hand, it wasn't difficult for the teeth to hit bone. The spot was pretty reddened already.

He grunted and disinfected his hands with sanitizer. With quick, skillful movements, he squeezed the punctures to drain, cleaned them out with peroxide, applied antiseptic, and wrapped her finger with enough padding to go ten rounds with a prizefighter.

You okay? he mouthed.

It stung like hell. "Just a bite. Not my first." Wouldn't be her last.

The way he was looking at her said he thought otherwise. Still cradling her hand in his large calloused ones, he brushed his thumb over her palm, eliciting a shiver. His mouth firm, he watched the movement as if in a trace, his gaze distracted and concerned.

Sunlight streamed through his strawberry blond hair. His scent of light woodsy aftershave rose up over that of damp earth and humid spring air, so comforting and familiar she almost didn't notice. He was standing close, mere inches away. Near enough to absorb the heat from his body, to count each of his pale, long lashes framing the most sincere hazel eyes. He had perfect facial symmetry. High cheekbones, wide jaw.

Her pulse thrummed heady. She eyed the dark blue scrub shirt covering his lean, athletic body and wondered what it would feel like to be held against all that hard. She hadn't been intimate with anyone in quite some time. As a chilly breeze swept through the meager space between them, she wanted to climb inside his warmth and let the rest of the world fade. Be touched by someone who cared.

God. No. *Bad, bad, Gabby.*

As if sensing her thoughts, he swallowed. Once. Twice.

She almost asked him if *he* was okay, but he pulled back suddenly. He glanced over her shoulder, shook his head, and rounded the car, climbing in the passenger seat.

Shaken, she popped a precautionary antibiotic they kept for bites, stowed their gear, and got behind the wheel.

Chapter 5

Flynn checked his watch for the tenth time. It wasn't like Gabby to be late for work. He sat back in the chair in his office and debated texting her. She was only ten minutes late, and they were scheduled in-clinic today on a light load, but in all the time they'd worked side by side, he couldn't recall her ever being tardy.

Maybe she'd called in sick. She'd seemed fine yesterday. He couldn't remember her calling in sick before either. Not even the time she had pneumonia two years ago and he had forced her to go home. She'd put up a stink.

Worry clawed at his gut. Shaking his head, he slid his phone closer and thumbed a text. She was probably hung up in traffic or something. But when another ten minutes dragged by and there was no word, he rose and headed to the front desk. No matter what, she always texted him back. Didn't matter the time and didn't matter what she was doing. She always responded.

He waited for Avery to finish signing out a patient and then turned to her. *"Did Gabby call in sick?"*

Confusion worked her brows. She glanced at the answering machine. "No. She's not here?"

He shook his head as his temples throbbed.

"Did you try calling her?"

He nodded, biting back the urge to snap at Avery. It wasn't her fault he was a breath from freaking out. It's just…this wasn't like Gabby. At all.

Avery held up a finger asking him to hold on and picked up the desk phone. After a few beats, she hung up and dialed another number, only to repeat the process. "She's not answering at home or her cell." Avery scooted her chair back and pulled a file from the cabinet behind her. She skimmed what he assumed was Gabby's chart and picked up the phone.

He watched her lips move, trying to pick up the conversation, but she was talking too fast for him to follow. Impatient, he focused the cutesy cartoon murals of dogs and cats simulating human activities that Zoe had painted on the walls when they'd remodeled, then eyed the semi-full waiting room. Most of the people were here for Cade or were Drake's surgical cases.

Avery shot to her feet. "What?" Her wide brown eyes met his in a panic. "Okay, thanks." She hung up and wrung her hands before signing and speaking simultaneously. "I got a hold of her mom. Gabby's in the hospital. Something about an infection."

His stomach sank. Hell. The cat bite yesterday. He thought he'd cleaned it out well and she'd taken a preventative antibiotic, but the tissue had been pretty irritated. He should've checked on her last night, but he'd figured after the awkward moment outside of Mrs. Crosby's house a little distance was needed.

He pointed to the door, indicating he was heading out. *"Reschedule my appointments today, would you?"*

Avery nodded. "Text me when you get there. Give me an update."

He strode out, drove across town and into the next county to the closest hospital. Redwood Ridge had an urgent care clinic, but emergent cases were directed to the bigger cities, a fact that never bothered him until this very second.

Infections were nothing to sneeze at, but his stomach settled by the time he walked through the front doors knowing Gabby would've sought treatment at the first sign of a problem. Hopefully, her hospitalization was just a precaution.

The front desk nurse didn't understand sign language, so he scrawled Gabby's name and date of birth on scrap paper so she could look up Gabby's room.

"Are you family?"

He stilled, wondering if she was in ICU. Typically, that was the only time they'd ask. Knowing the bureaucracies of healthcare, he lied and nodded.

Letting out a relieved breath after the nurse handed over a room number, he strode down the hall. Gabby's sister Rachel was in the room when he finally made it up. She flipped through a magazine from a corner chair, seemingly irritated to be there. She looked up and spotted him, rolling her eyes.

Rachel and Gabby couldn't be from further ends of the gene pool and still have the same DNA. Where Rachel had dark hair and olive skin like their father, Gabby was fair like their mom. Rachel was crass and selfish. Gabby's superpower was tact and gentleness.

Rachel began flapping her mouth, but Flynn had never been able to read her lips. As if knowing that irked him, she smiled, offering him an expression which indicated she thought he was stupid instead of deaf.

He focused on a sleeping Gabby instead. Her cheeks were a tad flushed, but other than that, she looked all right. An IV was hooked up to her right arm. Her left was bandaged. And...swollen from fingertips to elbow. Jeez. She got it but good. The monitor indicated her vitals were normal. He scanned the IV bag. Just saline for fluids and a heavy antibiotic.

Her lashes fluttered open and she offered a wan smile. "Hey."

His stupid heart thudded in happiness. He skimmed his gaze over her caramel hair spread out on the pillow and then on the blue of her eyes as she fought to wake up. *"How are you?"*

She motioned to sign, forgetting her arm, and winced. Her cheeks paled five degrees.

Gently, he set his hand over hers and tapped his mouth, directing her to talk instead.

"I'm fine. Just a little sore and tired."

"When did you get here?" And why hadn't she called him?

She shifted a little in the bed and patted the mattress by her hip. He obediently sat on the edge. "My hand started swelling around midnight. I was running a fever, so I went into the ER."

Uneasiness tightened his throat. *"Did the infection hit your bloodstream?"* Because that would be bad. Very, very bad.

She shook her head. "Labs looked good. If I stay fever-free, I can go home this afternoon." Her gaze shot over his shoulder to Rachel. She frowned. "I said you didn't have to stay. My car's in the lot. I can drive myself home."

The hell she would. He turned to face Rachel, who was waving her hand at him and talking a mile a minute. Shaking his head, he refocused on Gabby. *"What's up?"*

The irritation erased from her forehead. "Mom dropped Rachel off this morning. She had to call in sick to sit with me." She looked pointedly at her sister. "Which you didn't have to do. Take my car and go to work. It's fine."

Gabby's hand fisted under his, her eyes narrowing. "You know why. Because he needs to read my lips. I can't sign right now."

No doubt, Rachel was wondering why her sister was speaking more slowly than usual. Rachel starting a snit had knocked Gabby's pulse higher according to the monitor.

"Tell her to leave or I'll kick her out. Swear to God. I'll stay with you and drive you home when they release you."

She eyed him and swallowed hard. "What about your patients?"

"Light load today. They're being rescheduled."

Though she still looked hesitant, her chest rose and fell with a deep breath. Her gaze traveled to Rachel. "Flynn's off the rest of the day. Take my car. Go to work. I'll come pick it up tomorrow." She closed her eyes as if seeking patience. "Tell Mom I'll call her soon. Thanks for staying with me."

Flynn waited until Rachel left the room before leveling Gabby with a stare. *"When you didn't show up for work, you scared me. Avery's worried. You should've called me."*

Her pretty pink lips parted. "I'm so sorry. I—"

He was an asshole. Swiftly, he shook his head and wiped any anger from his face. *"You're fine. That's all that matters."*

"You really don't have to stay."

He smiled. *"Shut up."*

"I mean it. I'm in the hospital. I don't need a babysitter—"

"Gabby."

"Yes?"

"Stop talking."

His grin widened when she sighed and grabbed the remote with her good hand. All flustered, she fiddled with the thing as the cord got caught in her IV.

He texted Avery to give her an update.

And then Gabby switched the TV to closed captioning. For him. Because she always did shit like that. For him. Until Brent had brought it up the other night, Flynn had barely registered those little things. Now he was noticing them everywhere. Like in the car yesterday when the radio readout displayed the song lyrics. He'd bet his bank account the SUV hadn't come with that feature.

His gut retracted as if being punched. He'd been taking her for granted for years. Nearly his entire life. She had other friends outside their circle. So did he. But they spent a great deal of time together and he couldn't help but question if that was why she was still alone. Perhaps Brent had been right.

He had to find a way to get some distance between them without her catching on to him. Eventually, the day would come where some guy would notice how great she was, how…irreplaceable, and Flynn would have to start figuring out how to go day-to-day without her doting.

He stood and dragged the chair Rachel vacated over to the bed and sank into it.

Gabby held out a package of Jell-O, wiggling it when he didn't take it from her.

"I'm pretty sure you're supposed to eat that."

"I hate Jell-O. If you eat it, they'll think it was me and maybe spring me sooner. I haven't had much of an appetite."

It hardly seemed like decent payback for all she did for him, but he took the package from her. Before digging in, he opened her applesauce and jerked his chin at the cup.

She scooped a spoonful and focused on the TV. Two bites in, she set the cup aside and changed the channel from some gushy girl drama on Lifetime to the Discovery Channel. If reading material or television viewing had any kind of romance or feelings, she was typically all over it.

Which made him eye her suspiciously.

She looked at him. "What?" He lifted his brows and tilted his head toward the wall-mounted set. "You prefer *Deadliest Catch* to bawl-your-eyes-out anything."

See? There was the problem right there. He'd bet she wasn't even consciously aware she'd changed the channel until he'd pointed it out. Hell. She was the one in the damn hospital.

He grabbed the remote, switched the station back, and tucked the controller out of her reach. His balls shriveled from all the estrogen on the screen. Ignoring her attempts to get his attention, he shoved gelatin in his mouth. His guilty gut rejected the stuff, but he ate it, anyway.

An hour passed before a doctor strode in. Young, possibly thirty, the guy looked like he'd walked off the set of *Grey's Anatomy*. Which Flynn only knew because Gabby liked the show. Doc's bright blue eyes zeroed in on Gabby. He flashed her a charming grin that made Flynn want to growl.

His chest rumbled, and when Gabby shot wide eyes at him, he realized he had growled. Out loud. Oops.

Doc's gaze drifted back to her. "How are you feeling?"

She set her megawatt smile to blinding. "Good. See? I ate."

Dr. Pain-in-the-Ass dropped a hand on her shoulder and inspected her arm. He eyed the monitor. "I think you're good to go home today. Let's have you finish this I. first. I'll write you a script for some oral antibiotics. You'll need to come back in seven days to have the stitches out."

Stitches? What stitches?

"If you develop a fever, get right back here. Do you need a work excuse for the next couple days?"

She shook her head. "That's my boss."

Boss. Not friend. He tried not to get insulted because she was just weeding out the unnecessary, but his temples throbbed at the title.

Dr. Needs-to-Leave-Now laughed and squeezed her shoulder. "Gotcha. Okay, you feel better soon."

Flynn narrowed his eyes on her when the guy left. *"What stitches?"*

She held up her hurt arm, showing him three black sutures on the fleshy part of her underarm. "They put in a drainage tube last night and removed it this morning."

What to the what? A drainage tube meant she had been worse off than she'd indicated. The excess fluid in her arm, barely swollen now, must've been massive when she'd arrived. Christ, another hour and she could've wound up with the infection in her bloodstream.

"Breathe."

"What?"

"You're not breathing. I'm fine. So breathe."

Obliging when he wanted to throttle her, he sucked in a lungful of air and pulled her clothes out of the room cubby. Two hours later, he had her home in a recliner, tucked under a blanket with hot cocoa and soup on the table next to her, and the remote in her hand.

He ignored her adorably confused expression, plus her invitation to stay, and hauled ass out the door to start putting that much-needed distance between them.

Today.

Chapter 6

Two days without Gabby at work and Flynn was rethinking the distance thing. It had become blatantly obvious that he'd taken her for granted.

Brent was no idiot, and he was damn good at his job. Yet, he'd been primarily Cade's tech for years and knew those patients better. He and Gabby alternated as Drake's surgery assistant when needed, too. But working with Flynn was a far cry from working with his brothers.

Most of the time, Flynn didn't get down on himself or hope for things that could never be. Such as ears that worked. However, the past forty-eight hours had stretched his patience thin and had him wishing to be normal.

Because damn. Brent wasn't Gabby, and the situation only forced him to realize his wayward…attraction to her had to stop. He could not go another day like the last two and avoid a homicide charge. And if he gave in to the urge to make a move, to shove them over the friendship line, everything as he knew it would fly to Kingdom Come.

While on the road yesterday, his schedule had the senior citizen complex on the agenda. Flynn had to remind Brent to interpret sign language for the clients in order for Flynn to ask routine questions. Brent was also unaccustomed to listening to bowel sounds, lungs, and heartbeat, as Cade typically did that in his exams. Even routine vaccinations and nail trims had been a clusterfuck of complicated. Brent hadn't known where to find supplies in Gabby's travel bag, and spent too much time digging through it to acquire what he'd needed. What should've been a six-hour day had turned into nine.

If he hadn't watched the tech struggle so much, Flynn would've sworn Brent had done the disconcerted routine on purpose just to mess with him.

This morning had been significantly smoother, but nowhere near as fluent as when Gabby was with him. He guessed he'd just never noticed the little things. How she always automatically signed so he could follow along, how she knew to use the stethoscope to listen while he did the physical part of exams to calm the animals and distract, knew the clients and what questions to ask.

Mostly, she knew *him*. She could interpret his signals, deduce what he needed, and act without hesitation. She was irreplaceable. And that was just the work aspect of their life.

Personally, spending forty-eight hours not seeing her was akin to withdrawal. He'd had to force himself not to head to her place after work to check in on her. Resorting to pacing, bad TV, and scrolling the Internet, he'd hoped she had enough sense to call him if she needed anything. So, he'd not visited. The much-needed boundaries were never going to hold if he didn't stand his ground.

Then again, all this might be some screwed-up fantasy in his head. Gabby had never shown any signs of sexual interest in him before. Just because he was losing his marbles didn't mean she was.

Brent waved to get his attention in the small exam room. That was a problem, too. Flynn's head hadn't been in the game. He kept drifting out of focus at odd intervals. If he didn't start paying attention, he might hurt one of the animals.

And, of course—*of course*—today had to be the day Mixey was scheduled for her yearly visit at the clinic. The German Shepherd was not fond of Flynn and seemed to like Brent even less. Even as a pup, the dog had been skittish. She kept darting her how-could-you-do-this-to-me eyes between Flynn and Brent, her body language giving Flynn pause with every move. She didn't have a red flag in her chart, meaning she'd never bitten anyone, but after today, Flynn figured that was just a matter of time.

Two minutes before, he'd asked the owner to leave the room in order to get the shots over with. The dog appeared more anxious with her owner there, and this was going to suck donkey balls just getting Mixey to hold still long enough to inject her. The poor dog kept looking at the door like she expected Gabby to walk through.

Because the dog loved Gabby. Who didn't?

Flynn sighed and looked at Zoe, who he'd asked to come into the exam room for an extra set of hands. *"We need to do this fast. Brent, you lift her onto the table. Zoe, help hold. I'll inject. In and out."*

They nodded, and Flynn moved to the counter to draw the syringe, keeping his back to Mixey so she couldn't see. He quickly capped the needle, dropped it in his pocket, and nodded to Brent and Zoe. They sprung into action.

Hell broke loose.

* * * *

Gabby grinned as she walked into Animal Instincts just after lunch and found a full waiting room. She was supposed to be off the rest of the day, but she couldn't sit around her house anymore crying over movies and eating ice cream. Her scrubs wouldn't fit if she stayed at that rate. Besides, the swelling in her arm was completely gone and she'd been fever free.

She'd missed the noise and wet dog smell. Zoe, Brent, and Avery had popped by after work the two previous days to check on her. Drake and Cade had called. Flynn had been unusually absent, but she figured he thought she'd be resting. It wasn't the same, though, being away. She'd even missed the stupid clinic bird, who was perched on top of his cage behind Avery's desk.

Squawk. "Knocking on heaven's door."

Yeah. Gossip only spoke in song titles and lyrics. The cockatoo's former owner had ditched him four years ago and Gossip had become their…uh, pride and joy. She-rah, the clinic cat, was mounted on her throne on top of the printer, sending looks of disdain about the room. Thor, their giant Great Dane and the biggest wuss to dogkind, was probably under Avery's desk, hiding from She-rah. Or its shadow.

Missed this so hard.

Spotting Mrs. Hinderman in reception, Gabby made her way over. "Hey there. Is Mixey in for a checkup?"

The fifty-year-old woman pressed her hands to her ample chest and let out a gale-force wind. "Thank God you're here. Mixey doesn't like anyone but you and she's so nervous."

Aw. "Brent is wonderful with animals. I'll bet Mixey is just fine. I was heading back there, anyway. I'll go take a peek."

"Thank you so much!"

Gabby *oomphed* as the woman hugged her in a vise. She briefly met Avery's amused gaze over Mrs. Hinderman's shoulder. Oh look, their client had missed a spot when she'd colored the gray out of her black hair. Right there, over her ear… "Gotta let me go if I'm gonna check on the dog."

"Yes. Sorry. Really happy to see you."

Squawk. "Love is a battlefield."

Grinning, Gabby made her way down the hall to Flynn's exam room and stopped short. Brent's voice was raised to holy-shit level and Zoe— *Zoe?*—was squealing like a pig. Zoe was their groomer. Sure, she helped in the clinic on occasion, but what was she doing in there if Brent was assisting? When her tone increased to something close to banshee, Gabby opened the door. And froze.

Mixey was belly down on the exam table, her nose buried in Flynn's crotch. Zoe straddled the dog backwards with her ass in Flynn's face. Brent was hunched over the German Shepherd's rear end looking, by all accounts, like he was humping the animal. Tufts of brown and white fur flittered down like confetti.

They stilled and turned slowly to look at her.

"Hi." Gabby waved awkwardly. "I didn't mean to interrupt your foursome. Should I give you some privacy?"

At hearing her voice, Mixey whined and wiggled. Brent cursed a wicked streak, attempting to hold tighter. Or hump more adamantly. Flynn winced, and Gabby realized the dog was not only nose-deep in his junk, but had her teeth sunk into his pants.

Oh boy.

"You're a riot, you know that?" Zoe blew green strands of hair off her face. "Help us, would you?"

Unable to stop herself, she laughed. "Mixey, drop!"

The dog unhinged from Flynn and shot up off the table, knocking Zoe to the floor with a squeak. Brent's hands shot up in surrender, possibly prayer.

"Come here, pretty girl." Gabby knelt on the floor and accepted the dog in her arms. "Who's a good girl?"

Over the dog's back, she wiggled her fingers for Flynn to pass her the syringe. When it was in hand, she uncapped it, injected the dog, and handed it back to Flynn backwards all while cooing to Mixey. She never even noticed the vaccine amongst her tail wagging and licking.

Standing, she turned to Flynn. Though irritation edged his eyes, the corners of his lips curved as if fighting his happy response to see her. His wavy strawberry blond hair was sticking up in a rat's nest and his jaw sported a shadow just shades darker than his head. Poor Flynn had a rough morning.

Their gazes locked, and she could've sworn desire grappled with longing in his eyes. But that was silly. She'd convinced herself what had happened during their dance lesson had been a fluke. And then again when he'd bandaged her hand at Mrs. Crosby's.

"Don't mind me. I'm fine." Zoe rose from the floor where Mixey had knocked her and smoothed her hair.

"Shh." Brent waved his hand. "They're having a moment." He pressed his fingers to his lips as if sonnets might spontaneously burst from within.

Gabby opened her mouth to deny the accusation, but when she returned her attention to Flynn, the atmosphere around her shifted. A charge of awareness.

All too conscious of his height as he looked down at her, his perfectly angular face, she attempted a swallow, but her throat wouldn't work. Wide shoulders, solid thighs, and a narrow waist rocked a pair of scrubs. The muscles in his arms coiled and bunched as he kept his hands low on his hips. Her heart pounded until all she could make out was the roar in her ears.

God. They *were* having a moment. Dizzy with the feeling, she ran her gaze over him again, wondering what in the hell had happened to normal. Because her and Flynn sexually aware of each other? That was nowhere near the realm of normal.

Flynn's gaze only left hers to dip to her mouth and up again. The intensity in those hazel depths had the oxygen seeping from her lungs. He really was a very handsome man. And smart. And kind. And...

With her cheeks hot, she dropped her gaze to his naughty zone. But that only made things worse. Because now she was picturing him naked. And liking it. She slapped her hands over her eyes.

The entire crotch of his light blue scrubs was damp with Mixey's drool, looking as if he'd wet himself. Damn it. She'd looked again. *Bad eyes.*

"Um." Her gaze shot back up. And wow. It was hot in here. "Are you okay? Did she hurt any of your...man bits?"

Flynn's brows rose and his expression indicated he had issue with her terminology. "*She had a hold of my pants, not the goods.*"

Goods. Yes, goods. She'd bet they were very, very...

"*Happy to have you back.*" He closed the few feet of distance between them, cupped her cheeks, and smacked a fast, hard kiss to her mouth. It was about as sexual as a hurricane, but just as shocking. He pulled away swiftly, leaving her reeling. "*You're never allowed a day off again.*"

With that, he strode from the room, Mixey at his heels.

Silence hung. And hung.

"Oooh, girl. What was that about?"

Snapping out of her shock, she eyed Brent. Shook her head to clear it. "Nothing."

Zoe crossed her arms. "That come-hither smolder he was directing at you wasn't *nothing.*"

"Sweet baby Jesus. I didn't imagine it, did I?"

Brent tsked. "Not unless it was a group hallucination."

"When did you guys start...?" Zoe held out her hand as if unable to pull the words from her mouth. The idea of her and Flynn together did seem quite odd, especially if one took the last five minutes out of the equation. "No. Nothing happening. Honest." She ran her hand over her forehead, torn between the giddy bubble in her belly and panic in her chest. "I think the Battleaxes are messing with us. Kinda threw us off-kilter."

Zoe shrugged. "That explains it."

Brent made a sound of noncommittal. "What are you wearing to the Spring Fling? It's next week. And you need to bring it for the kissing booth, sister."

Damn it. The thought of just what population of Redwood Ridge would show up to kiss her had an involuntary shudder ripping through her. She kept replaying her non-date with Tom and knowing he wasn't the only one who'd skimmed right past her as if not there. "No one's going to show up, anyway. It doesn't matter."

Brent cocked a hip. "Not if you wear your pretty little sundresses or jeans, they won't. You need to snazz it up. Make them see you differently. We're going shopping after work."

She closed her eyes and sought patience. If she couldn't be herself, would she really want a guy noticing her when she wasn't? "The last time we went shopping, I wound up with a drawer full of see-through panties." Which no one saw but her. Her love life was a sad state of affairs when her cat and her gay friend were the only ones who viewed her undergarments.

"And those are hot. We're going to buy you an outfit to ensure someone has the desire to take it off."

Sounded like a lost cause. "Fine. But I draw the line at miniskirts."

Brent frowned. "You take the fun out of everything." His gaze skimmed over her as if plotting. "We need to do your makeup, too. Slut you up a tad." She opened her mouth to argue, but he turned to Zoe. "You can do it."

Zoe fisted her hands on her hips. "And what makes you think I know anything about slutty makeup application?"

Brent's eyebrows shot up in an *oh please* move.

"Okay, I totally do." Zoe sighed and looked at her. "One come-fuck-me makeup job, coming up. I'll be over Saturday morning. Buck up. My cartoon caricature booth is right next to yours. We can make fun of people behind their backs."

Zoe had done all the murals inside the clinic. Though she never called herself an artist, she was pretty great. For most of the town events, she was parked at a booth selling quick caricature sketches. Maybe the Spring Fling would be less sucky with Zoe to hang with.

They opened the exam room door and she followed them down the hall. "I can dress myself and do my own cosmetics, you know."

Brent laughed so hard tears trekked his cheeks.

Chapter 7

A fine mist of saltwater from the Pacific rose over the western-facing cliffs at Redwood Ridge Park, mingling with a thin fog across the damp grass. On the south grounds, a few kiddie rides were in full dizzying effect. Game tents had been set up not far away. Local food vendors were lined up along the fenced cliff ledge, sending the scent of popcorn, salted nuts, and roasting meat into the humid air. A cool breeze knocked the mild temperature to chilly, despite the rare sun appearance.

Flynn crossed his arms and scanned the park. The north grounds were where he and Gabby were supposed to participate in the activities soon. How he got suckered into that, he hadn't a clue. In years past, local businesses had two representatives compete. Gabby, Zoe, or Brent had always done it for the clinic.

And speaking of... Where were the booths? The park was crowded. Townsfolk mingled around and waited in lines for food, tickets, or rides, making it hard to figure out what was what. An odd twist of nervousness wrecked his gut. He'd been stuck between worrying no one would show at Gabby's kissing booth and concerned they...would.

He ran a hand down his face.

Avery frowned. "What's wrong?"

Everything. Ignoring the question, he squatted by her feet to Hailey's eye level. Flynn had a soft spot for the kid. Avery's eight-year-old daughter was a nonverbal autistic and seemed fascinated Flynn couldn't talk either. *"Having fun yet?"* he signed.

Hailey flapped her hands in excitement.

The look on Cade's face was priceless. A cross between pride and joy, his brother smiled at the girl who had him wrapped around her pinkie. Not long ago, Cade had transitioned from woman to woman with no intention of settling down. Then Avery had moved to town. And if Flynn was a little jealous of what his brother had, no one needed to know.

He refocused on Hailey. *"Another month and you'll officially be my niece. I think you should call me Uncle Awesome."*

This earned him another hand flap and, grinning, he stood.

Avery held up a finger, gaze focused on Drake, who stood a few feet away talking to a couple of women from the salon. Or rather, listening to them with a withering expression. "Be right back. I need to save Drake."

When she stepped away, Flynn turned to Cade. *"She got him to come to yet another town function."*

Ever since his wife Heather died almost four years ago, Drake had kept pretty much to himself. They'd grown up together and there wasn't an area of town that hadn't held memories for him. But Avery had slowly worked him out of his rut, and his eldest brother was looking less and less like a ghost and more like the guy he used to be.

Cade nodded. "Took almost no coaxing, too. She asked if he'd be here. He stared at her for less than a beat and shrugged. Oddest damn thing."

Like the rest of their family and friends, Flynn had been concerned Drake would never claw his way out of his grief. Though Drake's body language didn't exactly scream cordial, he wasn't stalking away either. Progress.

Flynn glanced around again. *"Any idea where they have Gabby's kissing booth?"*

"Next to Zoe's caricature booth." When Flynn narrowed his eyes, Cade grinned like the asshat he was. "Why? You gonna stand in line?"

"No."

Cade's grin shot from amused to mocking. "How's it going with the...feelings?"

Flynn sighed, wishing he'd never told his damn brother a thing. At the time, he'd thought it might help get his head on straight, but all it managed to do was acknowledge the attraction. *"I'm ignoring them. They'll go away."*

Cade tipped his head back and laughed. "Good luck with that. You mean to tell me you're not wondering how many men are lined up right this minute waiting to kiss Gabs?"

As if he needed the reminder. *"Nope."*

Cade's gaze darted over Flynn's shoulder, his smile slipping. His brother closed his eyes and shook his head. "Battleaxes. Three o'clock."

Flynn froze. Though his mother and aunts' presence seemed to send others running for safer ground, their conniving didn't much bother him. They meant well and hadn't targeted him in their schemes. But what Gabby had said in the car last week about the Battleaxes trying to set them up had him not only wanting to bolt, but lock himself in a room for a few weeks until they found another victim. After all this time, what made them lock onto him and Gabby? And why?

Aunt Marie stepped to his right, dressed in her usual black pantsuit and in full mayor mode. "The competition's going to start in about twenty minutes. You should find Gabby and head over."

That was the plan. If only someone would point out where in the hell her booth was located.

Aunt Rosa grinned, sending Flynn's stomach near his shoes. Her unnaturally short red hair shoved back from her face with a wind gust. "I hate to pull her. She's getting quite the turnout. Raised a lot of money so far."

And nope. This wasn't helping. He schooled his features neutral. *"Where's she at?"*

Mom kissed his cheek, her familiar scent of cotton swirling around him. "She's on the other side of the food tents. Remind her to put up the *Be back soon* card. The guys will be disappointed, but they can return when she's done with the games."

Guess that answered his question on whether she was seeing any action. He shot his brother a *no thanks* look and headed toward the food tents. Since the vendors were lined up along the fenced cliff, he could only assume his mother meant Gabby was farther down the bluff.

He veered right and there she was, tucked between the sheriff department's Say No to Drugs booth and Zoe's caricature sketch. The makeshift plywood box and awning reminded him of an old *Peanuts* cartoon, and was one of many in a neat row. Zoe had a decent line about ten deep with kids, as did the sheriff's department. But Gabby's booth? Her line stretched all the way to the copse of trees and kept going. Easily fifty guys. And...some boys. Like ten- and twelve-year-old boys. Hell.

Brent appeared to be directing traffic, or pimping her out, and looked up from his perch by the corner. When he spotted Flynn, he made his way over. "Look at our Gabby." He waved his hand in front of his face as if getting misty. "Can you believe that line?"

No, he couldn't. The kissing booth had always turned out good numbers, but this went beyond what he'd expected. And to think, she'd been worried no one would show. Christ, half the male population was in attendance. He wondered how she was handling all the attention. His view of her was blocked by the booth's side flaps.

Brent tapped his chin with a finger. "I'm so glad I spread word around town before the event. Made a difference, don't you think? Telling people Gabby was single and on the prowl worked."

Flynn ground his molars. *"She's not a piece of tail, man."*

This earned him an exaggerated eye roll. "Relax. I merely alerted the public that she wasn't attached." His gaze skimmed down Flynn's body and back up. That she was attached *to him*, even if by assumption, went unsaid and implied.

Point taken. Was that all it took to change how guys viewed her? True, she hadn't dated much, and as of late, it had bothered her, but was that on him? Perhaps Brent was right and he'd been inadvertently standing in her way. Guilt churned his gut.

Brent's shoulders sagged with an exhalation. "Too bad most of the guys in line are..."

Flynn couldn't understand the last part and shook his head.

"F-U-G-L-Y. Fugly. Means fucking ugly."

Knowing Gabby, she probably didn't care much what a man looked like. With a heart like hers, she'd see past physical attributes to the personality. Which was another reason he felt like shit for possibly being her problem in the dating department. She was such a good person. Kind, sincere, pretty. Any guy would be lucky to have her.

"The outfit helped, too. She wasn't too happy with me, but I made her show a little skin." Brent made a clawing motion with his fingers. Like a gay cat.

Flynn swiped a hand down his face and strode around the back of the booth, stopping only when he had Gabby in sight.

And there went the damn air from his lungs. A little skin? *A little skin?* Try all of it. Nearly every creamy, smooth, delectable inch of her. A black lace corset-style shirt barely covered her midsection and a matching black skirt rode up the back of her shapely thighs as she bent over to kiss the next person in line. He couldn't tell who because his gaze was locked on that pale patch of skin just inches shy of the jackpot.

He wondered if her panties were black lace, too.

Shit. He was semi-hard with one glance. He shoved his hands in his pockets and adjusted himself as subtly as possible. Though Gabby wasn't exactly conservative in her clothing style, that outfit was as North Pole from her typical choices as she got.

He followed the curve of her spine to her bare shoulders as her muscles shifted. Her caramel hair was wavy and swept over to one side, more full than usual. She looked soft—her skin, her curves. As soft as her heart.

Her neck, a spot just below her ear, was of particular interest. It was his favorite part of the female body. He could kiss, lick, or suck all reason away and bury his face right there while his hands got to work on other areas.

Most men went for ass or breasts or legs. Not that her legs weren't groan-inducing. In fact, he had a nice little fantasy going about those legs wrapped around his hips and...

He looked up to find her blue gaze pinned on him, eyebrows quirked in question.

He glanced at Brent, hoping to hell she hadn't said something while his eyes were otherwise occupied from her hands, and rubbed his chest. Damn ache wouldn't go away. When Brent's amused expression offered no assistance, he returned to Gabby.

And if he'd thought the rear view of her was fantastic, her front put that to bed. The milky white swell of her breasts peeked out of the top of the corset, and damn if he could remember why he'd never checked out her chest before. Her breasts were perfect, what he could make of them. Perhaps a C-cup, they were large enough to be a handful, but not detract from the hourglass curve of her waist.

He was staring at her chest. With half the male population watching. So not gonna help her cause. Forcing his attention up, he swept past her glossy painted lips parted in surprise and zeroed in on her eyes. That wasn't a hardship either. All that blue framed by pale lashes. Except today they were lined with coal or some other cosmetic term. He'd never seen her wear that much makeup.

Pity. He preferred her without. She'd gone from girl-next-door to Hooker Barbie. Patent pending. Where the hell was his Gabby?

She startled and spun to the line waiting for her as if someone had called her name. Front and center was Tom, the douchebag who'd hit her up for a date with her sister a couple weeks ago.

Something ugly filled his chest, had his hands shaking as he fisted them. A pounding headache began behind his eyes. He strode over to the counter, slapped the *Be back soon* sign up, and pulled the grate down to close her booth.

Her eyes shot wide. "What are you doing?"

As if he knew. *"We're needed for the competition."* He paused and...to hell with it. *"You're not kissing Tom. Not now or when we get back."* Or ever. The guy had played on her sweet side to get to her sister, and now that Rachel seemed done with him, he'd moved on to Gabby. She should never be someone's second choice.

She lifted her hand as if to reach for him and drew it back. "Are you all right?"

Since there was no way to logically answer that, he looked around, spotted her jeans on a nearby chair, and tossed them to her. *"You can't do the games dressed like that."*

With a furrow between her brows and her confused gaze set on his, she kicked off her knee-high leather boots and stepped into the jeans, sliding them under her skirt. By the time she'd removed said skirt and had the boots back on over—God help him—skinny jeans, her expression was growing pissy.

She grabbed the cashbox, passed it to Brent, and stalked out of the booth.

Flynn had forgotten Brent was there, and if his grin was any indication, Brent was entirely aware of that. "Did I mention she's got five dates lined up?"

He should've stayed in fucking bed. Too late now, he went after Gabby and caught up to her angry strides halfway to the north grounds.

She stopped and spun to face him, her cheeks flushed and sapphire eyes blazing. It was a rare sight, her worked up, but damn if it wasn't one of the hottest things he'd ever seen. "Why couldn't I wear what I had on?"

He had a fleeting image of her bare thighs exposed for the town while they competed in a relay, and shook his head to clear it. *"You really want to do a three-legged race wearing that skirt, be my guest."*

She tilted her head as if considering that, then nodded. "And why can't I kiss Tom? Not that it's up to you."

He sighed, finding it hard to look at her without wanting to haul her to his chest, so he focused on the ground instead. *"You're no one's leftovers."* When her hands didn't move to sign, he made himself meet her eyes. That look on her face, like she thought she'd never been anyone's main course either, made his heart trip in his chest. *"Never mind. I'm sorry. Do what you want."*

Her teeth worked her lower lip as she studied him. "Are we okay? You seem off lately."

If anyone would know, it was her. She understood his every nuance and tic as if they were her own. And he was a really crappy actor. Plus, the distance thing wasn't working. Maybe he should just talk to her about the shift in him so they could move past it. She'd probably laugh her ass off at any rate, and things could return to normal.

But now wasn't the time. *"We need to go. They're getting ready to start."*

Taking her hand, he led her to the open field where spectators were gathered on either side of a long strip of damp grass. Other competitors from local businesses were paired up near a makeshift check-in point. His Aunt Marie nodded to them and lifted a mic to her mouth.

Unable to read her lips at that distance, he turned to Gabby, who automatically signed for him. Apparently, they were to do some kind of egg toss first, moving a foot apart with each turn until only one couple remained. He recognized several of the other participants from Shooters, restaurants, the library, and small businesses. Aunt Marie's secretary passed out eggs, directing the women to one side and the men on another.

Facing Gabby two feet away, he grinned, cradling the egg. "We got this. You're a vet. You've got good hands."

He shook his head, not caring one iota if they won or not. Knowing her, she probably didn't either. For her, it was the fun factor.

She turned to look at Aunt Marie and counted off with her fingers to tell him when to start. At her thumbs-up, he gently tossed the egg underhand. She caught it with cupped palms and reciprocated. They took a step back and repeated the process several times, surviving this round longer than most of the others.

Until she missed and the egg broke. On her chest. Right between her breasts, where yellow yolk disappeared behind her corset-like shirt. Hell. He'd never eat eggs again without thinking about that. Her hands froze at her sides as if unsure what the heck to do. He curled his lips inward to avoid grinning.

The couple next to them, employees of the hardware store, cheered their victory. Gabby said something to the woman and, after a beat, she passed Gabby her egg. Turning to Flynn, Gabby narrowed her eyes and smiled. It kind of reminded him of their sophomore year car wash fundraiser when she'd dumped a bucket of soapy water over his head after he'd set the hose on her.

Hell. No. *"Hey, you're the one who missed—"*

The egg hit him and broke. Over his crotch. Cracked shell and yellow goo plopped to the grass by his feet. He dropped his hands to his hips and waited until she was through laughing. Damn pretty sight that was, too. Watching her, he wished, for just a moment, he could hear what she sounded like. He'd bet her laugh was as light and musical as her eyes.

She sobered. Sort of.

He sighed. *"Feel better now?"*

She closed the distance and patted his shoulder, snatching a dry towel midair someone threw to them. He stared at the bystanders while she wiped herself off, and he swore he caught Brent high-fiving Aunt Rosa. Why?

Gabby flung the towel at him and he attempted to remove the egg from the fly of his jeans. Still looked like he'd pissed himself.

A three-legged race was next. He had better scenarios for being physically tied to Gabby and it didn't involve their legs. Regardless of the heat and awareness coursing through his bloodstream having her sidled right next to him, their arms around each other's waist for balance, the relay went off without a hitch.

Mostly. They came in last because the couple next to them got tripped up and took them down. Flynn was trying too hard not to react to Gabby landing on top of him, her hair a waterfall of blond around their faces, to care about getting back up and finishing. Her honey scent was the craziest aphrodisiac.

One more event and he could call this crap over. He missed half the instructions staring at the now overcast sky and praying to a higher power. God grant him the serenity...or something. It didn't work. He still wanted Gabby horizontal again, sans the witnesses and clothes. He was an asshole of the first order for even thinking it.

Gabby set a pink water balloon in his hands. He stared at it, then her. Karma was a cruel bitch if the next competition involved her, that outfit, and water. He looked at her in question, and when she explained what they were supposed to do, he could do little more than grind his molars.

He watched the others place the balloons between their bodies, chest high, and get into position to waddle to the finish line, the object being not to break the balloon or let it drop. Or use their hands. Maybe he should just "accidentally" drop theirs now.

Gabby pressed up against him, thigh to thigh, chest to chest, and positioned the balloon between them, looking all chipper and cute while his breath stalled. Desperation—for this attraction to end or evolve, either would do—closed his throat.

She must've sensed his tension because her cool fingers wrapped around his forearm and her tender gaze searched his.

They had to talk. There was no getting around it anymore. Through the years, they'd been able to discuss most anything. Surely, this irrational blip would be no different. Right?

He hadn't realized the others had started the race or that he'd involuntarily moved closer to her until his shirt was...wet. Great. They hadn't even started and he'd prematurely blew.

She shivered as goose bumps pebbled her skin. Bits of pink rubber from the balloon tangled in her hair, her mascara slid south, and she swiped water droplets from her lips with her fingers, making him desperately wish he were that hand.

Reaching back, he pulled his sweatshirt off and yanked it over her head.

Chapter 8

With Flynn on her heels, Gabby walked into her small ranch house and set the keys on the entryway table. She eyed her big, cozy blue chair by the living room window with longing and then frowned at her clothes. Shower first. Drop dead after.

She turned to tell Flynn she'd be right back, but the tension in his shoulders and around his eyes gave her pause. He'd been acting strangely for two weeks. And she was no idiot. Between the heated stares and his attempt at avoidance, she was past suspecting his attraction.

He shoved his hands in his pockets, making his T-shirt stretch over his biceps, and studied her hardwood floor as if he'd find the answers to solving world hunger between the dark-stained planks.

Tired, she toed off her boots and kicked them near the door. It had been a long day. Brent had dressed her like a prostitute, Zoe had done her makeup in drag fashion, she'd been forced to kiss every available male in Redwood Ridge, and then compete on behalf of the clinic in a silly set of games. She was over it. She wanted a hot shower, a cup of cocoa, and two hours of uninterrupted reading.

Present company or not. She didn't care. Hanging out with Flynn had always been easy. Lately, not so much. She missed...them.

At least the next five Friday nights looked hopeful. Her kissing booth a success, she'd been asked out on a date many times. But instead of relief or giddiness, disappointment tightened her chest. The guys in question never would've made a move if she hadn't dressed differently or if Brent hadn't pimped her out. She wanted someone to see her as she was, without the muss or frills. Which, let's face it, hadn't happened since puberty, so why bother hoping?

And the man in front of her? Her best friend? For some unknown reason, he suddenly began noticing her not as his buddy, but a woman. She could tell in the way his breath rasped, the dilation of his hazel eyes, and the bumbling conversation whenever they got within ten yards of each other that he was fighting his desire. As if wanting her was wrong.

She'd admit, she didn't know how she felt about the shift, had barely slid past denial on the matter to know if she wanted him, too. He was an incredibly attractive man, both physically and his personality. But that was moot. Because when push came to shove, at the end of the day, she deserved a man who wasn't ashamed to want her. To be with her. Someone who didn't act like he had to fight off his feelings.

And it was blatantly obvious Flynn didn't want to want her.

Her chest squeezed and his form blurred as tears misted her eyes. Drawing a deep breath, she shoved down the ball of hurt.

Finally, he met her gaze, apology and regret in his eyes. *"Can we talk?"*

Worst phrase in the history of the spoken language. It was right up there with *let's be friends.* Except they already were. That was the hardest part. He was her best friend, knew damn near everything about her, and he was ashamed of his desire.

She jerked her chin toward the hallway. "I need a shower first. Give me five minutes?" She grabbed the hem of his sweatshirt he'd loaned her at the park and pulled it over her head, handing it to him.

His throat worked a swallow and he nodded, taking the shirt from her while managing to keep his distance. For all his James Bond stoicism, he sure looked not only shaken, but stirred to boot.

She shuffled down the hall. Avoiding the mirror, she quickly showered, not lingering under the hot spray as she would've liked, and put on a pair of boxers with a T-shirt. Feeling more like herself, she reached for the doorknob and hesitated.

Flynn wanted to talk. She didn't know if he planned on coming outright with the truth or if he intended to feed her a line, but either way, her heart couldn't take the blow. Not from him. She gave herself a moment to think of what she should do and then opened the door.

After she made her way to the living room and saw him, it confirmed her decision to evade. Sitting on her couch, hunched over with his head in his hands and her tabby cat, Popsicle, doing her damnedest to get his attention by kneading his rigid back, Flynn was apparently in full guilt mode.

Was it too much to ask to have a man want her guilt-free, too?

His head jerked up, gaze colliding with hers. The impact hit her square between the ribs. The sheer honesty alone was staggering. It was hard separating him as a man from the friend she'd known too long, hard to imagine they were the same person. If possible, he seemed even more wary than before. Which gave her an idea on a way to dodge their much-needed conversation, at least for tonight. Tomorrow, they could deal with things.

"Are you still nervous about the first dance for Cade's wedding?"

He rose, but came no closer, his expression indicating he didn't know how to answer. His strawberry blond hair stood on end from his fingers fisting the strands moments before and his jaw was ticking to the beat of her heart.

Maybe she hadn't thought this through. Okay, definitely hadn't. She could pinpoint the exact moment things went screwy between them and it had been when she'd tried to teach him to slow-dance. Getting all up close and personal again was about as good an idea as skiing the Klamath in December. Naked.

Popsicle pawed at his pant leg, little attention whore that she was, and he bent to pick her up. His large hand stroked her back, gaze focused on the movement, and Gabby could all but hear the gears turning in his head.

After a beat, he set the cat back down and tentatively looked at her. The ten feet between them shrank to one without either taking a step. "*I think we should talk.*" He winced as if realizing what he'd said and raked a hand through his hair. His eyes fell closed. "*I'm about three seconds from losing my shit.*" He opened his eyes and sighed, imploring her to make this right.

And just like that, the tension evaporated and he was her best friend again, wanting to discuss a problem. Regardless if she was the issue. Talking about it wouldn't change anything because he obviously still didn't like the idea of being attracted to her. But she softened. Right then, he needed her, and she'd never deny him anything.

"I know. We don't need to dissect the situation, though, do we? Just understand that...I'm aware." She'd meant it as an out, a way to acknowledge what was there without him having to rake himself over the coals. Give them some time to adjust and see what happened.

But...hurt clouded his features as if he thought she'd dismissed him. Slowly, his brows drew together, understanding filling his eyes and firming his lips. She had a sinking suspicion his version of understanding and hers weren't on the same dictionary page. She stepped forward, the need to comfort fierce, but he looked away and she stilled.

He ran a hand down his face. "*What do we do? How...?*"

She closed the distance and took his hands, waiting for him to look at her so he could read her lips. It seemed to take an increasing amount of effort, but finally, his gaze drifted to hers and lowered to her mouth.

"We dance. That's what we do. Dance."

A little V formed between his brows. His shoulders dropped like a tremendous weight lifting, and he stepped flush against her. His heartfelt sigh teased her hair as he pulled her in, one hand behind her head and the other low on her back. She pressed her cheek to his chest, breathing in his scent of soap that mingled with the outdoors from their day.

She wrapped her arms around him, palms flat on his warm back, and they stayed that way for a few moments until he gently set them in motion. A careful sway as if he were tentative to move. Following his lead, she shifted with him. A step left, another one back, all while he kept her secure against him.

There was no music, but something close to magic wafted around them. Through them. The rest of the world faded, leaving only him and her. If she believed in such things anymore, she'd think it was almost fairytale-like the way he seemed to be protecting her, even if from himself. His arms banded tightly around her, cocooning her between two solid biceps.

After a couple of minutes, she became readily aware of two things. One, he didn't need dance lessons. And two, her girly bits were cheering at his nearness. They'd never been close like this, where she could feel every ridge of him, burrow into him.

With her breasts crushed to his hard wall of chest, her nipples pebbled at the stimulation of moving with him. An ache. A burn. His chin rested on the top of her head as if holding her were the most natural thing. Their thighs brushed, his denim to her bare skin, and she eased closer when one of his legs worked its way between hers. The muscles in his back shifted under her hands, a delicious play of strength, and need coiled in her belly. Heat sizzled a path from her core to between her legs.

That answered her question on whether there was any spark on her end. He'd obviously been feeling...something, but she'd kept denying what had been in front of her, thinking she'd read too much into nothing.

This wasn't nothing. And she had no idea what to do.

"Gabby..."

Oh, *his* voice. He didn't speak often, and due to his lack of hearing, her name sounded more like *Gob-bee*. But the strain, the need riddled in that one word, tore a shiver from her roots to her toenails and didn't bother passing Go.

They'd stopped dancing, she realized. Her hands were fisted in the back of his shirt, clinging for dear life. She'd unconsciously pressed her forehead against his throat, her mouth millimeters from his warm skin, and when he swallowed, her lips grazed him.

He stilled at the touch, all but his fingers clenching in her hair. Then, as if testing the waters, his other hand moved from the small of her back to her waist, a slow yummy glide. Her breath hitched and, taking that as permission, he slid his palm over her ribs and splayed his fingers so that the tips caressed the underside of her breast through her shirt.

Her lids fell closed and she went molten in his arms. Liquid fire. Nothing else mattered, not her reasons for refusing to act on the desire, nor the rift that could possibly split their relationship. All that filled her head was him against her, making her heart stutter and her body crave. Ache. No man had ever made her want like this, left her mind spinning and her knees jelly.

He dipped his head to brush his cheek against hers. The rasp of his five o'clock shadow grazed her and she moaned. Rough against soft. He must've felt the rumble in his chest because he let out a groan in response. His chest expanded with a sharp, shallow inhalation Hot, erratic breath skimmed her ear, her throat. His mouth whispered against her flesh, a ghostly caress hovering...so...close.

Yes. God, yes. She buried her face under his jaw, parting her lips and darting her tongue along his throat. He smelled so good, like warm aroused male. The salt from his skin had her wanting to taste him everywhere. He clasped her neck as if needing to hold her against him or afraid she'd stop. The fingertips over her ribs dug deep, branding her with heat. His hips jerked forward, his thick erection thrusting against her belly, and...

He pulled away.

She reeled at the sudden loss and the rush of cool air hitting her skin.

Hands on her shoulders at arm's length, he held her away. His breaths soughed like a man dying. He glared at her like he'd never seen her before. Wide hazel eyes that held of myriad of emotion. Then his lids slammed closed, heavy as a door shutting her out, and a pained expression twisted his face.

Rejection punched her stomach and she wrapped her arms around her middle in an attempt to hold herself together. Trembling, dangerously close to tears, she stared at his chest because looking at the regret on his face a moment more would drop her to her knees.

God, did that hurt. She'd been passed over countless times. Had been in a room full of people and rarely seen. Shoved into the good girl friend zone. But Flynn dismissing her like he'd just made the largest error of his life thrust the lump of pain from her chest into her throat. They'd barely done anything and she'd been reduced to...a mistake.

He straightened, ramming both hands through his hair and stalking away, only to come right back and cup her cheeks. Rigid desperation radiated off him. Shaking, frustration marring his brow, he stared at her through pleading eyes. As if realizing he was touching her again, he lifted his hands in surrender and took two steps away.

He rubbed the back of his neck. Glanced around. *"Christ. I'm sorry. I'm so sorry."*

Yeah, she got that. How pathetic was it that the only thing she was sorry about was that he'd stopped? She tried to draw in a ragged breath, but she could still smell him in her space and it made things worse. Her stomach cramped and her stupid, stupid arms wanted to be around him again.

"I won't..." He stepped forward, dipping his chin to look in her eyes. *"It won't happen again. I promise."*

She nodded like an idiot because what was she supposed to say?

Popsicle wound her way between her ankles as she stood frozen on the precipice of shattering to millions of tiny pieces. Only when the front door closed quietly she did realize he'd left.

Stumbling to the couch, she plopped down and rubbed her forehead. Numb shock settled in, and she had no idea how long she sat there with Popsicle butting her arm to be petted and her staring at the sweatshirt Flynn left behind. She blinked.

Her phone rang and she jumped, startling the cat and earning a hiss. Hoping it was Flynn, she reached for the cell on the table and checked the ID.

Brent. Any other time she would've answered, but tonight she needed... What? Something. One of the girls. Avery or Zoe to talk out what just went down because she didn't know her ass from her elbow right now. How were she and Flynn going to work together? Would it be awkward? And what about their friendship?

With trembling fingers, she ignored Brent's call and unlocked her screen to scroll through her contacts. She passed Avery, thinking she might be putting her daughter Hailey to bed. Choking back a sob at Flynn's name, she kept going and hesitated over Rachel. Her sister had buckets of experience when it came to sex, but nada when it pertained to friendship or dating. Zoe's mother had been diagnosed with early-onset dementia four years ago. Her mental state was rapidly declining and poor Zoe was doing everything she could to keep her mom at home. Since they'd been at the Spring Fling all day, Zoe was most likely attempting to put order back at home to keep her mother calm.

She scrolled back up. Avery was relatively new to town. Maybe she could offer Gabby a fresh perspective, a new set of eyes. Avery had moved into Cade's house last month, and Cade was very active in Hailey's life. Perhaps Gabby wouldn't be intruding if she reached out to Avery.

She couldn't sit around all night in this state or she'd climb the walls. Or hold up the Ben & Jerry's plant. *Give me all your brownie batter ice cream or else...*

"Hey. Am I interrupting anything? You got a minute?"

Avery made a sound of dismissal. "Not interrupting at all. What's up?"

She barely held it together long enough to tell her friend what had happened. After a thought-filled silence, Avery said, "Wow."

"Yeah."

"If I'm being honest, I'm surprised something hasn't happened before now. You guys are...I don't know. There are sparks. Definitely."

Sparks, an inferno. Tomato, *tomahto.* And up until recently, if there had been anything romantic, she'd been oblivious. Had the rest of the town seen something she hadn't?

Avery sighed. "Aside from the obvious, what's keeping you from acting on the attraction? I mean, I can't see you guys hating each other if it doesn't work out."

Hate? No. But the friendship and close working unit, never mind their circle of friends, could collapse. "He acts like this chemistry is the worst possible thing."

Avery laughed. "To him, it probably is. Face it, Gabby. You've known each other since kindergarten, you work every day together, and he depends on you more than you realize. And for a guy, that last part's pretty emasculating to admit. I'm willing to bet he's kicking himself thinking he's ruined everything."

That much she understood. But she couldn't be with a man who felt guilty for touching or desiring her. And since that man happened to be Flynn, everything as they knew it had changed. Because he wasn't just anyone. If they acted on their feelings, there was no going back. Out of everyone in her life, he had the potential to truly hurt her bone-deep, not on the superficial level others had inflicted.

She petted Popsicle and stared at Flynn's sweatshirt. "What do you think I should do?"

Avery blew out a breath. "You got asked out a lot today, right? Go out with someone else. Flynn hasn't really seen you with another guy in a dating sense, not since realizing he's attracted to you. Maybe being with someone else will show you both what you want. Who knows? Maybe there is nothing there between you two and you're getting worked up over what amounts to little more than interest. Either way, it'll force him to act."

She chewed her lip, not wanting to force him into anything. She just wanted...what Avery and Cade have. What Drake and Heather had before she'd died. She wanted to be loved, to mean something to somebody.

"And Gabby? In my opinion, ignoring the situation is only going to cause an implosion."

Chapter 9

Cade set down his beer. "Wait. So you mean to tell me she wasn't into it?"

Huddled up to the bar at Shooters, back facing the rowdy Friday night crowd, Flynn shoved his ball cap lower on his forehead and tried to figure out how to answer. Truth was, he didn't know if Gabby had reacted to him or if he was just that damn delirious.

Flynn shrugged. *"I don't know."*

From the stool next to him, Cade whipped him a disbelieving look. "How do you not know? I mean, she responded or she didn't, yeah?"

That was the thing. He'd tried to talk to her and she'd...blown him off. She'd never done that before, not once. Proving whatever he'd been feeling was one-sided. She'd stood in front of him in her living room and acknowledged she knew he wanted her, and then acted as if they'd discussed the weather.

Right then and there, he'd decided he'd gnaw off his arm before making another moment uncomfortable for her. He was the stupid ass who'd crossed the line. No way would he punish her for that. Determined to go on, business as usual, he'd find a way to get past it.

But then she'd pressed her soft curves against him and hung on like a woman starved. Talk about a mind fuck. There was no mistaking her hard nipples, her shallow breathing, flushed cheeks. And her open mouth against his jaw, tongue darting out to...

Lick. Him.

Any other woman and he would've had them horizontal, halfway to satisfied before doubt even registered. It had been awhile, but it wasn't as if he'd forgotten how. But Gabby wasn't any other woman.

He'd pulled away to look into her eyes, get some kind of confirmation, and instead he'd found... Shit. He'd never erase her gutted expression from his memory. As if he'd *betrayed* her.

"Things seemed pretty heated between you two at the Fling."

Flynn rubbed his eyes and took a long sip of beer. *"Guess not."*

Cade studied him from the corner of his eye, then pulled out his phone and clicked an app. A few swipes of his thumb and he turned the screen toward Flynn.

"You have a Pinterest app on your phone? Man up, little brother."

Cade frowned. "When you have the Battleaxes gunning for you and meddling in your life, you will, too. Then again, you're already there." He wiggled the phone.

With a sigh, Flynn took it and froze. There, in one of the boards, was a picture of him and Gabby from the Fling—her in his arms, their faces close right after the balloon had popped. If he didn't know any better, he'd swear they'd been posed for some sensual perfume ad.

"No chemistry? You need a better lie."

He passed his brother the phone, pulse pounding. *"We're just friends. Same as we've always been."*

"Are you okay with that?"

He'd have to be. What was the alternative? Lose her? *"I'm fine. We're fine."*

Last Monday morning, she'd acted as if nothing had happened. They went through the motions at work, everything as easy and fluent as always between them. Except there were the little things. How she hadn't sung along to the radio, rarely made eye contact, and had failed to inform him of her date. Tonight.

Gabby and one of the local deputies they'd gone to school with were exactly three tables behind him. She was wearing a sundress the color of her eyes that tied around the back of her neck. One pull of that knot and the thing would slip off her body, drift to the floor.

From what Flynn could gather by watching them in the mirror above the bar, Wyatt had been very attentive to her, leaning in when she spoke and casually touching her hand. Gabby, for her part, had her smile cranked and laughed on cue. They seemed to be getting along swimmingly. Hooray.

He ground his molars. What asshat took her to Shooters for a first date? And why the hell was Flynn still here torturing himself?

"Fine, eh?" Cade shoulder-bumped him. "That's why you're shooting daggers in the mirror, because you're fine? You haven't gone five seconds without looking at her. Hell, you haven't even noticed Emma Jane has been checking you out the past hour."

Flynn's gaze lifted to the bartender. Emma Jane was a petite brunette who he'd quietly hooked up with on a few rare occasions. "Quietly" because she had a three-year-old daughter and "on occasion" for the same reason. The last time they'd connected had been at least eight months ago.

Neither had an interest beyond sexual release and, really, it was more trouble than it was worth. He'd spent more time watching her face for cues she'd liked what he was doing than enjoying himself. True story with all his lovers. A lot of females tended to get creeped out he kept his eyes open. But because he couldn't hear, and he was a good guy determined to leave them satisfied, he relied on sight. If a partner, at any time, wanted to change her mind or wasn't into a particular move, he wanted to know.

Sex had become too much work. Not that he'd planned to give it up.

Emma Jane turned from pouring a tap and smiled. After wiping a wet spot on the bar and sliding an ale to Frank from the hardware store, she made her way over, towel slung over her shoulder. "How have you been?"

She knew just enough sign language to get by, so he kept his answers simple. *"Good. You?"*

"Another day in paradise." She grinned at Cade. "Need a refill?"

"I'm done after this. Thanks, though."

She nodded, gaze back on Flynn. Her mouth opened like she wanted to say more. No doubt, she was trying to figure out a way to hook up later without alerting his brother to the fact. Another time, Flynn might've texted her for a semblance of privacy while they made plans, but he wasn't up for sex tonight.

Instead, a glutton for punishment, his gaze found a certain blonde in the mirror again. It was her birthday tomorrow. He had her present in his car. With the awkwardness between them, he'd been unsure whether to give it to her at work today or not. They'd always spent her birthday together, either with their group of friends or just them and takeout on her couch. At this point, he wasn't even sure if he'd be welcome.

"She was interested."

Flynn forced his focus from Gabby and onto his brother. At first he thought Cade meant Gabby, but then realized he was talking about the bartender. Emma Jane had left to refill orders and he didn't want to talk about her, so he changed the subject to Cade's upcoming wedding.

They discussed nonsense another twenty minutes before he called it a night. Flynn left Shooters, Gabby still immersed in her date, and went home alone.

By the next morning, he hadn't slept an iota and disturbingly graphic visions of what Gabby might've been doing with Wyatt burned his retinas.

Gut twisting, he turned his head toward the window and the murky rays of light peeking through his blinds. Frustrated from lack of sleep and what he was beginning to refer to as The Gabby Effect, he rubbed his chest.

Fletch shoved his cold, wet nose against Flynn's arm, a silent demand to get moving. The golden retriever had been his solid companion since Flynn adopted him five years before. Originally trained as a therapy puppy, he'd been too skittish around elders to stick.

"I suppose you need to go out."

Fletch tilted his head, ear twitching. The only time Flynn spoke aloud was when they were alone and sometimes Flynn thought the dog preferred sign language. Not that he understood either form of communication.

He scratched Fletch's scruff and procrastinated. Getting out of bed meant deciding what to do today. And if those plans included Gabby. She turned thirty today. He was on call for the clinic this weekend, but his pager hadn't gone off. Wondering if his luck would hold out, he rose to start a cup of coffee and, while it brewed, he showered.

As he took his first sip of caffeine while leaning against his kitchen counter, Fletch already let out and fed, he stared at his cell screen. No missed calls. Gabby always texted to tell him how a date went. Though it was only eight, she was an early riser. Perhaps Wyatt had worn her out? Or they were still in bed...

He tossed his phone aside and rubbed his eyes. Hell to the no, it wasn't his damn business who she hooked up with. He'd promised her what happened last weekend wouldn't happen again. And he meant it. Even if she had responded to him, and he was still uncertain if she had, they couldn't cross that line.

But damn it. He missed her. The entire week she'd been distant, remote. And she shouldn't spend her birthday alone. Her family wasn't big on celebrating, so if he didn't head over, she'd probably eat a pint of mint chip while watching some girl drama on TV.

Unless Wyatt had spent the night.

Shoving off the counter, he tapped his thigh for Fletch to follow him out. He'd do a drive-by to check for another car outside her house. If she was alone, they'd do their thing. Hang out. Talk. Eat cake or what the hell ever. He was determined to whittle the tension away and force normal down their throats.

Five minutes later, he was standing on her porch, Fletch next to him with Gabby's gift bag dangling from his mouth. There were no cars outside her house or in the driveway, but he pulled his cell out anyway and shot off a text.

You awake?

Gabby: *Yes*

Are you alone? For the love of beef jerky, please let her say...

Gabby: *Yes*

He let out the breath he'd been holding. *Open your front door.*

Caramel hair up in a high ponytail, face fresh and wearing jeans with a sweater, Gabby swung the door wide. Her smile came as if an afterthought. Which wouldn't do.

He stepped inside, Fletch on his heels, and shut the door behind him. *"Happy birthday."*

The smile upped a notch, but didn't hit her eyes. She glanced at the dog and...Christ. There was the smile he'd missed all damn week. At least Fletch got one out of her.

She knelt in front of the retriever and scratched his ears, taking the gift bag from his mouth. She looked up at Flynn from her position and did a double-take. And here he thought he'd schooled his face neutral.

"What?"

He shrugged. *"You turned thirty. I was expecting gray hair and sagging breasts. At least a massive amount of crow's feet. You look the same."*

She laughed and rose, holding the bag up in question.

"Open it. You know you can't wait."

He hadn't finished signing and she was tearing through the tissue paper, pulling out an eight-by-ten frame. The tradition started sometime back in high school when he'd noticed she had an adorable fixation for fairy tales. Every year since, he'd searched for photos of castles and gave her a different one for her birthday. Her living room and bedroom walls were adorned with them.

She pressed a hand to her chest, studying the print. "I love it. Where is this one from?"

"Scotland." Not that he was into that sort of thing, but this one was his favorite. It was a castle partly in ruin with the lush green backdrop and mountains. Inside the castle walls, a warm yellow light illuminated. The photo was taken near dusk. Very whimsical. He saw it, thought of her, and bought the print in two clicks.

She set the frame down on a table and launched herself at him. He barely had the wherewithal to catch her and stumbled back a step before wrapping his arms around her. Any residual strain from the past week dissolved with her against him. Her honey scent and soft curves so close brought his heart aching relief.

She eased her head back and cupped his cheek. "Thank you. I love it."

Because his hands were occupied, he mouthed, *You don't say. I couldn't tell.* Smile still in her eyes, she stared at him while he tried to find a logical way not to let her go. She made no attempt either. His own grin slipped from his face as the blood roared through his veins. His damn Gabby, heart in her eyes. *I'm sorry,* he mouthed. Sorry his stupid actions nearly pried a wedge between them and that he'd been too weak to let it go.

Her tender gaze swept over his face, pausing on his mouth. "You're attracted to me."

Since she was stating the obvious and he had no idea where she was going with this conversation, he didn't respond.

More silence stretched until she—fuck him dead—slid down the length of him, rubbing their good parts together in the process and creating enough friction to stall his lungs. With her feet on the ground, their bodies aligned toe to toe, chest to chest, and her warm hand still cupping his cheek. Her thumb traced his jaw and it dawned on him he forgot to shave. He wanted to close his eyes and savor the touch, but he settled for fisting the back of her sweater.

"We should talk about it."

What changed her mind? He'd wanted to get it out in the open a week ago so they could move past it, go back to the way they were, but she'd blown him off. The ache in his chest returned with the memory because the Gabby he'd known most of his life would never have done that, proving this might be something they couldn't come back from.

"You said you didn't want to discuss the matter." He was pretty sure if they did now it would make the situation worse.

"Things are uncomfortable between us. I don't like it." She chewed on her lip and a bead of sweat broke out on his back with the restraint not to lick that spot. "I've had some time to think about things." She gently pressed her hand to his chest and stepped back, pointing to the couch.

She may as well have put the Grand Canyon between them. That's how this "talk" felt. Like more and more distance between them, and they'd hadn't even begun. But this Dr. Phil step was more like them. They'd never held back from whatever was on their minds, so he took a seat on the couch.

Popsicle strutted past Fletch, flicking her tail in the dog's face. Fletch, used to the cat's antics, lay down, one eye watching her. It took less than a blink for the cat to curl up next to the dog and both fell asleep.

Gabby sat right next to him instead of on the other side of the couch. She twisted to face him.

He sighed, bone-deep tired. *"How was your date last night?"*

She propped her head in her hand, elbow resting on the back of the couch. One shoulder shrugged as if to say *meh.* "We spent most of the night reminiscing about school. It felt more like a class reunion, party of two, than a date." Her smile was self-depreciating. "We smacked foreheads when he leaned in to kiss me."

He laughed. *"No second date in the future?"*

She shook her head, smile gone, gaze distant. He knew the moment her thoughts shifted back to them because a tiny wrinkle formed between her brows and she was hesitant to meet his eyes.

He waited her out and glanced around her living room. Her house was a cookie-cutter two-bedroom ranch which, unlike his color schemes of cool gray and green, she decorated with warm yellow and red. Her furniture was big and cozy, littered with accent pillows. She had glass figurines and vases where he had naturist art. It suited her, the house.

In Gabby fashion, she eventually looked him dead on and spoke her mind. "When did you start feeling this way about me?"

High school, not that he'd admit it to her. Back then, he'd been able to lock the emotions away and live in blessed denial. Why now the lock busted, he hadn't a clue. He shook his head, at a loss. *"I don't have any answers for you, Gabby."*

"It bothers you that you're attracted to me." Not a question. A statement.

Hell if that didn't look like hurt in her eyes. For a woman who'd stood in front of him and acknowledged his feelings, but in no way reciprocated, what right did she have to look so gutted? Unless his initial vibe was correct. She *had* snuggled up against him and pressed her face to his neck. There *had* been other more subtle signs as well. He thought he'd been delusional, reading too much into it at the time. But now, he wasn't so sure.

"Am I alone in this, Gabby?" Not the direction he'd expected the conversation to take, but if she was even halfway near the place he was hovering at, then things just got lethal.

Her gaze lowered to her hands and she seemed to be fighting for an appropriate answer. His heart all but leapt out of his chest, cracking ribs and tearing tendons along the way. If she had to think this hard, then he wasn't alone. He stopped breathing, waiting for clearance from her, but when her gaze met his, the floor dropped out.

Tears shimmered in her eyes and she drew in a ragged breath. "I'm having a hard time accepting that all of a sudden you're seeing me in front of you. I've been here all along, Flynn."

Did she seriously doubt he'd never known she was there? Didn't recognize that nearly every waking minute she was wrapped around him, entwined in all aspects of his life? So much so that untangling them would cause massive bleeding. *That* was why he'd put his desire in a box years before and stored it away. *That* was why, now, when the box got dumped onto the floor, scattering the fragmented pieces, he was fighting so damn hard not to act. She was goddamn everywhere. Work. Home. Family. Friends. In dreams. Awake. In...his...head.

And she still hadn't answered his question.

"It doesn't matter how I feel. You don't want this. Not really. You wouldn't be this upset if—"

He stood so fast her cat toppled to the floor. He hadn't noticed she'd jumped in his lap. Tufts of orange fur floated down.

Was she serious? He didn't really want her?

He froze, staring at her wide, holy hell blue eyes and fisting his hands to keep them off her. Keep himself from dragging her to the nearest flat surface and demonstrating just how much he disagreed with her assessment. Air burned through his lungs. His temples throbbed.

And screw it. She wanted answers. He'd give them to her.

Taking her elbow, he pulled her to her feet. "*My car. Now.*"

"What? Where are we—?"

He cut her off with a deadpan glare and then looked at the dog and pointed for him to stay.

Chapter 10

Gabby chewed on her lip as Flynn drove them through town, her gaze focused out the window at the passing storefronts. The rain had cleared, leaving heavy humidity and light fog. From the driver's seat, cosmic waves of frustration emanated from Flynn, making her stomach cramp harder. A thousand questions flittered through her mind, never connecting to her mouth.

All week things had been off between them. She figured talking it out would cure that, but whatever had tripped his mood wasn't abating. And she had no idea where he was taking her. He'd just ordered her to get in the car and he'd peeled away. He hadn't spared her so much as a glance since.

A few quick turns off the main street and he pulled into the elementary school lot, cutting the engine. Gaze straight ahead, his jaw ticked. His fingers fisted the wheel before finally letting go to sign. *"Room 10."*

She glanced at their old school, a two-story tower of red brick and wood, and then back to him. "I don't understand."

He shook his head, a slight movement she wouldn't have noticed if she hadn't been watching him so close. *"That's where we met. Kindergarten, room 10, right inside that building. Your father had just been transferred from Portland and you were the new kid. You had your hair in pigtails and a nervous smile painted on your face."*

Slowly, he turned to look at her, and her lungs quit working. The anger was gone from his eyes, replaced with wary fondness and a plea of understanding. His gaze skimmed over her face as if comparing the girl she used to be with the woman before him.

One corner of his mouth quirked in a half-smirk. *"We were standing by our cubbies getting our coats for recess when you first noticed me. You*

thought I was being rude, not talking to you. And when you found out I was
deaf, my dad told me you made your parents enroll you in sign language
class at the rec so you could learn how to talk to me."

He paused, affection softening his hazel eyes. *"Outside of my family, no*
one had ever done that before. Or since. They try by reading lips or using the
app communication on my phone, but no one ever went balls out like you."

Reminding herself to breathe, she swallowed hard. She couldn't believe
he remembered the first time they'd met. She had vague pieces of memory
from that time, but nothing that gelled like it had in his mind.

Her fingers tightened around the seatbelt strap across her chest. She
stared at the school, the scent of glue and chalk filling her nose as if she
were inside, then she looked at the surrounding grounds. Oak and maple
trees were breaking past their seedlings and into full spring bloom. The
lights in the building were off since it was Saturday, leaving the area quiet.

Flynn opened his door, motioning for her to get out and follow. She
trailed him around the east side of the school, breathing in damp grass
and pine as they made their way to the playground. She had no idea what
he had planned or why they were here, but she smiled being back on their
old stomping grounds.

He stopped in front of the monkey bars and gave them a once-over.
Raising his arms, he gripped the top rail and leaned into his hands. The
muscles in his shoulders and biceps strained against his black T-shirt, all
delicious hardness coiling. A slight breeze took his strawberry blond hair
from a tad disheveled to unruly.

Staring at her, his expression unreadable, he opened and closed his
mouth several times as if trying to form words. "In first grade, you were
crossing these bars and Jimmy Valez pushed you down."

She sucked in a harsh lungful of air. Whether out of self-consciousness
or too much effort, he almost never spoke. She'd heard him enough
through the years to recognize his voice, but it floored her every time. A
deep rumble mixed with odd dialect. When he did use his mouth instead
of signing, he talked like he did everything else—in leisure with careful
assimilation and thought behind it.

His throat worked a swallow. "I ran to see if you were okay. I was too
worried you were hurt to realize I'd spoken aloud. Some of the kids made
fun of me." Even now, the embarrassment tinged his cheeks and made her
chest tight. Kids were stupid, didn't know how much words could hurt. "To
this day, you and Fletch are the only ones I talk to. Not even my brothers."

Drake and Cade would never do anything to make him feel different.
Flynn was exceptionally close with both of them and, despite their banter

and joking around, there was so much love between them it closed her throat. Because she and Rachel? They barely tolerated each other as sisters, never mind as friends.

But she got what he was saying. Tears burned her eyes and she had to blink repeatedly to clear them before he misunderstood. She didn't pity him. She cared on such a deep level that when he hurt, she hurt. And he'd been hurt a lot.

He glanced heavenward, dropped his arms, and strode back toward the car. She took a moment to collect herself and followed.

They didn't speak as he drove them two blocks down the road to the high school, once again parking in the empty lot. By now, she had a clear understanding of what this little trip down memory lane was about, but she didn't stop him. She'd forgotten all about the monkey bars and the day they'd met, but he hadn't. Those things were cemented in his mind for a reason and she found herself more than interested in seeing his side of their coin.

He sighed, staring at their old high school, so similar in design to the elementary that it could've been its twin if not for the extra floor. *"You used to take notes for me in class so I didn't miss anything. Most of the teachers were conscious about facing the room so I could read lips or signed if they knew how. But you took notes, anyway."*

His gaze slid to hers and held. Intense. Determined. *"Three out of four homecoming dances and both proms, we went together. By then, everyone saw you as the sweet girl not to be touched and I was the last resort for anyone. If my brothers didn't have the same lunch period, you made sure I never ate alone. You were there, including me."* He drew in an unsteady breath and closed his eyes. *"High school was bearable because of you."*

She couldn't remember their classmates ever treating him like an outcast. Drake, Heather, and Zoe were a grade ahead of them and Cade one grade behind. Avery and Brent hadn't moved to Redwood Ridge until later. Besides their close circle, there were others. Flynn had been on the baseball team all four years. He'd had a lot of friends. Back then, he'd been tall and wiry, not filled out like the man he was today. Still, he'd gotten quite a few batted eyelashes.

The female population may overlook him a lot for being deaf, and part of that was due to Cade having been the town's playboy before settling down, but Flynn wasn't hard up. That she was aware, everyone thought he was a funny, handsome guy. Then and now. But...maybe there were instances she hadn't known about, ways in which kids had been cruel to him?

And he was making her out to be some kind of saint. She didn't always do the right thing, and if he thought those examples from high school were noble, they weren't. It had just been her, being a friend. Anyone would've done the same. His brothers, Heather, and Zoe had.

He'd obviously forgotten about all the ways he'd helped her, been there for her, too. Staying up late, cramming for biology and chemistry tests because she'd sucked at science. Or going out of his way to drive back from baseball practice before class to pick her up for school because Rachel refused to be seen with her. Or the way only he seemed to remember her allergy to roses. Countless times he'd cut off deliveries at the clinic from clients or warned her dates not to give her roses. Heck, he'd probably boycott Valentine's Day to save her buying antihistamines.

He didn't get it. He was no more replaceable in her life than she was in his. She looked at him, all hard edges and rigid spine, wanting him to understand. Her stomach knotted as she reached for his arm.

He shoved the gear into drive and tore out of the lot, their field trip apparently not through.

Over the next hour, he took her past the bowling alley, the ice cream shop, the park, and Shooters—all with a different reason for why they meant something to him. The clinic was particularly hard for him judging by the frustration in his eyes and the way he relayed how difficult the job had been while she'd been recovering from her infection.

But when he drove through the cemetery gates and wound the car slowly on the curved path, her heart dropped into her stomach. As he parked and stared at the headstones, her hands shook and a lump of grief wedged in her throat.

He got out and she followed, standing quietly by his side as he read his father's grave marker. It would be ten years this summer since he'd died. Flynn had been a senior in college when he'd passed. Of all three O'Grady boys, the loss had hit Flynn the hardest. His father had been Flynn's first champion. And Flynn had been the one to find his dad's body after a sudden heart attack.

"You remember the day he died?" Flynn didn't face her, but she could tell by his profile just standing here was bringing it all back.

"Yes." She'd heard the news from her mother moments after the ambulance had taken the body away. Word spread quickly in small towns. Gabby hadn't waited for more details, just bolted out the door and ran to Flynn's parents' house. "He'd be so proud of you."

He closed his eyes and shook his head, his laugh humorless. *"You said the same thing the day of the funeral when I wanted to quit college. Quit everything."*

She'd meant it then, too. Flynn had pushed past his handicap and into a chosen profession that most said he'd never be able to do. He got around the challenges of not using a stethoscope, incorporating other equipment and his keen observation skills instead. Even his professors couldn't find fault when he'd accurately displayed the ability to diagnose and treat animals, despite being deaf. It was exactly what his father would've wanted for him. His dad had started Animal Instincts from the ground up and left it in his three sons' capable hands.

"I wouldn't be a vet if not for you." He turned to face her. *"You listened to me talk nonsense that whole week, laid in bed with me and pretended not to see me cry, then made my ass go back to school to finish."*

"You would've done it without me."

The doubt in his eyes said otherwise. He swallowed, intently watching her face as if trying to decide something. Finally, he glanced off into the distance. *"I didn't know what was wrong with me. Grief, I suppose. But I couldn't stand all the well-wishers and mourners, couldn't stand to see my mother bawling her eyes out."* He looked at her. *"You grounded me when I was spinning out of control, wanting to chuck it all away."*

"You give me too much credit."

He shook his head, shoving his hands in his pockets as if to say he was done with this conversation. His jaw ticked a steady beat, his brows furrowed, and pure pissed-off male shone in his eyes.

She stepped into his space, crowding him. "You gave as good as you got, Flynn. For every time you think I saved you, I have a memory of you. We were there for each other because that's what friends do. They lean on each other and pick up the pieces. And I'll still be here tomorrow, the day after, and the day after that, picking up your pieces. Same as you will for me."

A thousand and one emotions filled his eyes, there and gone in a blink. He didn't move a muscle, but he was around her, inside her, taking up space and filling the dark crevices. Comforting, soothing. And for the first time, it wasn't only that. It was more. A sexual charge of lust, an ache so deep she hadn't known it existed. She wanted his lips on hers, his arms around her. Wanted to know what his skin would feel like against hers and how good it would be to have him buried inside her.

That. That was what she'd been missing from her previous relationships. Hunger. Heat. The driving need to take and be taken. A good man on the surface, in his heart, but an animal behind closed doors. They hadn't kissed, had done little more than touch, so she had no idea if this combustion would last. If either would feel anything sexual if they crossed the line.

But, damn. She wanted to find out.

Her breathing grew shallow, her face hot, her belly quivering. His eyes widened in recognition and he leaned forward, desire dilating his pupils. He hovered in the small space between them, breath mingling—only to jerk upright and take a step back. Like he'd done before. Denying them both. Rejecting her.

But this time, she understood his reasons. Valid reasons. And he was right. After everything he'd said today, all the places he'd taken her, they probably shouldn't act on their attraction. The consequences were too great.

He pressed his palms to his eyes and put more distance between them as if trying to do the right thing and powerless to proceed. A growl rumbled in his throat as he turned to face the headstone.

After several deep breaths, he squatted by his dad's grave marker and brushed the fresh grass clippings from the face. His head bowed, she imagined he was having some kind of internal talk with his father.

She gave him space and walked down a ways to Heather's grave. Drake's wife had died after a short, brutal battle with ovarian cancer. It had left them all wrecked, especially Drake, and staring at her tombstone only made her realize how short life could be. The people she loved could be taken from her at any given time. There one minute, gone the next.

"Miss you." She blew Heather a kiss and made her way back to the car, tears burning her eyes. By the time Flynn returned to the driver's seat, she had herself under control.

She thought he'd take her home, but instead, he pulled up to his house and got out. Maybe after all the memories he'd forgotten Fletch was still at her place. But the minute he unlocked the door and went to stand in the middle of the living room floor, she knew he wasn't done.

She closed the door and leaned against it, letting it hold her upright. Flynn's tormented, desperate gaze found hers from across the room and exhaustion claimed her. Best and worst birthday ever. She needed cake. And wine.

She preferred an orgasm, but that was looking as likely as Ryan Gosling sweeping into town and claiming his undying love.

Flynn glanced at the fireplace. *"You and Zoe helped me decorate the house after the build was complete."*

She nodded. "We helped Cade with his house, too. What's your point?"

He ran a hand through his hair. *"My point is, even in my home, you're here. You're on the couch, watching movies. In the kitchen, whipping up margaritas for the hell of it. In pictures on the wall and accent pillows I can't stand, but refuse to get rid of because you gave them to me."*

Someone needed to snap them out of this circle, so she brought out the funny, too tired to do any more. "I'll take the pillows back."

"It's not about the pillows!"

"You just said it was." She never considered herself a pyro, but this playing with fire thing had its merits.

He bared his teeth, fists clenched in front of him as if wishing her throat was in them. Veins protruded from his arms. His biceps strained against his shirt.

Her panties went damp. "I'll make daiquiris instead next time since margaritas bother you so much."

On a dime, he froze. Glared at her. Swiped a hand down his face and... laughed. *"Christ, Gabby. This isn't funny."*

"It's a little funny. And you laughed." Strained as it may have been.

He sat on the arm of the couch, legs stretched out before him and shoulders sagging. He clasped his hands in front of him and stared at the floor. That was the real reason he'd brought her here, to point out the exact spot where things had changed for them. She was positive.

"You forgot something." She took a step closer and then another. His eyes narrowed in warning, but she kept going until she stood between his legs, his face level with hers. "You forgot about this area of the floor where we danced and—"

"Gabby," he growled.

And oh, her girly parts cried. "I understand why you're hesitant, why you're fighting whatever this is between us. Everywhere we went today, everything you said, it makes sense. I get it. But did it ever occur to you we built this up in our heads? What if we kiss and don't like it? What if we have sex and it sucks?"

He stared at her deadpan while his chest rose and fell so fast it belied his expression. His lids grew heavy, eyes glazing with lust. Lips parted, he brought his hands up to her waist. Squeezed. Electricity zinged through her bloodstream. He sucked in a harsh breath like he'd felt it, too.

"And what if it doesn't suck?" He stared at her, a question in his eyes, almost like a last hope. As if him speaking aloud was supposed to turn her off even if the words weren't meant to.

Torn, she studied him. If they kissed and nothing was there, problem solved. But, if there was a spark, if the chemistry went beyond what-if, then...

He splayed his fingers, hands moving from her waist to her lower back and nudging her forward. Her pulse tripped, shooting up somewhere in the vicinity of a spastic, sugar-induced child. Her nipples pebbled behind her bra just at the mere brush of his hard chest against her sweater.

Heat. So. Much. Heat.

Aroused male and the scent of his soap surrounded her, had her head spinning. She gripped his shoulders, his...firm...shoulders, then slid her hands around the back of his neck, fingertips weaving into the strands at his nape. His hands jerked on her back, dipped lower, nearly grabbing her backside.

"Decide," he said, gaze focused on her mouth as if he'd already made up his mind. A lazy blink and then his eyes lifted, met hers. A sea of green and brown enclosed in long, pale lashes. A travesty to the female species, those eyes. Beautiful, expressive, they drew her into his vortex. "I'm losing it, Gabby." His voice, a low, coarse rumble, caused a tremor to tear through her body. "Decide."

A whimper—hers—and then the miniscule centimeters between them vanished.

Chapter 11

Flynn fisted the back of Gabby's sweater as she leaned in, hovering a whisper from his lips. He'd told her to decide because he didn't know what else to do to fend off this desire anymore, and it seemed she was all systems go. He'd taken her throughout town, not only showing her but telling her all they had to lose by crossing the line.

And here she stood in his arms, smelling like honey and sweet torment, throwing the past twenty-five years of friendship out the window.

Her soft, full lips brushed his and her eyes drifted closed on a sigh. He felt the rush of hot breath all the way to his groin and back. His heart beat a staccato rhythm, his body tensed between *hell, yes* and *don't do this*.

She barely touched him, her actions tentative and hesitant as he fought for some kind of guidance she was just as affected. Grazing her lips back and forth across his, she increased the pressure from ghosting to a caress and parted her lips.

And there was his sign. He tilted his head, sealing his mouth over hers, going deeper, seeking more. He darted his tongue past her lips, stroked his with hers...and that was lights out.

Her fingers clenched the short hairs at his nape, dragging him closer than the holy ghost and crushing her curves against him. She settled between his thighs, arching into him, cutting off his blood supply on everything south of his navel. He slid his hand under her sweater to the soft, warm skin of her back and higher until he drove his fingers into her hair, holding her to him.

It wasn't enough. Raw, primal need coursed through him. Blinding. Fierce. He'd never known anything like it in his life. He grabbed the back of her thigh, lifting it to wrap her leg around his hips. She ground against him. He thrust up in response, seizing her hip in his hand to encourage more.

The kiss went from hot to scalding to he-required-life-support. She sucked his tongue into her mouth, nipped it, and stroked to ease the slight twinge of pain. Holy hell. He tilted his head the other way to draw in a quick breath, only dive right back in.

Her hands gripped his shoulders and he went flying. His back met the couch cushions and every...single...curve of her aligned perfectly with his. Their kiss never broke, but his sanity did. Her weight settled on his chest, between his legs. The strands of her hair teased his cheeks as she ran her fingers down his sides.

His hands went everywhere at once. Her hair, her jaw, her waist. Finally, he settled on her hips to hold her as he rocked against her.

A rumble battered his ribs. Whether the groan was his or hers, he hadn't a clue. And she'd actually questioned whether they would like kissing each other. Had been worried they might...what word had she used? Sucked? He almost laughed, but that would require breaking apart for air.

Doubt niggled in his brain. This was too good, the need too intense. Christ.

He threw his head back, severing the connection, heaving in air. Shit. She'd kissed him blind. Wait. He opened his eyes, gaze landing on the ceiling.

He'd closed his eyes. Lost in her, he'd shut his eyes and succumbed. He'd never done that before. Always, *always* his focus stayed on his partner, hyperaware of their cues. But...he was flat on his back on the couch, Gabby sprawled over him, her hair a curtain around them, his fingers kneading her hips and hers tangled in his shirt. And he had almost no recollection of how they'd wound up this way.

Panic clutched his chest. He whipped his gaze to hers, hoping like hell he hadn't pushed too hard. He couldn't formulate an errant thought to save his life at the moment.

Her eyes were dilated to twilight and beginning to refocus. Her lips were red, swollen from his mouth, and her cheeks had stubble burn from his jaw. Her chest heaved in the same desperate attempt as his to bring in oxygen.

They stared at each other a suspended beat, until a wrinkle formed between her brows and her gaze dipped to her hands bunching his shirt. She unclenched her fingers and sat up as if still in a daze. A frisson of regret hit her eyes, pushing away the shock. Or maybe embarrassment? He lay frozen under her, having the sinking suspicion his world just began and ended right here in his living room.

Slowly, she scrambled off his lap and pressed her fingers to her lips. Her gaze darted around the room and settled on the floor. "Can you take me home?"

His heart pounded for an entirely different reason than lust. *"Gabby..."*

"Please?"

He got to his feet and stood in front of her, his hands itching to pull her to him and fix this somehow, erase the bewildered, tormented expression on her face. She wrapped her arms around her middle like she was trying to hold herself together.

At a loss, he nodded and pulled his keys from his pocket. She was out the door and in the passenger seat before he'd even made it to the other side of the room. Anxiety ripped through his gut as he climbed in the car and started the engine. His brain was functioning just enough to drive on autopilot to her house and park.

She reached for the handle and he stopped her with his hand on her arm. Except he didn't know what to do from there, what to say. She turned to him, gaze roaming his features. He had no clue what she saw because a numb state of shock was the only thing registering.

Her shoulders slumped like he'd disappointed her. "For the record, I'm not upset you developed feelings for me." She drew a ragged breath and his heart turned over behind his ribs. "What bothers me is that you don't want those feelings."

No kidding. Didn't she get it? After everything he'd said, all the places they'd gone today, how could she not be as fucking freaked out about losing him as he was about her? Not be worried about disrupting the natural order of *both* their lives?

"That's the thing that can destroy us, Flynn. Not the attraction or acting on it. We'd bounce back if it fizzled out or didn't work. We always do." He wasn't so sure, and her expression said the same, but her eyes shimmered, so he didn't respond. "But you not wanting to feel things for me... You, of all people, not wanting to be with me, even though the potential for something great is there? I can't recover from that."

Christ. He'd never thought of it that way. Was that really how she viewed things?

"You keep getting close, almost make a move, and then you..."

He so did not want her to finish that sentence. He thought he'd been an idiot for crossing the line, but somehow his good intentions to rectify that had twisted in her mind and he'd hurt her.

She wiped her tears before they could make much progress. "Every time, you back off like you regret it." She bit her lip. "Regret me."

Fuck, no. *"Gabby..."*

"Even after that kiss, and you know I was into it, you retracted."

That's not how he remembered it. He'd resurfaced for air to check on her... His chest cracked wide open and he cupped her face, desperate to make her understand. Tears trailed down her cheeks. He swiped them with his thumbs, and because he didn't want to let her go, he used his voice. "I wasn't rejecting you. I don't regret you. But you know what's at stake. I tried to show you, to tell you today. You are everything to me." He paused, at a loss. "I don't know what to do here."

She swallowed and wrapped her fingers around his wrists, gently removing his hands. "When you figure it out, let me know." She drew a deep breath. "You asked me to decide. I have. Don't toy with me unless you're all in." She turned toward the door. "I'll send Fletch out to the car."

And then she was gone.

* * * *

Gabby had needed girl power in the worst way, so after Flynn had dropped her off, she'd called in reinforcements. Zoe had gotten Gayle to watch her mom and had shown up with margarita mix. Hailey was with Cade, so Avery had come with brownies. Thank God.

Two drinks in, Gabby leaned back on the couch. "Men suck."

From next to her, Zoe lifted her margarita in a mock toast. "Got that right."

Gabby shifted to look at her, the tequila making her lose focus for a beat. She was nearing tipsy, but not there yet. Since Zoe and Avery had to drive home, they were taking it easy. "You don't have any dating prospects, I thought."

Snorting, Zoe ran her hand through her bright orange hair. She'd changed it again this week. "Ergo, their suckiness."

Avery sighed, shaking her head, and curled her legs under her in the chair across from them. "You know, not all men suck."

"Ha." Gabby swallowed a mouthful of frozen concoction and pressed a hand to the icy headache in her temple. "Says the happily engaged woman who's getting some nightly."

A contented, dreamy expression crossed Avery's face. "Yeah." She sobered and waved her hand. "I don't understand. You and Flynn talked, right?"

"Maybe that's the issue." Zoe grinned. "Too much talk, not enough action."

Gabby agreed. Yet... "We're not like other people. We can't be a one-night stand, and a relationship could ruin things. We always talk to each other. It was necessary to discuss...things."

"True, dat." Zoe set her glass down. "But I don't get it. I mean, sure, Flynn's not as alpha as Drake or flirty as Cade, but it's not as if he doesn't have game. Why is he keeping it zipped? You're a cutie. He's a hottie. Why not release a little stress? Go for it?"

Gabby thought back to Flynn's field trip today. Everything he'd said made sense. She couldn't put up a decent argument for his hesitation. Half of what he'd shown her she hadn't a clue he'd felt that strongly about until he'd put it right in her face. There was a lot at stake.

She'd also meant what she'd said, too. If they went for it and things didn't work out, they could get past it. She hoped, anyway. But she couldn't live in the constant what-if state. If he decided not to take the step, then they'd go back to what they were. It might be awkward for a while, but so be it.

The problem was, she feared Flynn was denying them both something that could wind up being really great just for the sake of their friendship, something that had always been there. He wasn't seeing the potential, just one possible outcome.

Either way, she'd promised him he wouldn't lose her. She didn't know what else to do. The ball was in his court. If he could act on their attraction, yay. If he couldn't, she'd bend over backward to put them right back in their normal routine.

Avery cleared her throat. "How long do you think he's felt differently about you? I've never detected tension from either of you, not until lately."

"Me, either," Zoe said. "Honestly, I'm kind of shocked you guys have taken this long to notice each other. You already act like you're together, minus the sex and fighting." She leaned forward as if having an ah-ha moment. "That's the damnedest thing about you two. You never fight."

Rarely. Maybe that's what was eating her raw. The fact they were in disagreement. She rubbed her forehead. "You want the truth? Part of me thinks if it took him this long to feel something beyond friendship, maybe it's just a flash physical reaction and not meant to be."

Avery narrowed her eyes.

"What?"

"You haven't exactly jumped his bones before now either." Avery shrugged. "Just saying, don't put it all on him. This isn't easy for him."

Gabby's shoulders slumped. "I know. You're right."

Zoe picked up her glass and stared into it. "I think I need to drink the Flabby Kool-Aid."

Gabby blinked, looked at Avery, and back to Zoe. Yeah, um....no. She was still confused. "What? And no more tequila for you."

Zoe grinned. "Flabby. Your couple name. Combining Flynn and Gabby."

Avery threw her head back and laughed.

"That's so wrong. I'm cutting you off." Gabby took Zoe's glass and set it aside. "And what do you mean by *our Kool-Aid*?"

Zoe shrugged. "It would be nice not to fight with the oldest O'Grady. That's what I mean. I should drink your Kool-Aid. Live in harmony."

Gabby opened her mouth and quickly shut it again. She looked to Avery for assistance, but got none. Avery shrugged, looking this side of concerned.

"You and Drake don't fight." Okay, maybe a little bickering that led to a mutual...tolerance. But they didn't go at each other's throats. In Gabby's opinion, the two of them seemed to be flailing since Heather's death, trying to figure out where they fit in one another's lives.

Zoe closed her eyes and breathed a laugh without mirth. "Right." She shook her head. "Where's Brent? If we're having a hate men party, he should be here."

Gabby shared a *ruh-roh* expression with Avery and let Zoe's comment drop. "I'm mad at Brent."

"Do tell." Zoe rubbed her hands together. "What did gay Batman do?"

Because she was annoyed and not nearly drunk enough, Gabby downed another mouthful of margarita. "I think he's in cahoots with the Battleaxes. They've set their sights on me and Flynn."

"Oh," Zoe said, stretching the word out to five syllables. "Sucks to be you." She patted Gabby's knee and then retracted her hand as if she might catch the Battleaxes' attention by touching her.

Avery had remained unusually silent, watching the interaction. Gabby chewed on her lip. "Thoughts, Avery?"

After eyeing each of them, Avery set her elbow on her knee and her chin in her hand. "You're not going to like it, but I don't think it's a bad thing. Face it, if they weren't spot on, you wouldn't be upset. There's obviously something between you and Flynn. They just shoved you along. The kiss *was* good, right?"

"No, it wasn't good." Gabby slumped back against the couch, her lips still tingling, her body humming. "It was panty-melting, moan-out-loud, holy-cow great." She pouted. "I might be underselling it."

Zoe laughed. "I'd kill to have my panties melted."

Gabby turned her head. "You're the town's badass. Every chick wants to be you and every guy wants to do you." It had been that way since high school. Zoe had always been confident and not afraid of anything. Even over the past couple years when her wattage had dimmed, Zoe was still someone Gabby aspired to be. "Go find someone to melt your panties. It should take you five seconds, tops."

"Pfft. Who has time?" Zoe glanced at her phone. "Speaking of, I gotta go. Gayle said she could only watch Mama for a few hours."

Gabby didn't know how Zoe handled working full time, taking care of her late-stage dementia-diagnosed mother, and still have time to work on her art. "Thanks for coming and bringing tequila."

"Happy birthday, babe." Zoe hugged her and took off.

Gabby eyed Avery after the door closed. "You're going to ditch me, too, aren't you?"

"Yep. Going to go home and have sex with my future husband." Avery slapped her thighs and stood.

"Show off."

Avery laughed. "You know the Battleaxes screwed with Cade and I to get us together." A statement, not a question, because everyone knew that. There was a Redwood Ridge Pinterest board dedicated to them. "Might not be a bad thing to let them, you know, prod things along."

Gabby tilted her head. "Should I call them? Tell them you need more help with wedding plans?"

Avery's eyes narrowed to slits as she seemed to fight a grin. "I will remove you as maid of honor."

"Brent would make a better MOH, anyway."

Bending down and pulling Gabby into a hug, Avery squeezed. "Hang in there. It'll work out."

"Love you. Have fabulous sex so I can live vicariously."

After Avery left, Gabby flopped back on the couch and stretched her arms overhead. Popsicle hopped up next to her and butted Gabby's breast. She eyed the cat. "At least my boobs are getting some action tonight. You're a little hairy for me, though. And the wrong species."

Meow.

"You're totally right. And we're not lesbians." She pulled the cat in, nuzzling her orange fur. "You were a little slut today, by the way. Cuddling up to Fletch, winding around Flynn's legs. You should play hard to get."

Meow. Purr.

"Yeah, that's not working for me either. I want to climb him like a scratching post, too." She sighed. "How about we eat all the brownies and watch *Sex and the City* reruns instead?"

Meow.

Chapter 12

By Friday, Gabby was almost convinced absolutely nothing romantic had happened between her and Flynn. Apparently having made his decision to keep them in the friend zone, he'd returned to an almost normal routine, leaving her not only a little disappointed, but frustrated, too.

They'd had two clinic days this week and three on the road for home visits. Everything had been in sync. Other than catching him watching her every so often, they'd talked as usual and had worked well together. Same old, same old. She'd promised him nothing would change between them, no matter what. She'd given him a choice, and he'd made his, if his behavior was any indication.

So why was her stomach in a perpetual state of spin-cycle and why was there this strange hollow ache behind her ribs? She'd gotten what she'd asked of him. She couldn't have it both ways.

Focusing on the job, she waited for Flynn to be done assessing a brown gelding before jumping into her part of the exam. Squatting, he ran his hands over the horse's abdomen, careful not to get too close to the rear of the animal and spook it. Flynn's dark blue scrubs stretched over the wide expanse of his back, his biceps bulging as he shifted. And holy hotness, his ass was a thing of fantasies. Especially when he was bent over, causing the material of his pants to become more snug, leaving nothing to the imagination.

She shook her head. He'd always been an attractive guy. Even as a boy, he'd been cute, but it wasn't until recently she'd noticed him as a...man. Someone other than her friend. Ever since their kiss, it had been hard to separate the two. Every time they were near each other, she couldn't see the Flynn she'd always known.

Instead, it was like looking at an entirely new person. A bombardment of sensory overload. Wide shoulders. Narrow waist. Hard muscles. Warm, tan skin. The scent of outdoors and soap. Full lips. The light five o'clock shadow on his jaw. Intense, observant hazel eyes. Large hands. Sexy bedhead hair.

God. Her face was hot.

She drew a slow breath when he reached behind him, holding out his hand in a silent request for an instrument. Good thing she knew him so well, had worked with him so long, or she wouldn't have a clue what he was asking for. She passed him the ryding tester, and he ran his fingers down the gelding's leg, holding the foot between his knees as he used the stainless steel jaw clamp to gauge the diagnostic pressure of the hoof.

Flynn shook his head and turned to look at her over his shoulder. A frown marred his brow, his mouth tight. Restrained agitation darkened his eyes. She understood without him signing a word. This horse, like the others, had not been receiving the care it needed. Though not in the range of full-out neglect, they were all slightly malnourished.

Flynn sighed and stood. *"Let's get fecal samples on all of them. Blood work."* He rubbed the back of his neck. *"Hold off on immunizations until we get those results."*

She nodded and got her supplies. After she finished drawing blood and obtained the samples, she labeled them and packed up the bag. She passed him hand sanitizer, waited for him to finish using it, then applied some herself.

"Ready to talk to the owners?"

He gazed heavenward and rolled his shoulders. *"Yeah."*

They were at a new client farm at the base of the Coast Range, deeply isolated and way north of town. A lot of their patients were farms like this one, and though the remoteness and seclusion wasn't new, her uneasiness was. A good portion of their clientele had been with the clinic for years. Perhaps she was just being paranoid.

Almost from the second they'd stepped out of the SUV, a niggling sense of restlessness had crept up her spine, making her impatient to leave. The main house was a tiny ranch and the grounds had two barns. Both were in need of repairs, but that wasn't uncommon being this close to the coast. Saltwater, humidity, and harsh winters, coupled with very wet springs, could do damage quickly to the exterior buildings.

One of the barns housed six horses, the other four goats and two cows. There were also two border collies and four cats on the premises. Though not the largest of their clients, a lot of time would be needed with the farm since they were new. Today, she and Flynn had assessed and examined one barn and the cats. Monday they were coming back for the other barn and the dogs.

Tucked way back on the property, there was another, much smaller structure which had probably been a large chicken coop at one point. The roof was near gone and the boards rotted through in several areas. At least, what she could see of it. The owners hadn't allowed them back there, and it wasn't necessary since there were no animals to treat on that side of the property.

Jose met them at the car. A brick wall of a man in his late twenties, he had two sleeves of tattoos and an unpleasant odor of stale tobacco. Though she'd seen other guys milling about, Jose was the only person they'd had contact with.

Gabby opened the back hatch of the SUV and set her bag inside. Before closing the door, she grabbed the satellite phone, just in case. Cell signal was nil in this area and she didn't know how Jose would react to Flynn's discussion. It made her feel better to have a lifeline.

She met Flynn and Jose by the hood, and when Flynn stepped closer to her, putting her slightly behind him, her anxiety upped ten notches knowing Flynn was concerned, too.

Maybe engaging in some friendly chatter first might ease the tension. She forced a smile. "How long have you owned the farm? It's a beautiful location."

Which was true. Situated between the rocky coastline and the mountain base, the air was rich with pine and saltwater. Greens and blues and grays collided for an array of color. Land in this area wasn't very fertile, so most farms were more like working equestrian ranches. Some raised goats for milk. One of the botanical shops in Redwood Ridge bought goats milk for making soaps and lotions.

"I inherited it from my grandfather a few months ago." Jose ran a hand over his buzzed head. "Haven't been up here in years. I'm going to be selling the livestock and tearing down the barns. That's why I called you guys to check out the animals so I can price them."

She nodded and shared a mutual should-we-trust-this-guy look with Flynn. If Jose was on the level, it explained why the animals were malnourished as he wouldn't know how to care for them.

Flynn, wasting no time, signed his concerns about neglect and the tests he planned to run. Gabby interpreted for him so Jose could follow along. Though the man's jaw hardened and his eyes narrowed, he did little more than nod when Flynn was finished.

Gabby swallowed. "We'll be back Monday for the other animals and we can discuss your options then."

Flynn took her elbow and walked her to the driver's door, waiting until she was inside before rounding the SUV and climbing in. Jose stood where he was, arms crossed, stance wide, while she backed out of the driveway, made a Y-turn, and headed for the road.

After a couple miles, Flynn turned in his seat to face her. *"I don't want you to go anywhere on those grounds alone while we have those people as clients. Stay with me at all times."*

Because driving the curvy, winding road down the mountain required her full attention, she nodded. Flynn wasn't the bossy, domineering type. His request was only because he was worried and not intended to be a controlling maneuver. Besides, Jose gave her the creeps. Staying near Flynn sounded just fine by her.

Back at the clinic, she unloaded the labs and samples, set them up for testing, and checked on their kennel animals before heading into Flynn's office to say goodbye. Everyone else had gone home for the day.

From behind his desk, he glanced up from his laptop. *"What are you up to tonight? Want to grab a pizza?"*

She chewed her lip, hesitating, then decided if they were going to keep things normal, she had to be honest. "I have a date with Mike Miller." He was one of the guys who'd asked her out at the kissing booth. He had been four years ahead of her in school and she didn't know much about him.

Flynn stared at her, his expression unreadable, then blinked as if snapping to. His eyes narrowed as his gaze wandered off, probably trying to place Mike's name with a face. *"The guy from the arcade?"*

She nodded. "We're going to the seafood restaurant down the bluff."

His eyebrow quirked as if to say, *you hate seafood.* Which she did, but there would be something on the menu she could eat, surely. Mike had picked the place.

Flynn rubbed his jaw. *"Rain check? Tomorrow?"*

Her sister had set her up on a blind date for tomorrow. Normally, Gabby hated blind dates and didn't agree to them, but Rachel had never done anything nice when it came to things like that, so Gabby had said yes. She was still a little suspicious who the guy was or why Rachel had arranged the meet in the first place, then she felt guilty for the thought. Maybe her sister was just trying to be kind.

"I have plans tomorrow, too." His eyebrows drew together like she'd hurt him, and since they were still fighting for normal, she smiled to show him she wasn't blowing him off. "What about a hike on Sunday? You and me, Cyprus Trail?" That hiking path had always been their favorite. It was a little off the tourist radar and had a great view of both the Pacific Ocean and the Klamath Mountains.

His jaw ticked as he stared at the desk between them, and she wondered what he was thinking. His body was tense, poised on the chair as if ready to pounce, yet distance and indecision registered in his eyes. He propped his elbows on the desk and pressed his palms to his eye sockets.

And she knew. He wasn't as okay as he'd appeared, as he'd made her believe. Even as worry ate at her stomach lining, the urge to climb over his desk and crawl in his lap was fierce. The friend in her wanted to soothe the tension, make everything all right. The woman in her wanted him. Naked. On top of her. Under her. Inside her.

Shaking, she ran her fingers through her ponytail and closed her eyes. No matter how hard she tried, she couldn't ever remember desiring someone so much. Consuming and almost violent in its need. Rattled, she opened her eyes, seeking the one person who always grounded her, only to find his gaze already on her and just as unnerved.

His hands fisted on the desk as if making a conscious effort to restrain himself from using them to talk. Or touch her. He didn't seem to be breathing, and for every second that passed, his gaze grew more intense, harder, until he resembled something more animalistic than man.

Holy hotness.

Slowly, he rose from his chair. *"This isn't working."*

No kidding. For clarification, she asked, "You mean the stellar job we're doing of ignoring the elephant in the room? I agree."

He swallowed, and it looked like the act took considerable effort. Reclaiming his seat, he kept his gaze locked to hers and white-knuckled the chair arms.

Okay, last straw. She wasn't aggressive by nature and she'd always considered herself pretty old-fashioned, but traditional wasn't cutting it. Out of some twisted sense of moral code, he thought he was protecting her and their friendship by not acting, but all he was doing was killing himself, one cold shower at a time. His pain was her pain. And she couldn't stand him beating himself up anymore.

Taking her time, she made her way around the desk, his gaze tracking her every step. She set her hands on his forearms to prevent him from moving and straddled his lap. He sucked in a harsh gale through his nose. Hope and interest and a little oh-shit rounded his eyes. The muscles in his forearms coiled under her palms. Her breasts grew heavy with desire, the apex between her thighs achy. His scent of outdoors and soap floated around her, the most unbearable turn-on.

Every instinct was telling her to lean in and kiss him, but she kept her face far enough from his so he could read her lips. What she had to say was more important. "You feel that, Flynn? Your heart pounding and that tightening in your gut? Me, too. That's basic need. Nature trying to tell us something."

His gaze shifted from her mouth to her eyes and back. His lips parted as if to speak, but only a shallow, desperate pant emerged. The back of his head hit the chair.

"I'm going to go on my date tonight, and the one tomorrow night because it would be rude to cancel on such short notice." He tensed beneath her and she smiled. Yeah, he didn't like that. "I'll be thinking about you the entire time. On Sunday, you and me will go to Cyprus Trail to go hiking. Our first date."

His ragged breath caressed her cheek, hazel eyes softening. His gaze swept over her face as if trying to take in each aspect of her expression, gauge her seriousness or search for a secret motive.

"We'll take it slow, ease into this new change between us. No pressure. Just us, like always, minus the denial." His chest rose and fell, and she imagined his lungs were fighting for oxygen. His eyebrows slammed together, gaze pleading, like she'd handed him everything and stripped him to nothing. "We deserve the chance to be together, to see where it can go. You will not lose me."

He closed his eyes and offered a slight shake of his head as if unable to deal with the struggle anymore. When he opened his eyes, he searched her gaze, and she knew he was looking for any sense of reservation. His last-ditch attempt to not upend their lives.

"You will not lose me," she repeated, and hoped to hell she was right.

His arms broke free of her hold and he reached up to cup her cheeks. His thumbs traced her jaw as he sighed. Gently, he pulled her in to kiss her forehead and eased her away again. He nodded and dropped his hands to her thighs.

"I don't want to tell anyone right away. I'd rather we keep it just between us until we know what we want."

His expression said he knew exactly what he wanted, and it involved her and him and no clothes. "*It's impossible to keep a secret in this town. You know that.*"

True. "If we go out and around together, most people won't think anything of it. We're together a lot. But I'd like to keep the public displays and actual romance quiet at first."

He ran a strand of her hair between his fingers before answering. "*Why?*"

"It'll be harder to go back to normal if it doesn't work out. It'll put a lot of pressure on us, too."

A deep breath, and then, *"Okay. Whatever you want."*

She grinned.

His eyes narrowed. *"Within reason,"* he amended.

"There's just one more thing." She bit her lip, and he groaned. "No sex. Not right away. Hold on," she said when his expression dialed to *hell no.* "If we jump right into something physical, we won't acclimate properly as we go from friends to more. I want us to have the best shot."

She'd thought about this a lot over the past week, and this was a hard limit. They'd known each other for so long there was very little they didn't know about one another. Except how to date. They needed an adjustment period, no matter how badly she wanted him naked.

He traced her eyebrow with his finger, ran it over her temple and down her cheek. His gaze followed the path, his expression contemplative. *"Be sure, Gabby. We're about to screw up everything."*

Her heart swelled. He still didn't see the potential, just the possible fallout. But he would. She'd show him they could do this. And that they should try. Years of insecurity had built up inside him because of his disability. His romantic entanglements hadn't helped in that regard. She'd seen it countless times until it was as if Flynn had resigned himself to a few physical releases and had stopped hoping for more.

She didn't know if they were compatible, if anything would come from attempting a romance with him, but they owed it to themselves to give it a shot.

"I'm sure."

Chapter 13

On Sunday morning, Flynn opened his front door to Drake standing on his porch, holding two styrofoam cups of coffee. Big Brother raised his eyebrows when Flynn hesitated.

"Sorry." He pushed open the screen to let him in. *"Everything okay?"* Drake hadn't popped over for a visit since... Hell. Since Heather died. Cade's fiancée, Avery, had been able to get him out and about more, but Drake was obviously still clinging to isolation.

Drake handed him one of the cups. "You tell me."

Damn. If his big brother suspected something was wrong, Flynn was screwed. He sighed and jutted his chin toward the kitchen. They walked out onto the back deck and collapsed into Adirondack chairs.

Flynn sipped his coffee and stared out at the yard. A thin riverbed wove through the thick copse of trees, glittering in the sunlight. The scent of pine and damp grass mingled with late spring rain that had fallen last night. The temperature was mild, perfect for a hike with Gabby soon.

The reminder had him closing his eyes and running a hand through his hair.

Drake tapped his arm to get his attention. "What's going on? You've been off all week."

Gabby had said she'd wanted to keep things quiet, but Flynn figured Drake didn't count. He'd always been able to talk to his brothers about most anything, and it wasn't like Drake was going to post this conversation to Facebook. He needed to talk about it. What he'd been doing sure wasn't working to settle his conscience.

He set his cup aside and faced the yard again. *"I kissed Gabby."* After a few beats, he looked at his brother and frowned when nothing but white teeth flashed him through Drake's grin. *"What in the hell are you smiling about?"*

Drake shrugged. "About time, man."

Flynn's heart started to pound and he had no clue if it was from excitement or anger. *"What does that mean?"* Drake owned a third of their clinic. At the very least, he should be concerned about a disruption in The Force.

Drake put his cup down by his feet to sign and speak simultaneously as if what he was going to say would come straight from the Obi-Wan handbook. "It means you've been joined at the hip since kindergarten and have been fending off your attraction to her since you realized she had breasts."

Screw it all to hell. Flynn sucked in a humid breath. Was he made of transparent glass? He shook his head in answer because it was all he had as a response.

Drake merely lifted his brows, shit-eating grin still in place. Four years since Heather had died, and Flynn missed his brother's smile enough to concede. A little.

"Don't say Gabby and breasts in the same sentence."

Drake laughed. "Okay. Should we discuss her baby blues or her long legs or her...?"

Flynn growled.

"Right. Breasts, then. She has them."

Flynn gave him the best shut-it-or-die expression he had in reserve as images of Gabby's curves floated before his mind. Not. Helping.

"What did Gabby think of the kiss?"

Flynn ran a hand down his face. *"She wants to...date."*

"And you don't?" When Flynn didn't respond, Drake dipped his chin. "Why? Because you're best friends and seeing her naked might unravel that bond?"

Hell squared. He closed his eyes, but...nope. Visions of Gabby underneath him in nothing but skin bombarded his brain. The breath stalled in his lungs. When he opened his eyes, Drake's wry expression indicated he was mocking him.

"Did it ever occur to you she's the best person for you? No games, no doubts about whether she can hack being with a deaf guy?"

Flynn stilled, part out of shock Drake picked up on his lifelong insecurity, and partly because...no. He hadn't thought of that. He'd been so wrapped up in everything that could go wrong he hadn't seen much else. To give his hands something to do besides shake, he picked up his coffee and took a sip.

Drake stood. "I'm out. Give the dating thing a whirl." He stepped to the patio door and turned. "Breasts." With that parting shot and a told-you-so smile, Drake left.

Flynn slumped and checked his watch, his knee bouncing in restless energy. Gabby had picked the best "first date" for them in going on a hike. They wouldn't have to hang around wondering what in the hell to do and he wouldn't have to question how close to sit to her or whether it was okay to hold her hand. They'd be in constant motion.

He leaned his head back. Gabby may be his best friend and he may have known her for years, but he didn't know how to date. He'd had a couple girlfriends in high school and college, but nothing lasting. The past few years had amounted to hookups on occasion. Namely, how was he supposed to date someone he knew everything about?

Shaking his head, he went inside. Grabbing a backpack, he shoved a few water bottles and granola bars inside along with a couple treats for Fletch, and then whistled for the dog. Gabby had the satellite phone and tranquilizer gun with their vet supplies in case they encountered wildlife. She'd be bringing it as usual. He checked to make sure a first-aid kit was in the side pouch as the dog strode in from the bedroom.

"Hike?"

The dog tilted his head as if to say *meh.*

"Go see Gabby?"

Fletch danced in circles.

"You're predictable."

Gabby had wanted to meet at the trail, so he headed directly there. The small lot was empty when he arrived. This early on a Sunday, most people were still asleep or church-going. At least he and Gabby would have some time alone. He got out and leaned against the trunk to wait, Fletch at his heels.

Was he supposed to kiss her hello? Hug her? He thought back to their usual encounters, but that didn't help. Nothing felt normal about today now that they'd put a label on things. Like throwing natural and twenty years out the window.

She pulled in a few moments later and exited her car. He smiled at her leggings and too-big Oregon State sweatshirt. One she'd stolen from him last year. It went past her knees. She had her hair up in a high ponytail and not a stitch of makeup. Now *there* was his Gabby, not the dolled-up version from the Spring Fling.

He scratched his jaw. "*Tell me again why I couldn't pick you up.*" Seemed stupid when they lived less than a mile from each other.

"Because I always drive myself on a first date. It's my back-up plan in case things don't work out or I need to escape quickly." Her mischievous grin hit him square in the solar plexus. She gave adorable new meaning.

He sighed, feigning disinterest. *"And you think you'll need escape from me?"*

She played coy and shrugged, then turned to greet the dog. Leading Fletch to a patch of grass, she knelt and scratched his ears. In seconds, they were rolling on the grass, playing. Sunlight hit her caramel hair and face, bathing her in soft hues and illuminating her eyes from navy to cerulean. Fletch pinned her and she laughed.

Flynn rubbed the ache in his chest, unable to look away.

When she made her way back over to him, he struggled for something to say other than she'd just leveled him. Again. *"How were your dates this weekend?"* Well, hell. Not that.

Her lips twisted. "Mike only speaks in third person. Yeah," she said at Flynn's shock. "He invited me to go to third base with the offer of a home run back at his apartment. Which is above his parents' garage."

Was he an asshole for being relieved? He pressed his lips together to avoid laughing and failed. *"What about the other guy? Saturday night?"*

The smile left her face in point three seconds. "That was a blind date courtesy of my sister. He was seventy years old."

Flynn straightened and crossed his arms. What in the hell was wrong with Rachel?

Gabby shook her head. "The guy was so embarrassed until I told him I wanted to meet because I had a lot of friends his age. I set him up with a few gals from the senior center. God, Flynn. I felt terrible she did that. We had dinner and a nice chat. I didn't want to just walk out, you know?"

Flynn ground his molars. *"I hope you chewed her out."*

"Oh, I so did. And then I told Mom."

He laughed. *"Good girl. Can I be honest and say I'm glad neither worked out?"*

Her expression softened into *aw, shucks.* "You can totally say that."

They needed to get moving or he was going to pull her into his backseat and kiss her senseless. He glanced around and jerked his chin, indicating the trail. *"You ready?"*

She held out her hand. He stared at it.

Her smile started in her eyes long before it hit her mouth. "It's okay to hold hands on a first date."

Damn, she slayed him. He took the satellite phone and tranquilizer gun from her bag, shoved them in his, shouldered the backpack, and tossed hers in the trunk. Then he took her hand and laced their fingers. She squeezed his and they were off.

They were immediately swallowed by cypress trees for which the trail got its name, and under a canopy of sequoia where the temperature dropped ten degrees. The base of the redwoods were wider than the two of them together, making him think of her as a tiny pixie in a gigantic forest. Peat moss mingled with pine to create a fresh, clean scent that settled the last of his nerves.

Relaxed, he walked with her, holding her hand like they'd done this a thousand times, Fletch at their heels. They were a mile deep when the incline narrowed. He let her go ahead of him, lest she slip, and climbed the rocky soil that would lead to her favorite view. It was damn near close to his, too, second only to the clearing by the bluff overlooking the Pacific.

She stopped at the top by an outcropping of boulders where the canopy ended, and streams of sunlight hit her from every angle. On impulse, he grabbed his cell from his pocket and snapped a picture of her while her back was to him before he legged the last few steps to stand beside her.

"God, I love this spot."

"Me, too," he signed, eyes only for her.

One of the greatest things about her was her ability to appreciate everything. Didn't matter what it was, grand or small, she found beauty in it all. Could be a scene he'd seen a thousand times and had taken for granted, and she'd make it seem like the first time he'd opened his eyes. In a world where people rarely stopped long enough to breathe in what was around them, Gabby found the details.

She slid him a side-glance, lips curved in amusement. "Look at the view."

"I am." But, to appease her, he forced his gaze off her and turned toward the cliff ledge.

Panorama spread out before him, shrouded in a fine mist of fog. To his left, he could scarcely make out the ocean in the distance around the bend, and to his right, the wall of the southern-facing Coast Range jutted rock and shallow ledges of spruce and foxtail pine.

"It's so quiet." She glanced at him and narrowed her eyes. "Don't look at me like that. It *is* quiet. You can't hear anything with your actual ears, but you can feel certain sounds. Don't you feel the stillness?"

She was right, completely right, but he couldn't wipe the smile from his face to save his life. She knew him, knew almost what it was like to be deaf since she'd inserted herself so deep into learning about the disability years before. She was in tuned to him and his nuances, and as comfortable as he was with her, she still had the capability of shocking the shit out of him with moments like this.

She sighed. "Nothing but the sound of nature. I wish you could hear it, compare it to town noises. It's different." Climbing up on a flat boulder, she turned toward him and sat, her legs stretched out in front of her.

He retrieved a treat for Fletch from the pack and used a hand motion to tell the dog to stay. He followed her suit and scaled the boulder, tucking a wild strand of hair behind her ear after he'd settled. *"Describe it to me."*

She blinked. "Describe nature sounds?"

Nodding, he pressed his hand over her heart and lightly thumped. *"That's what bass feels like from music. Now, tell me about the...quiet."*

She straightened and crossed her legs, scooting closer until they were knee to knee. "Well, when you first leave the city, it's kind of like a vacuum." She pressed her palms to his ears, creating pressure. "It takes awhile to adjust to the lack of noise."

He nodded his understanding.

"Then, when you're away for a bit, little things compute like small animals scurrying." She wiggled her fingertips across the back of his neck, sending goose bumps over his skin. "From up here, there's a faint sound of water trickling from the river." She zigzagged her fingers across his chest.

He grinned. *"Go on."* He liked this game. Not only was he getting her gist, but he liked her hands on him even in a nonsexual way.

"The ocean is a roar when you're close, but at a distance, it's more like a shush." She brought her fingers up to lightly brush his shoulders. "There's a crackling noise when the wind hits the leaves, a whir." Her fingertips traced the shells of his ears.

His heart stuttered behind his ribs and then caught rhythm, fast and insistent. His weak spot was his neck and his ears. One touch, lick, or kiss, and he was semi-hard. Every molecule inside his body became increasingly aware of her closeness, her caress. His skin heated and his hands itched to touch her in return, show her what it felt like relying on that sensory over the others.

"Wind against rock, or near the mountain, is a little different." She combed her fingers through his hair and gently tugged, sending a bolt of electricity straight from his scalp to his groin.

He lost sight of what she'd said next when he closed his eyes, just for a moment, to savor her touch. When he lifted his heavily drugged lids, her blue gaze locked onto his mouth as if she were having a hard time focusing as well. He had to concentrate on breathing because somehow he'd forgotten the simple act.

Every. Damn. Time. She knocked the wind out of him and brought him to his knees with one look.

"Thunder is the best part." Her gaze drifted from his mouth to his eyes, hers dilated nearly black with desire. She unclenched the short strands at his nape and set her hands on his knees, never unlocking her gaze from his. Slowly, she slid her hands up his thighs, inching closer to the promise land; and he decided breathing was overrated. A bead of sweat trailed down his back.

But then she stopped suddenly short of the target and removed her hands. "That's what thunder sounds like. Loud, like the blood rushing through your ears, heart pounding, and then an abrupt nothing, leaving an echo in its wake."

He never wished for a storm so bad in all his existence. Thunder? He'd show her thunder. And lightning.

Cupping the back of her head, he brought her mouth to his. Searing heat assaulted him the instant her lips met his and parted. Yes, *this*. Kissing her was like discovering unchartered territory and coming home in the same breath.

Without hesitation, she framed his jaw with her hands and wove her tongue against his. Soft, pliant. She rose to kneel between his legs, thrusting his head back and causing their chests to crash.

To hold onto something, he gripped her ponytail with one hand and fisted her sweatshirt with the other. He decided against the latter and drove his hand under her shirt to splay his fingers over the smooth expanse of her back, nudging her closer yet.

It was no use, this reason thing. He gave it his best effort. The ground dropped out and he fell, headfirst into oblivion.

She kept pace with him, frantic openmouthed kisses that bordered on desperate and shared retail space with endearing. He explored her mouth until nothing went unconquered and he repeated the process. Her scent of honey collided with the pine and seawater in the air, her warm skin a contrast to the cool breeze off the mountain. So soft, her every curve fit against his planes perfectly.

Nipping his lower lip, she said something against his mouth, her lips forming a word. Or several words.

He went rigid. For the second time, he'd gotten so wrapped up in her he hadn't paid attention to her signals. Pulling back, he looked at her. Lips swollen, eyes dazed. She seemed fine. He swore she'd spoken, though.

He cleared his throat and, unwilling to move his hands just yet, used his voice to grate out, "What?"

She brushed her nose with his. Smiled. Stole what felt like a good chunk of his heart. "I said wow."

Chapter 14

Suddenly a little nervous, Gabby unlocked her front door with trembling fingers and stepped back for Fletch and Flynn to enter. When she'd first arrived at Cyprus Trail, Flynn had seemed nervous, which had somehow calmed her. But now he appeared relaxed, confident, and she was a basket case.

On the trail, they'd gone from zero to panty-melting with that kiss. She wanted more, her body still humming, but she knew they needed balance to make this relationship work. If only she could find a way to temper her reaction to him just a smidgen, she'd be golden.

Fletch found Popsicle by the fireplace and, after several seconds of butt-stiffing, they curled up together on the floor and went to sleep, the cat under the dog's paw.

She eyed Flynn and smoothed her damp palms over her thighs. "What now?"

Amusement tilted the corners of his mouth, infused his hazel eyes. He shrugged. *"Am I supposed to go home now? Kiss you goodbye? You're the dating expert."*

Ha. She wrung her hands together, not wanting him to leave, but unsure if that's what he should do.

"How about pizza?" He lifted his brows in question.

Pizza. Yes, they could do that. She smiled and pulled her phone out of her purse. After ordering, she set her purse aside and looked at him. "Thirty minutes."

He was still standing near the door, but he'd shoved his hands in his pockets while she was on the phone. After him behaving strangely the past couple weeks, it was odd her being the antsy of the two. She was the one who'd initiated the date, and really, it was just Flynn. She drew a deep breath and glanced at the animals sleeping on the floor, trying to get her brain to make her body do something. Anything. Her wires were still scrambled.

He stepped closer. *"You're nervous."*

She bit her lip and nodded. Her cheeks heated in ridiculous embarrassment. Try as she might to play this off, the full ramifications hit her. Hard. This *was Flynn*. Best friend. Boss. Boyfriend?

That was just scratching the surface. If she dug deep enough, she'd have to acknowledge he might've been the reason for her disconnect with other men. Perhaps a buried part of her had been waiting for him all along. It explained the crazy gravitational pull, the way she responded on impact to him. And all the things that could go wrong, that had held him back, made a whole lot of sense.

He nodded as if she'd spoken. *"Now you get it."*

She sighed, shoulders sagging. Truth? He was the only guy who could break her heart, the only one who had ever been in there in the first place.

Without a word, as if he knew exactly what she needed, he closed the distance between them and pulled her to him. One arm banded around her, caging her in his solid, lean strength. He held the back of her head and pressed her cheek to his chest. Aligned perfectly, there wasn't an inch of space between them.

Closing her eyes, she breathed in his familiar scent and wrapped her arms around his back, gripping his shoulders from behind. Inch by inch, the tension drained, her anxious stomach settled, and she wanted to crawl inside him. Flynn was safety and reassurance.

He rested his chin on the top of her head and shifted to the side, keeping her wrapped tight. When he moved in the other direction, she smiled, realizing he was initiating a slow dance. Without leaving his embrace, she kicked off her shoes and placed her feet on top of his so he could control their movements.

They stayed like that a few moments, spinning in a slow circle until his Adam's apple bobbed and she tilted her head to look at him. His lips parted as if to speak, but they pressed right back into a thin line. Hesitation marred his brow while his gaze scanned her face.

"What is it?"

He gave a slight shake of his head and then sighed as if conceding to an act he didn't want to execute. "Sometimes I want to say something, but don't want to let you go to sign."

He studied her closely, and she got the impression her response would make or break him. Vulnerability shone in his eyes. His body grew rigid, poised on the edge of crumbling.

Holding his gaze, she hesitated, wondering why this was so important to him. He'd spoken to her before. Not often, and typically it was at work when his hands were occupied, but never in front of others. She knew he was self-conscious about his voice. Based off the reactions of some kids when they'd been young, he'd used mostly sign language ever since.

But...she wasn't just anyone. He'd said himself she was one of the only people he'd speak aloud to, so she wasn't spotting the problem.

She cupped his cheek, loving the rasp of his outgrowth under her fingers. "If you want to talk to me, then do it."

It was actually sweet he didn't want to let her go to sign. His dialect and pronunciations were awkward at times, and he spoke slower than the average person, partly due to being deaf and partly because he just hadn't practiced. But, wow. The deep rumble of his tone and the fact she was one of the only people who got to hear it made her chest swell and her panties damp.

He stared at her as if she hadn't spoken, then opened his mouth for several beats before forming words. "Does it bother you?" Again with the intense gaze like she might lie to him.

Was he serious? "No." For emphasis, she held his head in her hands. "No. I love your voice." At his blink of disbelief, he tried to turn his face away. She brought his gaze back to hers. "Where is this coming from? Have I ever given you the impression it bothered me?"

He shook his head.

"Then why hesitate? This is me, Flynn." When his chest rose and fell rapidly and the arms around her back clenched, her gut twisted. "Has it bothered other women you've been with?" That made sense. Getting physical with a lover wasn't optimal for signing.

His silence was answer enough. Anger shoved at her temples and she wanted to rip into anyone who made him feel like he couldn't be himself. Some woman, somewhere along the line, had made him feel like less of a man. Perhaps more than one woman. Her stomach bottomed out.

This conversation was doing a number on him. She could tell by his severe stance and the susceptibility exposed in his eyes. And talking to her about this had to be tearing into his pride, yet proved how much he trusted her. No way would she shatter that.

He glanced heavenward and drew a deep breath before meeting her gaze once more. "I usually don't talk at all. Almost never. Does it...turn you off?"

She was going to hunt down every female he ever dated. Hand to God. "Say my name."

His brows drew together in confusion as he shook his head.

She took his hand and placed it over her heart. "Say my name. Feel what it does to me."

His head reared back as he studied her. "Gabby."

The low, hoarse note skittered across the space between them. Her belly heated and her pulse went crazy.

He sucked in a harsh breath, eyes round and hopeful. "Gabby—"

Rising on her toes, she crashed her mouth to his. He paused a shocked beat and then dove in, finally taking charge like she knew he would. The tender side of him was what made him such a great man, a good veterinarian, an even better friend. But him barely restraining himself? Going after what he wanted?

Sweet Lord.

Perhaps because of their friendship he'd taken a moment to get out of the starting gate, but when he had, the results were explosive. Just like their last few encounters, he took charge and she could do nothing more than hang on for the ride. Though they'd done little more than kiss, he was the first man she'd been intimate with that had every thought dissolving into thin air.

His kiss was a direct contrast to his body. His mouth consumed, devoured, explored, while his hands remained gentle, reverent. Languid, diligent strokes of his tongue had her melting into him. Her knees shook and, as if sensing that, he drove his thigh between her legs and wrapped his arm firmly around her back.

She held his shoulders, the muscles shifting beneath her palms. Wanting to explore, she trailed her fingers down his pecs, nails raking over his nipples through his shirt.

He groaned and thrust against her hip, a significant bulge behind his zipper. He gripped her ponytail and tugged, tilting her head at a different angle so he could go deeper. His other hand slid to her ass, kneading and hauling her halfway up his body.

Fire licked under her skin. Her breath caught. Blood roared through her veins, her pulse pounding in her ears. Dizzy, she wrapped one leg around his hip and—

The doorbell rang.

Reluctantly, she pulled her head back and sucked air. His lids lifted slowly, pupils blown. "Pizza's here."

He looked at the door and nodded, then, as if an afterthought, he let her go and took a step away.

On unsteady legs, she answered the door and signed for the pizza. She went into the kitchen, grabbed a couple paper plates and two bottles of water, and headed back into the living room. Flynn was still standing in the same spot, hands tucked in his back pockets, his Henley stretched across his muscled chest and biceps.

Who needed pizza? She could eat him in one bite.

She crooked her finger at him, telling him to come closer. He groaned and took a seat on the couch. After the slices were dished out and he'd picked off the tomatoes, giving them to her, and she'd done the same with the black olives, setting them on his plate, they ate in silence. She reached for another piece and caught him staring at his second one as if in a trance.

She tapped his arm to get his attention. "What's up?"

He set his plate in his lap. *"You remember that party at Katie Marsh's house freshman year?"*

She searched her memory, vaguely recalling about fifteen friends getting together in Katie's parents' basement. Her birthday or something. Gabby wasn't that close to her and hadn't seen her much since graduation. "Yeah. I think so."

He signed while chewing. *"I smashed a piece of pizza into Luke Reint's face."*

She laughed and took a sip of water, remembering the incident, but not why. "We've had pizza on my couch or yours a zillion times since then. What made you think of that now?"

His smile fell a fraction and he shrugged. *"We played spin the bottle and, at my turn, it landed on you. We kissed in the closet."*

"That's right. I totally forgot." He'd been pretty nervous and the kiss had been short. Chaste. Neither had any experience really and she'd chalked the whole thing up as awkward.

He glanced at his plate and her stomach dipped, the look on his face indicating he hadn't forgotten one iota. *"Your turn meant you had to kiss Luke. You came out with a bloody lip."*

She tilted her head, staring distantly at the floor. Wait. "Yes. He had braces and we butted heads." She laughed. "He cut my lip."

He nodded, focus moving from her hands to his plate. *"I shoved my pizza in his face for hurting you."*

"It was an accident. He didn't really mean to hurt me."

Slowly, his gaze met hers, and a thousand emotions swam in his eyes, too fast to read or settle. *"And your cut lip was an excuse for what I did. I really did it out of jealousy."*

Frozen, she stared at him. Her heart did some kind of twist inside her chest and her lungs wrung dry. They'd been, what? Fifteen at that party? If he'd been jealous back then, that meant...

"You were my first kiss." His gaze roamed her face and he swallowed. *"I was upset someone else got to kiss you within minutes of me."*

Oh, God. Wow, wow, wow. And it had barely been a blip in her radar of scrapbook memories. She'd only kissed a couple boys before that incident, but she had been his first? And in such a meaningless way?

Her brain shut down as a lump wedged in her throat. "You...had feelings for me? Back then?"

He didn't respond other than to hold her gaze with a deadpan look of resolve. Not a muscle moved but the tic of his jaw.

Pressing a palm to her forehead, she stood and absently looked around, her gaze not settling on anything in particular. She'd never suspected, not once. Not until recently when everything had spiraled into a kaleidoscope of crazy. But she'd figured his attraction was a new occurrence, not something he'd been harboring.

"My feelings have always been there, Gabby. I shut them down to maintain...us."

She shivered at his voice. Immersing herself in the sound, she closed her eyes. When she opened them, he was in front of her, an inch away, not touching, but surrounding her just the same. Soul in his eyes, he left his gaze wide open for her to read.

And what she found gutted her. Affection. Nerves. Strain. He'd laid himself bare at her feet, fully disclosing everything for her to do with what she will. She'd been no better than any other woman from his past. He may have shut down his attraction, may have hidden it from her, but she should've seen. Worse, she had no idea how she would've reacted had she known back then. She barely had a handle on it now.

How long had she been inadvertently hurting him?

Drawing a breath, she knew the answer wouldn't appease her guilt. This had probably gone on since that stupid party, when they'd kissed. *You were my first kiss.* His words from moments ago slammed into her chest. He was the last person on earth she'd ever want to cause pain.

Frantically, she glanced around the room, gaze landing on her water bottle. She stepped away, putting the table between them. Tilting the bottle on its side, she flicked her fingers, spinning the bottle.

He looked at her, the table, and her again, understanding dawning in his eyes. Without removing his gaze from hers, he reached down and stopped the bottle, cap pointed at him.

Heart pounding, she strode around the table, grabbed the front of his shirt, and dragged him to her front hall closet. She opened the door, shoved him inside, and closed the door behind them. In the dark, she eased him backward, coats enveloping them, and reached for his face.

He shook his head. Hands on her hips, he spun her around until her back was to the wall and he pinned her there with his chest. *Yes.*

His lips grazed hers, barely a whisper, their noses brushing. His breath skated across her cheek as he nibbled her lower lip, then his tongue followed the path and she moaned. Heat coursed through her veins, made her breasts heavy and her core ache. His thighs pressed against hers as he moved in, and the thickness of his shaft pushed against her belly from behind his jeans.

He tilted his head, hovering, and then opened for her. Unlike their previous kisses, this one was sweet instead of hot, as if he was trying to pour emotion into the act. A conversation. Unrushed. Gratitude and affection and desire rolled off him, was evident by the tender way he moved his hands from her hips to her waist. His thumbs brushed her ribs, stroking, silently relaying he was savoring rather than pushing.

Fifteen years too late, but their game of spin the bottle had been renewed, this time with the outcome he'd obviously wanted.

Emotion welled in her chest, stung her eyes. This moment wasn't about demand, wasn't even about chemistry. He was telling her how much she meant to him. She knew it as well as she knew him.

He lifted his head with a harsh inhalation, his hand reaching out and slapping the wall. His fingers connected to the light switch and she blinked as eighty watts knocked out the dark. One quick scan of her and his gaze hardened, his mouth a firm line. Holding her jaw in both hands, he swiped her wet cheeks with his thumbs.

She hadn't realized she'd been crying. "I'm sorry."

He flinched. "For what?" Remorse filled his expression when she didn't respond. "Talk to me."

She drew a shuddering breath. "I wish you'd said something sooner. About how you felt. I—" *I'm sorry for being the first in a long line to hurt you. Sorry I hadn't seen what you were dealing with.* "I'm just sorry."

He studied her a long time and straightened. "*So I didn't push too hard? The tears weren't because you wanted me to stop?*"

Oh, God. "Of course not." Was that really what he'd been worried about? Acid churned in her stomach, ate away at the lining.

"*It was dark. I couldn't see.*" He ran a hand through his hair. "*You're okay?*"

"Yes." But he obviously wasn't.

Chapter 15

While Flynn finished his exam with one of the barn cats at the new client farm, Gabby ducked in the corners and in the stalls to search for the one they were missing. They'd examined the two cows and four goats, then the cats. She had scratches up and down her arms and a growing headache looming. One furball left, and they could get off this mountain and back to the clinic.

This place and the owner Jose gave her the creeps. At least he'd given them breathing room. Aside from meeting them at the car when they'd first pulled in, he'd left them alone. Thankfully, the other barn animals were in far better shape than the horses they'd encountered last week. She'd snuck in by them earlier and gave them some apples. Jose had said he'd planned to sell the horses, so there was that.

The adorable sheepdog who'd been following her around appeared at the barn door again. He wagged his tail, ducked out of sight, then came right back as if to say, *follow me.*

She turned to Flynn. "I'm going to go look for the last cat while you finish."

He frowned. *"Don't go too far."*

Nodding, she followed the dog. "Where's the kitty? Show me the kitty."

The dog took off at a lope toward what she thought was an old chicken coop. It was several yards away from the barns and behind the house. Last time she and Flynn had been out here, Jose had instructed them to stay only in the barns.

Figuring the dog was headed for the house—maybe the cat was hiding out under the back steps—she followed. Dried grass, straw, and gravel crunched under her shoes as she walked. Saltwater from the coast mingled with mountain snow. Damp earth reminded her spring was here, though it took its time. She couldn't wait for summer.

Her steps faltered and she bit her lip. The dog, who'd made a hard right away from the house, stopped and barked. He obviously wanted her to follow, but the hairs on her neck rose. The coop was very far from Flynn's location and he couldn't hear her if she called for help. Her cell and supplies were with him. Unease wove around her, made her stomach flip.

The dog barked again.

With a quick glance around, and after not finding anyone, she sighed. "Okay, but make this quick." She didn't like this one iota.

She trailed the dog to the edge of the coop. Roughly as tall as her and about six feet wide, it was more like a shed. Plywood slats boarded the windows on each side and the roof was rotted through in several spots. The precarious door had a padlock, but it was hanging loosely on the latch.

Hand on the knob, she paused, and the dog barked. "Shh. You'll get us in trouble."

This wasn't right. She eyed the door again, every ingrained instinct telling her to take off running. Something was wrong. Though the temps were mild and the breeze slight, a cold shifted through her to her bones. The clear skies and sunlight didn't chase the chill away. Unlike over by the barns, the scent of decay and feces hung in the air on this side of the property.

Just as she backed away, a whine sounded from the coop. Faint, but there. Shaking, she slowly opened the door. A creak of the rusted hinges tore a shiver from deep within her core.

The stench hit her first. Rotting flesh. Infection. Urine. Eyes watering, she squinted into the dark structure.

Oh God Almighty. *No.* She clasped her hands over her mouth, shock freezing her immobile for several beats.

Makeshift pine stalls were erected along three of the walls, five on each side, four in the back. Wire fencing covered each. And inside...inside *were dogs.* Pit bulls, all of them. A few looked up at her with pathetic, frightened eyes. Some didn't have the strength to even lift their heads. A couple didn't move at all. They were skin and bones. Gouges marred their fur. Large chunks of flesh were missing. Maggots and flies had burrowed into the wounds.

She gagged and ran outside, gulping in air. Retching, she fell to her knees, tears blinding her. Oh God. Who would do such a thing? Her throat closed and she couldn't drag in oxygen. A careening siren wailed inside her head as her vision grayed.

The sheepdog sidled next to her, whined, and nudged her with his nose. "Good, boy. You're a good boy." Her voice broke.

She had to get out of here. Get to Flynn and call for help. Panic clutched her chest as she carefully closed the coop door with a silent promise to the dogs she'd help them. For now, she just had to get away before Jose spotted her.

Wiping her face with her sleeve, she quickly glanced around and walked briskly toward the barn. Flynn was packing the bag when she got there. Alone.

Trying not to panic, she ran to him and signed what she found, not wanting to speak aloud in case someone was nearby. Flynn tensed, nostrils flared, an *are you serious* look in his lethal hazel eyes. She nodded, more tears threatening.

He fisted his hand in his hair and stalked away. Paced back. *"Call 911. I'll text Cade and Drake to meet at the clinic to help. When the authorities leave, we'll bring the dogs to Animal Instincts."*

She nodded. "What about the other animals?" There were four horses, never mind the cats, goats, and cows. They couldn't leave them.

He blew out a breath. *"When the cops get here, try calling some of our clients. See if a couple of them can board or take them in. Tell them they'll get free vet care for the next visit."* He swallowed. *"You okay?"*

She shook her head, but pulled out her cell. No signal. "I have to get the satellite phone."

"I'll be right behind you."

Once outside, she hauled ass to the SUV and sat in the passenger seat. After reporting the incident and assured the authorities were on the way, she slumped in her seat.

Flynn made his way over, stowed the bags, and stood next to her by the open car door. Silently, he ran his hand over her back in an attempt to soothe her, his body tense with his own shock and anger.

She couldn't quit shaking. By the look of those poor animals, they'd been part of a dogfighting ring. Once, years ago, she and Flynn had stumbled onto a puppy mill. That had been terrible. But those conditions, awful as they'd been, were not nearly as horrifying as what she'd seen today.

Flynn glanced behind the SUV. *"They're here."*

Stepping out of the car, she sucked in a breath. They had work to do, had to take care of the matter at hand before she could crumble. She didn't get to fall apart, not when those dogs were suffering. And God. She and Flynn had been out here on Friday. If she'd checked the coop then, maybe some of them wouldn't be in such bad shape.

As two squad cars from Redwood Ridge and another from State Patrol pulled in behind them, the screen door to the farmhouse snapped shut and six feet of murderous Jose vaulted down the steps.

"What the fuck is going on?"

Flynn straightened and shoved Gabby behind his back, but the officers were already between Jose and them. Jose threw a punch, landing wide of Flynn's jaw over the officer's shoulder. In seconds, the cops had Jose in handcuffs and sitting in the back of one squad.

The next three hours were a nightmare. The authorities had taken her statement, snapped photos of the coop, and escorted Jose away. One of the Redwood Ridge officers had remained to keep an eye on the scene. Cade and Drake had shown up and, after examining the dogs as best they could, came out of the coop where she and Flynn had been waiting.

All but two of the dogs had to be put down. The injuries were too severe. Not wanting to traumatize the poor animals more than they were, they'd euthanized right there, and Drake had taken their bodies back to the clinic for cremation.

Gabby, despite Flynn's protests, had knelt right next to each one while they'd administered the drugs so they wouldn't be alone. She'd cooed murmurs of comfort, petted their trembling bodies, and cried like a baby until her throat was raw.

Cade had dealt with the other animals. Avery, on his request, had contacted neighboring farms, and each goat, horse, and cow had a new home.

By the time it was all said and done, dusk had descended and the air was cool. Gabby was a mess. She'd never feel clean again. A layer of guilt and grime coated her skin, her clothes, and she couldn't take it.

Fidgeting in the passenger seat on the way down the mountain, she watched the scenery pass in a blur. Flynn, sensing her upheaval, put his hand over hers, gaze on the road while he drove. He hadn't said much of anything, but she knew he'd have nightmares, too. She tried to absorb his warmth, draw comfort from the weight of his hand, but it was useless.

* * * *

Gently, Flynn took the keys from Gabby and unlocked her house. Drake was dealing with the two Pitbulls they'd rescued and Cade was heading to Flynn's to take care of Fletch for him. Gabby needed him and, damn it, he needed her. So, regardless of her protests, he was staying with her tonight.

He'd never be able to scrub those images from his mind and, knowing Gabby and her big heart, she was probably a damn mess. Every tear she'd shed today tore a chunk out of him, and the detached, almost numb state she'd been in since was scaring the shit out of him. She hadn't muttered so much as a word in hours and she was still trembling.

He closed the door behind them, setting her keys and purse on the entry table. Popsicle wound around his ankles and, keeping his eyes on Gabby, he picked up the cat. Her purr of pleasure rumbled under his palm.

Gabby stopped in the middle of the living room as if unsure what to do. Her vacant blue eyes focused on the wall while she trembled.

Anger and grief warred inside his chest, not only for what Jose had done to those helpless dogs, but for what seeing them had done to Gabby. He'd never, for as long as he lived, be able to erase the image of her lying on the soiled floor of that shed. Her lips moving with words of consolation. Her shaking hands trying to soothe the scared dogs. Her tears trekking her face as Drake administered the euthanasia. Her biting her lip and crossing her arms protectively over her stomach while Flynn had to muzzle the two survivors, who'd put up quite the fight out of sheer unadulterated fear.

Hell, he needed to hold her right now more than he needed to breathe.

He set the cat down and walked to stand in front of her, but she snapped into a flurry of motion. Tears streamed from her already red-rimmed eyes and she clutched at her scrubs. Before he knew her intent, she'd stripped down to skin as if the material had burned. She stood there, shaking, naked...

Damn. He darted into her bedroom to get her a robe or something, emerging with a T-shirt that would cover her until she was in a better frame of mind. But when he'd returned to the living room, she wasn't there. Backtracking to the hallway, he found the bathroom door shut. His heart pounded so that every pulse point in his body ached.

Hand on the knob, he swallowed, wondering if he should open it. Worry took up commercial space in his chest. Concerned, he poked his head inside and steam hit his face.

Okay. Showering. He couldn't blame her. Slipping back out, he went into her bedroom to hunt up something better for her to wear now that there wasn't an emergent need to cover her.

Pink heart-designed pajamas lay on her comforter. Snatching them and a pair of panties from her top drawer—*don't look, don't look*—he eased the bathroom door open, quickly set the items on the toilet lid, and stepped out.

Wondering if he had enough time to scrub the day off himself before she emerged, he made his way to the SUV and dug around for the extra set of scrubs Gabby kept there for him. On his way back inside, he picked up her scrubs from the living room floor and emptied the pockets onto the coffee table. Hand sanitizer, pens, gloves, dog treats, scrap paper—Christ. Where was the kitchen sink?

Since she was still in the hall bathroom, he stripped in her adjoining one and threw her scrubs and his in the garbage, then showered.

The bathroom door was still shut when he emerged. Sighing, he lifted his hand to knock, but the door swung inward and she stood at the threshold, steam pillowing around her.

The boy shorts and tank top dotted with hearts—adorable, that—barely covered her good parts. Her skin was bright pink like she'd had the water set to scalding and had tried to incinerate the dermal layers off. Scratches from the barn cats ran up and down her arms. Though red, they didn't appear to have gone deep, nor looked infected.

Shoulders slumped, her watery gaze met his and...hell. Her lower lip quivered. "I'm sorry."

He shook his head and wrapped his arms around her, not having a clue what she was apologizing for. Chances were, whatever it was, it wasn't her fault. She sank into his embrace, face buried in his chest and shoulders shaking. Her fingers clutched his shirt and she teetered.

Before she could fall, he caught her, banding her tighter to him, and moved toward her bedroom. After she'd climbed in bed, he turned on the bedside lamp and followed, lying on his side to face her. The damn tears were gutting, but he stroked her hair until she'd finally, blessedly, stopped. Her honey scent clung to the sheets and he used the familiarity to calm the last edges of upset in his stomach.

Nose red, eyes redder, she studied his face. "I'm sorry."

Seeking patience, he shook his head. "Knock it off."

She blinked when he'd spoken instead of signed, but his voice didn't seem to repel or disgust her. It would take some getting used to, but he was trying. There were times signing just wasn't optimal and Gabby had never judged him.

The low light from the lamp made her features seem softer and he drank her in. She truly was quite pretty. Real in a way not found nowadays. A cross between sly sultriness and girl-next-door wholesome.

"Do you think you could eat?" No way he could, but they hadn't had anything since lunch hours ago.

She shook her head. A trace of a smile curved her lips. "I'll bet that was exactly how you imagined me taking my clothes off, right?"

He grinned because he couldn't help it. She was something else. "It was, actually. The sobbing while you stripped was an added benefit."

She slapped his arm.

"No, really. Such a turn-on when women weep while throwing clothes around. I'd work on your technique, though. I think you ripped the tabs off your bra."

She covered her face and laughed, shaking the bed. Some of the light was back in her eyes when she dropped her hand, and he breathed for the first time in hours. "I'll try harder next time." Her smile slipped a margin as she stared at him. "Thank you. For everything. Mostly for not putting me in a padded cell."

Christ. She killed him sometimes. "Fear not. The men in white coats are coming later." He brushed his knuckles down her cheek, needing to touch her. "I did get to raid your panty drawer, so I should be thanking you."

Covering her eyes, she laughed again. "Oh God."

"I like the red ones best. They go with your eyes."

Face in the pillow, she shook her head. When she resurfaced, her lips were pressed together, smile still in her eyes. Ah, there was his girl. Much better.

Leaning forward, she brushed his lips with hers, lids drooping. Her warm breath fanned his mouth and it took restraint not to push the kiss past gentle.

Allowing himself a moment to sink into her, he closed his eyes. Gabby was the only woman he'd ever been able to let go with, even as marginal a thing as not having to look at her. Heat fired through his blood as he pressed his mouth to her upper lip, then the lower. She brushed her nose against his and tilted her head, asking for more.

He cupped her cheek and increased the pressure. Her lips parted, tongue tracing the seam of his, and he groaned. She took that opportunity to slip past his defenses and stroked his tongue with hers. Careful, teasing, open-mouth licks that had his brain misfiring and his shaft hard. She pressed a hand to his chest, thumb circling his nipple, and he pulled his head away.

"Gabby..." Except he couldn't remember what he was going to say. Something about slowing down and reminding her she hadn't wanted to get physical right away in their relationship.

Her heavy lids lifted and blue desire look back at him. "Flynn."

What he wouldn't give to, just once, know what his name sounded like from her lips. Hear her voice. Her sleepy, wanton eyes and wet mouth were the ultimate turn-on, but he'd kill to hear her tone when she was like this.

"I could show you instead."

His gaze flicked to hers and he realized he must've said his thoughts aloud. Damn, she had him in knots. It wasn't like him to speak at all, never mind not be aware he was doing it. Then her words sank in.

Like always, she read his expression. Or his mind. "I'll show you what my voice sounds like. Close your eyes."

Reluctant, he did as she asked, and her soft plush lips grazed his jaw. Her mouth moved, speaking, and without looking he knew she was saying his name. Featherlight, she did it again, this time against his mouth and his heart tripped in rhythm.

His skin caught fire. His gut clenched in desire. Spreading his fingers over her back, he urged her closer. She dipped her head, moving her lips and continuing to level him by speaking against his skin. Down his neck. Across his throat. Behind his ear.

Against. His. Ear.

Christ, that was his erotic zone right there. He wanted her so bad he was shaking. His chest rose and fell in swift pants, and she...smiled against his cheek. The damn minx.

He shoved his thigh between her legs and cupped her ass, dragging her closer. Her eyes closed as her head fell back, caramel hair tickling his hand. Her heart pounded against his chest, the *thump-thump* increasing when she jerked her hips to ride his thigh.

He dipped his head to lick that patch of skin over the tendon on her neck, and encountered...fur.

He opened one eye and narrowed it on the cat. Popsicle stared back at him from behind Gabby's shoulder with a *pay attention to me* demand. His gaze dropped to Gabby when she shook against him. Lips pressed together, she laughed.

Right. He remembered Gabby had wanted this relationship to go slow.

Picking up the cat, he set her by their feet. Then he turned Gabby in his arms so she faced away from him, spooned her against his chest—which did not help calm his raging erection—and ordered her to go to sleep.

Face buried in her soft, sweet-smelling hair, he tried to follow his own orders.

Chapter 16

Gabby strode into the clinic and found Avery behind the desk, Brent sitting on the counter beside her. "Hey, you're both in early. I thought I'd be the only one here at this hour."

She'd decided to leave early to check on the dogs they'd rescued. She'd crashed pretty hard last night and hadn't gotten an update. And if her heart had sunk a little waking up alone, well...she was a big girl. Flynn had left a note by her coffeepot saying he'd headed home to get ready for work and didn't want to wake her, but it still kind of left her feeling abandoned. Which was stupid. He'd stayed the night and had all but taken care of her.

Avery leaned back in her chair. "With that mess from yesterday, there's a lot to do. I need to call the farms who took in the animals and get a status report, plus put them in Flynn's appointment rotation. The cops are asking for a more detailed report to give the DA. The paperwork alone is going to bury me."

Gabby offered a weak smile. "You live for paperwork."

"Not this kind." Avery rolled her head to stretch her neck. "How are you doing, by the way? That scene was dang awful."

She sipped coffee from her to-go cup to give herself a moment. "Yeah, it was. I'm okay." She glanced at Brent. "How are the dogs?"

"Better than expected." He hopped off the counter and uncovered Gossip's cage.

The cockatoo ruffled his feathers. *Squawk.* "Good morning, sunshine."

"Morning," they mumbled back.

"I looked over Drake's notes. No broken bones. Both of them are missing an ear. The flesh wounds were pretty bad. He had to do a lot of debridement work to get rid of dead tissue." Brent sighed and faced her, gutting heartbreak in his eyes. "Heck, sugarbuns. I don't know how you managed that scene."

Had Flynn not been there with her for the fallout, she didn't know how she would've either. "It was terrible." She forced the images from her mind. "How are their temperaments?" In cases like this, it was hard to tell if the dogs would adjust to a normal life. Trained to be aggressive, they might not be adoptable.

He shrugged. "Hard to say. Drake had to sedate them to treat, of course. They're on heavy-duty antibiotics. He's in the kennel room with them now."

Nodding, she set the billing statements from yesterday on Avery's desk and turned toward the hallway.

"Those don't go there."

Eyes narrowed, she faced Avery. "You are a Nazi, you know that?" God love her, Gabby didn't know how the clinic got by before she'd arrived. With a grin, she picked up the statements, set them in the proper tray, and lifted her brows. "Satisfied?"

"Very." Avery crossed her arms. "I just got a happy tingle."

"Speaking of happy tingles..." Brent dropped his hands on his cocked hips. "How's it going with Mr. Strong and Silent?"

About that... Gabby pointed at him. "Don't think you're forgiven for being in cahoots with the Battleaxes." She gave him a sly smile, keeping mum on the other part. Flynn didn't just give her happy tingles, he electrified her circuits. Let Brent stew and wonder. Served him right.

She leaned over Avery's desk and dumped out her pencil cup to mess with her, then spread them out for good measure. "Neener, neener. That'll drive you bonkers. Look, Avery, they're not even facing the same direction."

Face scrunched, Avery eyed the pencils, hands fisted. "That was just mean."

Brent patted her back. "It's okay, doll. We'll color coordinate them together. They'll be good as new."

Still pouting, Avery huffed. "Payback's a bitch."

Gabby laughed and headed down the hall. "I'm not afraid of you."

After dropping off her purse in Flynn's office, she made her way to the boarding room. They had low numbers this week. Only a few kennels were occupied, luckily with cats. They seemed to be contentedly sleeping for the moment in their cages on their side of the huge room.

She scanned the cheery space painted by Zoe a few years ago. One big mural of blue skies and green grass, it was meant to make the boarding animals feel more welcome. Fire hydrants and trees were scattered amongst the background. The scent of Lysol floor cleaner and fur made her smile.

Closing the door behind her had accidentally startled their clinic pet, Thor, and the chickenshit Great Dane leapt to his feet. He bumped into her with a *harrumph* and skedaddled to Drake's side, cowering by his feet.

Standing in front of the crates along the back wall, Drake glanced down at the dog. "Yeah. Gabby scares the crap out of me, too." His droll tone pulled a laugh from her.

Pausing next to him, she checked out the Pitbulls. In side-by-side kennels, they lay sleeping. One had grayish-white fur and the other tan with black markings. They had cones around their necks to keep them from biting the bandages. And there were a lot of bandages—around their heads, along their flanks, on their feet.

"You okay, kid?"

She sighed at the nickname and the question. Drake was only a year older than her, but he'd affectionately been calling her that since sometime in middle school. "Better than yesterday. Sorry for being a sobbing mess."

Heat flamed her face as she recalled blubbering while Drake had euthanized the other dogs. Fourteen canines and only two had survived. It was beyond sad. Two had already been dead by the time she'd found them in the coop.

"Never apologize for emotion." He crossed his arms and turned to face her, his shoes squeaking on the linoleum. In Drake-like fashion, his expression was unreadable. "Flynn told me the whole story from before I arrived. You did good out there."

"Thank you. I wish we could've saved more." She eyed the dogs again. The gray one started to stir. "We're not going to have to put them down, too, are we?"

"I hope not. It was hard to gauge their behavior. They were in pain and did little more than the expected fight-or-flight." He rubbed his jaw. "I've got them on painkillers and sedated."

Their food and water bowls were full, indicating they hadn't woken through the night. Or were afraid to eat. "How old are they?"

"Best guess? Under two years."

Poor little guys hadn't had such a great start in life. "Did you name them?"

"Saved that for you."

Aw. She studied them, head tilted. They were both males, but she thought they should have gentle names, unlike the life they'd had so far, but also something that implied strength of character, endurance. Perhaps nature-like.

She pointed to the tan one, "Cedar," and then the gray, "Cyprus."

Drake bit the cap off a marker he dug from his pocket and wrote their names on the kennel tag. Thor headed for the other side of the room and flopped by the door.

The gray Pitbull, Cyprus, opened his eyes. Confusion and a little pain radiated through his hesitant gaze. Without lifting his head, he blinked up at her, and her heart twisted. She crouched and reached for the latch.

"Take it easy, kid. Go slow. We have no idea how they'll respond."

She nodded as Drake stepped back to give them space. Chances were, the dogs would be intimidated by men since their owner was a male. Tension radiated from Drake, but Gabby kept her mood calm. Animals could read people and she didn't want to alarm the dog.

Opening the latch, she unhurriedly scooped a small handful of food and, leaving the cage open, scooted back, setting the food down as she went. She sat on the floor, legs spread, hands in her lap in a nonthreatening pose.

Cyprus lifted his head and eyed the trail of kibble from the kennel to her feet. His eyes had a dazed look from the drugs, but he was awake. He licked his chops.

"Shh, it's okay. Come here."

The door to the room opened and closed behind her, but she kept her gaze on the dog. Sudden movements or lack of eye contact might spook him. From her peripheral, she caught Flynn step beside Drake. Cyprus eyed the brothers.

"Maybe you guys should sit down?"

Drake signed to Flynn. They each took a gradual step back, still staying within ten feet just in case, and sat cross-legged on the floor. All three O'Grady men were wonderful vets, compassionate and caring. They knew animals and their temperaments. But right now, they were in overprotective friend mode, not veterinarian.

Cyprus watched their every move. Since he wasn't paying her any mind, she glanced at Flynn. His jaw was set, his eyes round with concern. His gaze flicked to hers and his nostrils flared. Worry wrinkled his forehead, but he stayed put, reluctantly trusting her.

She turned back to the dog. "Hey, boy," she cooed. "Who's a good boy?"

Cyprus tilted his head and struggled to his feet.

Flynn flinched out of the corner of her eye, his hands flexing.

Her heart pounded, but she forced her body to relax as Cyprus sniffed at the first piece of kibble just outside the kennel. He looked up at her as if to ask, *can I?*

Aw, man. Eyes watering, she smiled. "Go ahead. It's okay. Good boy." Gaze on her, the dog ate the piece and licked his chops.

As he focused on the next one, the door to the room opened. Quiet footsteps walked toward them and Cade came into view. The dog—and man—froze.

Drake quietly cleared his throat. "Gabby's doing her dog whisperer impression."

Without a word, Cade sat next to Flynn.

It took five minutes, but Cyprus eventually ate the next piece, and then the next until he made it all the way to Gabby's feet. Flynn's breathing had grown louder with every move from the dog until his inhalations were this side of panting.

When there was no more kibble left, Gabby carefully offered her hand palm down for the dog to sniff. Flynn made a sound of duress, all but hyperventilating. Cade set his hand on Flynn's tense arm.

"Drake," she said quietly, eyes on Cyprus, "sign that I'm okay. Remind Flynn to breathe." More worried about her friend than the dog, she smiled at Cyprus as Drake complied. "Shh. Come here, good boy."

Less than a foot away, the dog watched her hand. The stump of his tail was up as was his one ear, indicating he didn't feel threatened. Nothing about his demeanor showed aggression, including his fur, which was flat on his flank, not raised.

A moment passed and then Cyprus licked her hand. She breathed a laugh, eyes filling, throat tight. "Good boy. That's a good Cyprus." At her praise, he licked again. She repeated his name so he'd start getting used to it.

His stump wagged and she gingerly lifted her hand, giving the dog ample time to understand she was going to pet him. Flynn wheezed, but she ignored him and set her hand on the short, wiry hair of Cyprus's neck, leaving it there. His stump kept wagging and, after a beat, he tilted his head toward her touch.

She laughed, scratching his scruff. "Drake, grab a few pieces of kibble and come over here. Flynn's too tense. He might scare Cyprus. Cade, assure Flynn I'm okay before he strokes out."

While Drake moved to obey and Cade quietly laughed, Gabby kept praising the dog. Flynn continued to hyperventilate, and Cade set a hand on his brother's shoulder, not that it seemed to help. Cyprus watched Drake out of the corner of his eye, but showed no signs of distress.

From next to her, Drake held out his hand, offering the food. Unlike with Gabby, Cyprus took the kibble right away from Drake's palm. After giving his hand a thorough tongue bath, Cyprus all but climbed in Drake's lap, kissing his face. Mindful of the bandages, he petted him, a relaxed grin on his face Gabby hadn't seen in too long.

"I think he remembers you're the one who took him from that awful place." She wiped her eyes. "Looks like you have a friend. A new pet?"

He grunted, still smiling. "Maybe. We'll have to see how he does, let him hang out with Moses for a while when he's healed." Moses was Drake's German Shepherd and had an easygoing submissive personality. They'd probably do great together.

Poor Cyprus started to show signs of fatigue and went back to his kennel. Cedar never stirred, so she let him sleep. Maybe she'd try with him over her lunch break.

Just as Gabby closed the latch on the kennel, Cade's hand slapped her back. Hard. "Nice job."

Flynn strode out of the room, the door slamming as an exclamation point. She stared after him, worry tightening her chest. Surely he knew she'd never do anything she didn't feel was safe. If Drake hadn't been in the room, she never would've attempted to engage the dog. She'd wrestled canines bigger than Cyprus.

Cade grinned. "You scared the crap out of Flynn. He might need a shot of whiskey."

Drake rubbed his hand over his dark hair. "Hell, I might need two shots. You had me concerned for a while, too."

Cade glanced at his watch. "And we're open. Time to see patients. Good job, Gabs."

Drake nodded his agreement and she followed both men out.

She and Flynn had clinic today. Their first patient wasn't for another hour. She stood in the hallway, wondering if she should give him some time to decompress or go check on him. He'd been really worked up and obviously concerned. After a quick debate, she headed toward his office.

He had his arms crossed and head down while standing in front of his desk. His dark, reddish blond hair was mussed and sticking up on the right side. Stance rigid, he didn't seem to see her at first.

He wore dark blue scrubs that fit his lean, muscular frame. The drawstring waist was low on his hips and the cuffs of the top strained against his biceps. She recalled the way he'd held her last night. Gentle, despite the hard planes of his body, and his touch had been soothing.

Until she'd kissed him. Then he had her damp and desperate with the switch in chemistry. She wondered why she never paid attention to his quiet sexuality before. Flynn was a great combination of confident and humble, of boy-next-door and yum.

His chin jerked up as if he'd read her thoughts and his gaze locked on hers. Before she could blink, he was across the room. He shoved the door at her back closed and pressed her against it. Hunter versus prey, and the look in his eyes told her, in no uncertain terms, eating her alive was a distinct possibility. One hundred and eighty pounds of tense, hard male invaded her space. A jolt of pleasure rocked through her. With his palms on the wood beside her head, he crushed his mouth to hers.

Holy wow.

He devoured her, left no crevice of her mouth unexplored. Demanding strokes of his tongue swept against hers, fraught with strain and hot with hunger. Complete and utter domination. He pinned her to the door with his body, her nipples pebbling behind her bra, his erection snug against her belly. Every available inch of his body was in direct contact with hers.

She grabbed tufts of his hair, arching into him, and moaned. The vibration must've tipped him off because he responded with a growl, kissing her harder, deeper, until it seemed like he'd climbed inside her.

A fast thrust of his hips and he wrenched away, staring down at her through narrowed eyes with breaths soughing. "So damn proud of you. Scared a decade off my life in that room, but hell. That was a really good thing to see this morning after yesterday."

His voice was lower, more guttural than the tone he'd used before. She was still trying to get used to hearing him without swooning. There was no chance. She was a goner. Not to mention, using that timbre while issuing compliments? *Uhn.* She could straddle him like he was a horse right now.

The strain left his body and he relaxed against her. His hazel gaze swept her face, a smile teasing his mouth. He brought his arms around her back, easing her onto her toes with the embrace. "How long are we doing the no-sex thing?"

She opened and closed her mouth. "I didn't, uh...I don't know."

"I want you, Gabby. Soon." A contented sigh escaped her lips as he nuzzled her neck. "Never been like this before," he whispered against her mouth.

And then he kissed her again, softer, and she felt it all the way to her bones.

Chapter 17

Desperate to finish the workday, Flynn inspected the abdomen of a Westie who'd come in for a growth check. Last patient on his exam table, and then he could talk Gabby into dinner at his place. Between the dog-fighting ring and her trying to people-orientate the rescued Pitbulls, the past couple days had left him more than a little unnerved. And she was better than any damn therapy.

Gliding his hand up the thoracic exterior, he gently pushed along the edges of the Westie's fatty tumor. Without measuring, it didn't appear to be larger than the last check a couple months ago, but the client's owner was paranoid, so he pulled out his small flex ruler.

He looked at Gabby. *"No change in size. Looks good. Does it seem to bother him?"* If that were the case, they could surgically remove the mass, but these tumors were noncancerous and typically caused no issues.

Gabby interpreted for the client—one of Cade's former patients who'd been devastated by the news his brother was off the market—and turned back to Flynn. "She says he doesn't seem to notice it."

He nodded and, with a smile, rubbed the dog's ears. Snowden, being a small breed, danced in spastic circles trying to play. Setting the white fluffball on the floor, he turned to relay orders to Gabby to have them return in a couple months. But the owner was all up in his space.

A bat of her eyelashes, and the woman stroked a long fingernail down the front of his scrub top, making no ploy of hiding her come-on. Her shiny brown hair caught the light when she flipped the locks over her shoulder, sending the overpowering scent of her perfume right up his nostrils.

He forced a swallow. How had Cade dealt with this day in and day out? Before proposing to Avery, single females of all ages had made bogus appointments just to launch an attempt to be his next conquest. He'd had to fight them off. Things had died down since committing to his fiancée, but Cade still got the occasional suspect appointment. A few of them had moved onto Flynn's roster.

Nothing like the runner-up position to inflate a guy's ego. And none of these dates would ever pan out to potential, even if Gabby weren't a factor. After one evening, the women would realize the communication barrier and grow frustrated. Story of his life.

He stepped back, but Ms. Keller followed. "Do you have plans for Friday night? I make a mean lasagna."

Was there such a thing as a nice lasagna? His gaze flicked to Gabby's, who smiled with her eyebrows pinged to her hairline. Lovely. His girlfriend was amused he was being hit on. Right in front of her.

He signed for her to interpret. *"Tell her I'm seeing someone and, I swear, we're coming out as a couple before Cade's wedding."*

Grinning wider, she looked at the woman. "He says he's flattered, but he's involved with someone at the moment."

Yeah, that. Very diplomatic.

Ms. Keller pouted. "You sure?"

He nodded emphatically, then breathed when she stepped away. Christ, to have an eighth of Cade's charm right now...

She clipped the leash on her dog and headed for the hallway toward the front desk.

After she was out of sight, Gabby laughed. "You looked like a deer in headlights. So cute."

He narrowed his eyes. Most women would've been jealous. But no. Gabby thought it had been...cute to be molested by the owners.

"Not kidding. We're coming out. Soon." Not just to deter the single population of females, but because he wanted the world to know he was with her. It might have taken a bit to adjust and move past all that could go sideways by being romantically involved, but he'd never been so glad to be wrong. This thing between them was damn near perfect.

Her shoulders moved with a sigh. Smile engaged, she kissed him lightly and too quickly before stepping away. "I'm okay with that."

"How about you be okay with dinner at my place tonight?"

Head tilt. "Really?"

"Yeah." Why was his wanting to spend time with her so shocking? Especially after the past couple days, he needed her after hours. They'd done it as friends, why not as a couple?

She shrugged. "Okay. I need to run home and shower."

He silently thanked her for putting that visual in his head and made his way to his office to finish up a couple electronic charts before leaving.

On the way home, he picked up Chinese takeout. After he let Fletch out and had his own shower, Gabby walked in the door looking adorable in jeans and a pink T-shirt. Even better, she kissed him hello.

He eyed the cartons and thought about setting up dinner on the kitchen table or in front of the TV, but it was a nice night. His deck hadn't been used all winter.

He jerked his head toward the patio doors in question, but she stepped forward and pressed her soft curves against him. Wrapping her arms around his waist, she tilted her face up to his. "I know you were concerned with me and the dog this morning, but thank you for letting me do my thing without interfering."

He studied her face, recalling the outright panic from before clinic hours. He'd had to remind himself about a thousand times she knew what she was doing in order not to go ballistic. Guess the fear hadn't abated because there went his pulse again.

Focusing on her body pressed to his instead, he framed her face with his hands and gave her a brief kiss. "Concerned is not the word I'd use. You put me in cardiac arrest."

A thought slammed into him with the force of a twister. As her friend, he'd always been severely protective of her, but this new shift in their relationship had amped that to all-consuming. Had thrown everything about their dynamic, in fact. They were still them, except there was this added element that altered the air around them, hummed under his skin.

Truth be told, relationships weren't supposed to be this easy. He'd had other lovers. She'd dated other men. But none of his previous experiences had been in the ballpark of being with her. They hadn't even been in the same league considering the language barrier on his end.

Yet he and Gabby had transitioned from friends to dating as if it were an inevitable outcome. Their bodies seemed to recognize the touch, their minds in sync, and it left him wondering when the coin would flip. Because, damn. There had to be a flaw here somewhere. Great chemistry, similar likes, mutual respect. Nothing was this perfect.

They hadn't made love yet and perhaps that was his grating issue. Sex had always been stressful for him and much less rewarding than he figured it should. Part of that was his fault and the paranoia of making sure his partners were satisfied. Eyes open, attuned to every facial expression, worrying about whether he was being too gentle or not hard enough. Exhausting.

Gabby was the first woman he'd ever kissed with his eyes closed, the first woman he'd allowed himself to let go with, and he'd been telling himself it was because he knew her so well he'd be in tune if something were wrong. He wondered if making love to her would bring perfect crashing down.

She pressed her cool fingers to his forehead as if smoothing out the worry lines. As always, her touch was a balm. He stroked his knuckles down her cheek to tell her just that very thing.

"Where did you go just now?"

He shook his head. "Nowhere." And their food was getting cold. "Want to eat on the back deck?"

Her smile could stop wars. It was just that damn genuine, that addictive. "Sure."

While he brought the food out, she tossed a ball for Fletch in the waning light. Flynn sat in a chair on the deck watching them, the cartons on the table before him. His dog, like himself, had a thing for Gabby. The retriever could recognize her name as easily as trigger words like "walk" or "treat."

She turned toward the deck as the last of the pinkish-purple light dipped behind the horizon. Stars winked in the navy sky as the full moon illuminated the yard. In a couple months, summer would be around and they'd have more daylight, but he didn't complain. The temp was mild for spring and the breeze slight. Pine wafted from the dense woods behind the clearing, mingling with damp grass and moss. Not a half-bad way to end the day.

When he turned back to her seated in a chair next to him, she had the takeout dished onto paper plates and was picking the broccoli out of her meal to add to his, then the carrots from his onto her plate. He shook his head, grinning.

She looked up. "What?"

"Nothing." She was adorable, that's what. Her aversion to broccoli and his to carrots, and the way she automatically divided the vegetables was, well... Yeah. Cute.

She rolled her baby blues and handed him a plate.

They ate taking in their surroundings, and though they'd done this a million times, he wanted to keep doing it a million more. He pictured her here every night, eating dinner together and winding down from work. Making love to her and waking up to her face each morning. In time, maybe there would be a couple of blond-haired kids running around chasing the dog. Kids with her infectious smile and huge eyes.

His heart pounded as he stared at her. Pert nose, round cheeks, long lashes. Caramel hair up in a ponytail, her skin catching the moonlight.

She'd set her plate aside and was having some kind of conversation with his dog. And shit. He was more than halfway in love with her already. Probably had been since kindergarten.

"What? Something wrong?"

He shook his head. More like things were so damn right. His brain disconnected from his mouth and he told her what was on his mind. "Just a heads-up, I'm falling for you. Don't have a clue what to do about it either." He'd never had feelings this strong for someone, never been in love. Wasn't even sure he'd recognize it if it weren't Gabby.

Her lips parted, emotion swimming in her eyes. The shock of awe mingling with an *aw, hell* had him scrambling to distract her from his stupid almost-declaration.

Rising, he wrapped an arm around her and lifted her from the seat. Making his way down the deck stairs to the grass, he sank into a lounge chair and plunked her between his knees. Her back to his front, he wrapped his arms around her and dropped his chin on the top of her head. Her scent of honey collided with nature and settled inside him.

A few beats passed before she relaxed against him and he closed his eyes. His chest rumbled, indicating she was talking, but he kept his eyes shut, not wanting to know if she wasn't at the same emotional level he was or, worse, that she might brush him off in order to save awkwardness.

Undeterred, she turned in his arms and he conceded. Her dark blue eyes searched his. She stared at him so long he had the urge to squirm.

Finally, her gaze moved overhead. "Beautiful night."

He smiled, not disagreeing.

"I used to wish on stars when I was a kid."

Didn't surprise him one iota. "What did you wish for?" No doubt fairy tales and unicorns. Gabby loved happy endings, ever the optimist.

She sighed. "It doesn't matter." In Gabby-code that meant they hadn't come true, thus she pretended her childish secrets didn't matter. As he was about to tell her everything mattered, she looked at him. "What about you? Ever wish on stars?"

His grin spread. Christ, how could a guy not fall for her? "No. Since I have a penis and a Y chromosome, it's not in my DNA."

Another eye roll. "Okay, what about stargazing? Ever do that?"

He had, a time or two. Not for years, though. Before he'd died, Dad used to take him and his brothers camping when they were younger and Flynn would stare at the sky. It usually wasn't the constellations that drew him, however. "You could lose sight of the moon counting all those stars."

Glancing up, he took in the clear night. Not a cloud in sight. "Everything else is an accessory."

"Hold up. Did you just call the stars bling?" Her incredulous glare pulled a laugh from him. "Does this mean I won't get some rhetoric about me being your brightest shining star?"

Foolish woman. "You are no star, Gabby. You're the sky. The rest of us are just circling your orbit." True story.

Slowly, she straightened, her round gaze locked on his. Ah, yes. His Gabby, heart in her eyes. "Heck, Flynn. You just might get laid for that comment. Wow."

Laughing, he rubbed his eyes. Laughed harder at her confounded expression.

Then she pressed her lips to his and the smile was nothing but a distant memory. Straddling him, she crushed her breasts to his chest and brought their good parts in direct alignment. Her tongue sought entry and he opened for her, letting her in to obliterate thought as he knew it.

She rocked against him and he sucked a ragged breath into his lungs, grabbing her round ass. He wasn't a hundred percent sure if he intended to encourage more or slow things down, but she kissed her way to his neck and he bucked.

Damn, her mouth was a weapon. His neck and especially his ears had always been his hot buttons, and she wasn't just pushing them, she was pounding. Her fingers drove under his shirt, lightly raking his abs, which concaved at her touch. Higher, and the pads of her thumbs circled his nipples, working them into peaks while her mouth tortured his restraint into snapping.

Lick. Suck. Nip.

Christ. If he didn't have her soon, he might combust.

An adjustment later, and he had her back on the lounger, her shirt shoved up to her chin. Kneeling between her legs, he kissed her belly in a path to her breasts and tugged the blue lace aside to get at the goods. His breath stalled as he stared at her under the moonlight and on display. Beautiful.

He closed his mouth around her nipple, gaze on her to watch her response. Her cheeks flushed and she arched, eyes closing. And he was harder than he'd ever been in his life. Increasing the pressure, he sucked, moving his hand to her other breast to work that one. Her fingers wove into his hair, clenched. He shifted to her other breast, and the cooling air against the wet peak he'd abandoned puckered.

She shivered and he stilled.

They were in his backyard, where anyone from his family could pop over and stumble onto what they were doing. Mom's cabin was just on the other side of Cade's next door, not visible through the trees, but close. Drake's place was in the other direction and also nearby. Private lane or not, she deserved better than possible exhibitionism. Never mind the fact that things were heading toward the point of no return, his first time making love to her wasn't going to be in his damn backyard.

Reality eked in and he quickly replaced her bra cups. She lifted her head with a *what the hell* in her eyes. Tugging her shirt down, he urged her to sit up.

"Not here." He smoothed his hand over her hair, trying to calm his erratic heart. He wanted their first time to be unrushed, where he could take his time learning her body and not be concerned with on-call or getting up the next day to work. It was Drake's rotation for the pager on Friday. "Spend the weekend with me?"

She studied him, seemingly absorbing his offer. The meaning was implied. He'd be taking her to bed. And if he had any say in the matter, they wouldn't be leaving said bed until Sunday night, if ever. It was she who'd put the stipulation on the physical part of things, wanting them to transition before jumping. Sex with him didn't appear to make her nervous and he was done waiting.

He wanted her. Period.

Closing her eyes, a smile ghosted her lips before she pressed them together. He had no idea what was running through her head, but if she didn't answer him soon, he'd—

"Yes." A heavy sigh moved her shoulders, warm breath caressing his chin. "I'll stay the weekend." She rose to stand and leaned over the chair to press a kiss on his mouth.

Chapter 18

Finally Friday. Holy cow, this day couldn't come fast enough. From the last stall in the Carsons' barn, Gabby wiped the sweat from her brow with her sleeve.

The rest of the week had been pure crap. They'd had to head to police headquarters twice to make statements regarding what she and Flynn had encountered in regards to the dogfighting. According to the district attorney, the most time Jose would get was five years in prison—likely out in two—and a two-hundred fifty thousand dollar fine. And that was *if* the judge tacked on animal neglect and cruelty charges.

Not nearly a long enough punishment. Flynn had been beyond irate, but law was law. It needed changing.

Avery had double-booked Flynn and Gabby's clinic hours on Wednesday to give them an extra day for home visits in order to check up on the rescued animals. Thankfully, all were doing well, including the horses they'd followed up with today. They'd required new shoes and some wound care on their hooves, but other than needing nourishment, they'd be okay.

Cedar hadn't fared so well. Drake had been forced to put the other Pitbull down. Unlike Cyprus, Cedar hadn't adjusted to human contact and had displayed major aggression. Gabby had tried so hard to work with him on her lunch breaks and a little after hours, but she never got farther than approaching the kennel before the dog snarled, baring teeth. Drake had been so concerned, he wouldn't let her change the food and water dishes. He'd done it himself.

With the dog muzzled and heavily sedated, she'd sat by his side, weeping buckets while Drake had administered the euthanasia. Flynn had stayed with her that night, holding her until she'd fallen asleep.

The whole thing kinda made her understand why some people believed in capital punishment. At least Cyprus was thriving. Able to lose the cone and most of the bandages, Gabby had worked with him in the kennel yard out back and he was very playful. Gentle. Drake planned on trying to incorporate his German Shepherd, Moses, and Cyprus together this weekend.

Blowing out a sigh, she stood just outside the last stall and glanced down the long passageway to the open barn doors. Rain came down in sheets, creating mud puddles and drenching the grass. Humidity hung heavy in the air and the temps were much warmer for spring than usual. Over snow, she'd take it.

In the stall beside her, Flynn worked on fitting the last horseshoe on their last patient. And thank God. In a few, they could head down the mountain, drop off their stuff at the clinic, and go home. She'd never been so grateful for a weekend in all her life. Especially because she'd be spending it with Flynn.

She shivered in anticipation. His initial hesitancy in changing their relationship seemed to have passed. He was open with her, with his desires, and it was obvious he wanted her. Oh God, she wanted him. Whether a flutter in her belly from his kiss or the lick of flames on her skin from his touch, he pulled so many visceral reactions from her. No one she'd been with had ever been as passionate as Flynn.

They were going to be so good together. Her girly parts zinged in expectation.

He wore dark green scrubs today that brought out the mossy flecks in his hazel eyes. His strawberry blond hair was this side of long and starting to curl a bit around his ears. A day's worth of scruff covered his jaw, adding to the laid-back sexiness. Hard thighs, narrow waist, ripples on his abs, bicep muscles flexing, corded forearms...

Yes, please.

Watching the wide expanse of his back and the way the muscles shifted under his scrubs was becoming her favorite pastime. His tight ass when he bent over wasn't an eyesore either. Not that drooling over his body wasn't fun, but it wasn't her only draw to him. It was in the way he held her or smiled or how he made her laugh. And the things he said sometimes? Holy Gawd.

You're the sky. The rest of us are just circling your orbit.

Her belly heated just remembering. Would this day never end? She was so ready to get him alone.

Checking his progress and noting he was about done, she bent to retrieve the supplies. She'd finished her immunizations, rewarding the horses with carrots, and was just waiting on Flynn. Most of their farms did their own care, but Flynn had directed the rescue owners not to do anything with the horses until he could better evaluate. Good thing, too, because two of the horses had wounds from embedded gravel.

With the bag packed, she straightened and rolled her shoulders. After she got home, she would quickly shower and shave before going to Flynn's. Maybe use that new perfume he'd bought her for Christmas. It had a light, airy scent that hinted at sexy without shoving it in his face. Subtle. She mentally went through her panty drawer, wondering if he would like her green lace or blue crisscross ones better.

Choices, choices.

She smiled. With any luck, she wouldn't be wearing them long. It had been so long since she'd had a partner that nerves swam in her belly, but she quieted them with a mental bitch-slap.

A few of the horses in the stalls toward the barn's entrance stirred. Pin prickles of awareness skittered up her spine. Unsure why, she paused to listen. The Carsons had five horses in addition to the four they'd rescued, and all but the one with Flynn seemed to be...agitated. Hooves scraped dirt. Whinnies rent the air.

As goose bumps rose on her skin, she exited the last stall doorway and stepped into the aisle to check on things. She froze mid-step, her heartbeat screeching to a stop. Roughly eighty feet were between her and the barn door, where a...mountain lion stood in the open space. Head up, it sniffed the air.

"Oh shit." She glanced at Flynn, but he was in the stall and focused on the horse, his back to her.

The clinic bag with her supplies was inside the stall, but the emergency tote was several feet to her left by the tack room. The satellite phone and, most important, the tranquilizer gun, were in the second bag.

Crap, crap, crap.

This was the danger in mountain visits. Though the wildlife typically veered clear of humans, it wasn't unheard of for them to prowl for game or come hunting near the farms. The closest she and Flynn had come to this scenario had been a black bear a couple years back who'd scared the owners when they'd fed chickens. Which had happened an hour before their arrival. She'd almost run over a bobcat last fall with the clinic SUV, and a herd of elk once blocked the road for thirty minutes four winters ago, but...

Holy shit. There was a mountain lion, and it was...looking...at...her. Its tan fur covered powerful, thick muscle that shifted as it turned its head, sidestepping. Huge, huge paws stopped in the dirt as it tilted its head, ears perked. Then...its yellow eyes resettled on her.

Her stomach bottomed out as her throat closed, body immobile. Her limbs locked as she stared back, fifty gazillion thoughts flittering through her head. Would there be anything left of her for an open casket? Would it hurt real bad or would she die fast? Would the red panties wash out her skin tone if she wore them tonight? Could she run fast enough from a wildcat to get inside a stall and lock the door? If she screamed, would it alert the owners in time to get a shotgun? Did she turn the coffeepot off this morning?

Okay. She forced air into her lungs. Aside from a cutout window on the doors, the stalls were floor to ceiling. The animals were protected. The lion would have to claw through the wooden doors to get to the horses, which would take time. It hadn't seen Flynn, so as long as he didn't make any sudden movements, he was good.

It was up to her to do something. Mentally, she scrolled through the contents of the emergency bag, trying to remember where, exactly, the tranquilizer gun was located. Main section, left side, in a black case. Crap. Besides needing to get to the bag, that meant unzipping said bag, opening the case, and removing the gun. Too many steps.

And damn. She'd only shot the thing once before. As practice.

Eyes on the lion, fine hairs standing erect, shaking arms held stiff at her sides, she chanced a slow step to her left. It followed the movement with his eyes, then sniffed the air again. Breaths rasping, she moved again. Its head jerked her way and a low rumble of a growl rippled to her. She whimpered.

Flynn's shoes shuffled in the dirt and she nearly shut her eyes in terror. *Please, please, please. Stay where you are, Flynn.*

"Gabby?" His feet stuttered to a stop—by the sound of it, inches outside the stall—but she didn't dare look.

Oh hell. The mountain lion glanced Flynn's way.

Pressing her lips together to muffle another whimper, she held her palm up, hoping Flynn got the message and stayed put. Then she pointed to the emergency bag, telling him her plan. Blessedly, he didn't move.

Her knees knocked and her legs shook, but she slowly inched closer to the bag, eyes never leaving the lion. Five feet. Four. She was almost there. Two. One.

In gradual degrees, she crouched by the bag.

Whinnies rent the air. Hooves banged against stalls.

Another low growl from the wildcat. It...stepped...closer.

No, no, no. She did not want to die. At least, not before she'd had the chance to have sex with Flynn. Maybe get married and have babies and... Screw that. She didn't want to die at all. Most assuredly, not by being eaten alive.

Flynn's exhalations were rough, short. He emitted a low noise of frustration and terror, which amped her fear to DEFCON. Her heart jack-hammered against her ribs and the breath in her lungs stalled when the thing set its sights on Flynn.

She fingered the tab on the bag and slid the zipper open. The sound of teeth releasing in the mechanism was like an air horn. Dipping her hand inside, she felt around for the black case and her fingertips brushed the cool metal. Working her hand down to the latch, she flicked the release and pulled out the tranquillizer gun.

The object felt foreign in her hand. Heavy. Awkward.

Uneven breaths hissed between her lips when she stood and pointed the barrel at the lion. Her movements jerked its attention back to her and Flynn flinched. In reaction, the lion growled, baring teeth. It prowled forward, one step, two, and Gabby released the trigger.

The pop echoed in her ears and the shot rattled her teeth. The lion roared, pissed off as hell, and whipped its gaze to where the tranquillizer dart protruded from its flank.

Well, shit. She'd hit him. First try, too.

The fur on its back rose and its ears lowered as yellow eyes narrowed to slits. Classic signs of aggression, which caused every red blood cell in her veins to chill thirty degrees.

To err on the side of caution, they'd dosed the gun with high levels to enact quickly should they ever encounter this scenario. Too high, and it would kill the animal. Too low, and it would do no good. She had no idea how long the sedative would take to be effective, but if her frazzled brain recalled right, it could be anywhere from seconds to minutes.

They didn't have minutes because the lion whipped its head around and crouched as if to pounce. Shit, shit, shit. Raising the gun again, she aimed.

Footsteps pounded from her right. Flynn launched into her side, careening them into an open, empty stall. She had the vaguest blip of him grabbing the door edge and dragging it with them before they landed hard in a loose pallet of hay, him sprawled on top of her. The breath whooshed from her lungs.

Hinges rattled as the door thunked closed. Snarling followed from the other side. Scratching. A thump. Then, silence.

Chest heaving, Flynn jerked his chin over his shoulder toward the stall door. He watched it for several beats, then stared down at her. His frantic gaze ran over her face, lower. "Are you all right?"

She nodded repeatedly, probably resembling a bobblehead on a snowmobile. She was shaking so hard her muscles locked around bone and squeezed. Air wouldn't pass through her airway...in or out.

Holy God Almighty.

Flynn collapsed on top of her, face buried between her breasts. His body vibrated, probably with residual adrenaline. After a moment of seemingly catching his breath, he groaned. "I should've been an accountant." He lifted his head. Fear, frustration, and anger shone in his eyes, twisted his mouth. "A fucking accountant."

Not that she'd been moving, couldn't if she wanted to, but she stilled just the same. Her brain tried to process his words. She stared at him as a bubble of laughter rose in her chest and...escaped. Giddy, frenzied giggles that were ridiculous and unstoppable. And then her eyes welled, turning her hysterical laughter to tears. Sobs.

His gaze softened and he cupped her cheeks. "Gabby, sweetheart." He kissed her eyes, her wet cheeks, her mouth. "I'm sorry."

She waved her hand to dismiss his apology, but he wasn't looking anywhere but her face. "I could've been your receptionist," she wailed. The past week's tension and stress caught up with her and she let go. Hot, outlandish tears dripped down her temples into her hair.

Pressing his forehead to hers, he waited her out.

After she didn't know how long—the spell didn't seem very lengthy, halting as fast as it began—she hiccupped through the last of the tears. God. She needed a drink.

"Dr. Flynn? Gabby?" Footsteps shuffled from outside the stall.

She tapped Flynn's shoulder and he rolled off of her onto his back, draping an arm over his face.

Mrs. Carson's expletives muffled from the other side of the door, then it opened to reveal all five feet of the farm's owner. Her gray hair stood on end. "Hell on wheels. You two okay in there?"

Gabby glanced at the woman's feet where an unconscious mountain lion snored. She dropped her head back in the hay. "Yeah. Fabulous. I just need to look for my heart, which is somewhere over there." She pointed in the general direction of the tack room. The adrenaline was beginning to wear off, a crash impending.

Flynn sat up. *"That tranquillizer won't hold long. Have her call the ranger service to collect the animal."*

She nodded and translated his request. After Mrs. Carson left, Gabby unsteadily got to her feet and brushed hay off her scrubs, eyes on the wildcat.

If Flynn hadn't barreled into her and shoved them into the stall, *and* managed to close the door, she'd be...dinner right now. The animal had clawed and fought another few moments once it had reached the stall. It had collapsed right where she'd been standing.

Screw this. She needed more than a drink. She'd take the whole bottle.

Flynn got to his feet, and by the look on his face, he was thinking the same thing. Hunching over, hands on his thighs, he shook his head. Sucking a deep breath, he straightened and hopped over the lion, grabbing the tranquillizer gun a few feet away. He checked the chamber, seemed satisfied, and then waved her over.

Gun pointed down, he took her hand in his other one and helped her out of the stall. "Get everything packed up. I'll watch him, just in case."

She eyed the main door down the long aisle. Oh, look. It had stopped raining.

With a sigh, she grabbed the bags, put them in the car, and called Avery from the satellite phone to tell her what happened. Humidity clung to her skin. The scent of saltwater and rain drifted in the air mixing with pine and damp soil.

"Crap on a cracker. You both are determined to bury me in paperwork so I don't have a wedding next weekend." She paused. "Are you sure you're okay? Cade's done for the day. I can send him—"

"We're good. Just rattled." She glanced up at the crunch of gravel. A white pickup belonging to the forest rangers pulled in the driveway and around the clinic SUV, followed by a yellow truck for the wildlife rescue. "I gotta go. We'll be back soon."

She headed for the barn and shook hands with Grant Carver, the wildlife guy. She took in his brown jumpsuit with a swift glance, noting he filled it very well. They'd gone to high school together, but she hadn't seen him around much. "Thanks for coming so fast."

He scratched his head, shifting his thick chestnut waves. "Not a problem. We weren't far away, actually. So. New pet?"

"Ha." She motioned for him to follow her inside where a forest ranger was standing beside Flynn and Mrs. Carson. Gabby translated the conversation about what happened.

Ranger Rick—she couldn't remember his name as he was a recent Redwood Ridge transplant—crossed his arms. "Food supply must be scarce. This guy here is pretty skinny and they don't tend to come toward civilization unless desperate."

Skinny? She glanced at the lion, what looked like all one-hundred and ten pounds of him, and shuddered. Flynn ran a reassuring hand down her back.

Before the feral cat woke up, the guys transferred him into a large steel cage and into the back of a pickup. Then Gabby checked the horses one last time and headed for the SUV.

Flynn was waiting in the passenger seat, fisted hands in his lap and gaze straight ahead. His jaw ticked like a drum. Since he seemed ready to snap, she started the car and pulled onto the road. He didn't move one muscle the whole drive back. She kept glancing at him, getting more and more concerned as they got closer to the clinic. When he still didn't budge after she'd parked, she shifted in her seat and faced him.

She waved her hand to get his attention.

He glanced at her from the corner of his eye, not bothering to turn his head. Was he...mad at her? "Are we still on for this weekend?"

A stiff nod was his only reply.

She lifted her hands to sign, but he was out of the vehicle. He stomped inside the clinic, leaving her confused.

Chapter 19

How he'd managed it, Flynn hadn't a clue. Somehow, he'd driven himself home from the clinic, showered, and opened a beer. He wanted whiskey, a lot of it, but he settled for a longneck because Gabby was coming over. Him falling on the floor drunk probably wouldn't put her in the mood.

The image of her standing in the barn, eyes wide, body trembling, shoved into his mind again. Setting the beer down on the kitchen counter, he pressed his palms to his eyes and cursed. But the memory kept assaulting his brain, one after another.

Her demanding he stay where he was as if she would handle the threat. The way she'd inched toward the emergency bag while the mountain lion had her in its sights. How she'd paled and seemed to stop breathing when she'd fired the tranquillizer. And shit. The point five seconds he'd had to react when the thing had gotten ready to attack.

Gabby, clawed to bits. Gabby, eyes fixed as the life drained out of her. Gabby, chest hitching with her last breaths. Gabby...gone. All of those what-ifs...

Fucking hell. He was so damn brittle with tension the slightest touch might shatter him. His muscles ached. His bones throbbed. His temples pounded. Christ. He just might lose his shit.

Fletch nudged his thigh. His poor dog, sensing Flynn's mood, hadn't left his side since he'd gotten home. Wide eyes laced with understanding implored him to get better, to calm down.

Sighing, he rubbed the retriever's ears, sinking his fingers into soft brown fur. "I'm sorry, boy." He glanced out the window speckled with rain from earlier. Maybe tossing a ball around for Fletch would help them both unwind until Gabby arrived. He looked at the dog. "Ball?"

Fletch's whole ass moved with a tail wag. *Yes, yes. Now!*

Outside, Flynn sucked gulps of humid air and threw Fletch's favorite ball around. Once pink and girly, it had been a gift from Gabby, thus why it was his dog's favorite. After repeated use, it was faded to near white and dirty with slobber.

Closing his eyes, he let the gentle breeze off the Pacific wash over his face. Saltwater tinged with rain and brine helped soothe him a little. Peat moss and pine from the forest mingled with the other scents, reminding him why he loved it here so much. The abundance of nature, coupled with the privacy tucked back in this area of Redwood Ridge, was perfect for his personality. The blend of colors, the changing seasons...yeah. He'd needed this breather.

Fletch returned from the copse of trees and into the clearing, dropping the ball at Flynn's feet. *I got the ball. I got the ball.*

"One more time."

After a last toss, they went into the house, where Flynn washed his hands and leaned on the counter. The bit of fresh air helped to settle his nerves, but having Gabby within reach would be better. On their way down the mountain, he'd had to physically force himself not to look at her in the car or he'd feared he would've hauled her across his lap, ripped the clothes from her body, and sunk into her right there in the passenger seat.

This week had been hellacious. Today, a nightmare.

Resting the back of his head on a cabinet, he eyed the front door from across the kitchen and through the living room, grateful for his open floor plan. Tight as he was wrung, a visual warning of her arrival just might keep him from pouncing on her the moment she walked in.

The universe was smiling on him because he didn't have to wait long. Carrying an overnight bag and wearing skinny jeans with a yellow T-shirt, Gabby stepped through the front door. She toed off her flip-flops as Fletch made a beeline for her and, grinning, she set the bag down to pet his dog.

She'd left her hair down, still damp from a shower, and the soft caramel waves drifted past her shoulders. Her lips were moving with a smile as she conversed with Fletch. About what, he couldn't tell from his position, but the dog was enraptured. Heat curled in Flynn's gut and spread, igniting his nerve endings as he watched her. So damn beautiful. And for some ungodly reason he couldn't fathom, she was his.

He'd watched his elder brother Drake fall for Heather throughout their teen years and, later, marry her. He'd grinned when his baby brother Cade had taken the plunge with Avery just a few months ago. All the while, he'd stood by and kept his jealousy bottled, wondering if he'd ever get his shot, even though he'd been happy for them. Turned out, all he had to do was open his eyes. She'd been right there all along.

His mellow didn't last long, though. When Gabby lifted her blue gaze to him from across the vast space between them, the memory of today slammed into him again. Full force. No warning. His heart beat a staccato rhythm and his airway closed. Tension knotted every muscle.

Shoving off the counter, he stalked toward her. She rose from her crouch with wide eyes, her pouty lips parted. He ate the distance, grabbed her shoulders, pressed her back to the door, and crushed his mouth to hers.

Finally. *This.* This was what he needed.

She froze a fraction of a beat and then kissed him back. He was lost to everything but the softness of her lips, the hot, wet cavern of her mouth. She tasted like peppermint and sugar. Groaning, he pinned her to the door with his body, hands on her hips so he could rock his erection against her belly. Her curves molded to him and he nearly wept it was so good.

Her fingers drove into his hair as her tongue wove with his, sending a static charge bolting through his body. Frantic became desperate. She licked and nipped at his mouth like a woman starving, thrusting her hips into his ministrations.

All but vibrating with carnal need, he shoved his hands under her shirt to the supple, warm flesh underneath and splayed his fingers. Her chest rumbled against his and he was unsure if it was from a moan or a protest. Dragging his mouth from hers, he stared down at her, breathless.

Her lips were swollen from his kiss, her cheeks pink from stubble-burn. Sleepy, wanton eyes opened and met his gaze through thick, pale lashes. Her breath mingled with his as they shared air.

A moan, then. Not a protest. But because he'd been uncertain, he slammed his palms to the door behind her and dropped his forehead to her shoulder. Air seemed in short supply and what he could drag in was infused with her honey scent. His heart wouldn't quit pounding.

He couldn't do this with her right now. Not when his emotions were jacked up and he was completely out of control. He had to get a grip or he might do the unimaginable and hurt her. He motioned to step away, but she grabbed his shirt, bunching the material in her fist, and kept him there.

"What just happened?"

He tried to swallow and couldn't. *"I'm too tense right now."*

Her eyes narrowed. "You want a cure for that?"

Christ, yes. *"I can't be alert to your needs like this. My head's not right and I might miss signs or signals of displeasure. And—"*

"Stop." She studied him, hard, and her irritation melded into understanding. Her gaze grew tender. "If you don't trust yourself, then trust me. There is no displeasure here and there won't be unless you walk away, leaving me turned-on and wanting you."

His shaft thickened, even as doubt remained. "Gabby..."

She unfurled her fist from his shirt and grabbed the hem of hers. Yellow cotton went over her head and sailed past his shoulder, leaving him to stare slack-jawed at the green lace covering her perfect breasts.

His shaft went from erect to pretty please.

Her fingers dipped to the button on her jeans, and he could do little more than pray she stop and keep going in the same breath. The snap opened. The zipper slid down. Thumbs hooked in the waistband, she shimmied out of the denim. The pants sailed over his other shoulder.

And have mercy, the panties matched the bra.

Forget ready. His shaft was throbbing and stiffer than the Klamath Mountains' northern peak. His fingers flexed at his sides, wanting to touch.

Slowly, he swept his gaze over her. Starting with her tiny feet and polished red toenails, he worked his way up to her shapely legs, the hourglass curve of her hips, toned belly, full breasts, and stopped at her throat working a swallow. She was...

Christ. She was magnificent. Fair, smooth skin heating with a blush. Curvy form that wasn't too lean. And that green lace? He groaned.

She stepped into him, tilting her face up to his, and the room spun. Her fingers were busy doing something, though he was too enamored with the lace to pay much attention. Until the gray of his T-shirt momentarily blinded his view as she worked it over his head, then her hands had his full concentration.

His lungs quit the necessary oxygen exchange once she flattened her palms over his pecs. Her thumbs traced the flat discs of his nipples and worked them stiff. Mary Mother, her touch was a current. As her hands descended, he became acutely aware of two things. One, his shaft was going to bust the seam of his favorite jeans. And two... Hell. Two was lost in oblivion. Because she stroked him through his pants.

The miniscule remainder of his blood supply headed for the southern hemisphere.

Cupping his jaw, she tilted his face to direct his gaze from her hand to her mouth. "If you don't screw me into next week right this minute, I'll never forgive you."

He choked.

Her brows lifted. "We clear, Flynn?"

Grabbing her waist, he hauled her flush against him. "Crystal clear."

* * * *

Flynn's mouth crashed against hers, and Gabby's back hit the door once more as his solid body pressed her into the wood. She had no clue where his previous misgivings about displeasure had come from, but she was going to quash them dead.

Her breasts grew heavy and the apex of her thighs achy as he assaulted her mouth in a detonating kiss. He conquered. He romanced. She ran her hands down the contours of his arms and he flexed at her touch like she'd electrocuted him. The kiss turned savage when she reached for the button of his jeans.

He grabbed her wrists, yanked them behind her back, and looked at her as if to check she was okay. After a quick study, he dipped his head, trailing his tongue down her neck. She shivered and arched into him, hot skin to hot skin. The light scattering of his chest hair tickling her flesh sent sparks of sensation zipping through her system.

He spun them away from the door and backed her to the hallway, releasing her wrists to shove his hands in her hair. Kissing her again as if he'd die without, one of his rough palms pressed the base of her spine and urged her closer. He trailed openmouthed kisses across her jaw to her throat and she flung her head back.

She'd never seen him like this. Fierce and skating the edge of reason. His mood in the car, the way he'd stalked her when she'd arrived, all made sense. His patience had been stretched. And he needed an outlet.

Holy cow. She was so turned-on. Her previous lovers had treated sex with her like they'd visualized her as a person—the good girl. Chaste kisses and missionary gentleness. Oh, how she'd longed for a man to just take her. There was a time and place for making love, but sometimes a girl just wanted...animalistic.

Solid arms kept her against him and he moved lower to suck one of her nipples into his mouth through the bra. His gaze flicked to hers as if to question whether she was enjoying herself. Then he bit her and she gasped. Tingles shot straight to her sex. With their gazes locked, he did it again, and she cupped his head to encourage him.

Suddenly, he leaned over and opened a drawer. She hadn't realized he'd backed them into his bedroom. Giving her no time to glance around, he pulled out a strip of condoms, set them on the nightstand, and eased her to the side of the bed. Her calves hit the mattress, but instead of lying down, she sat at eye level with his fly. The contour of his erection bulged the denim and her panties grew more damp.

She hadn't had much opportunity to explore his body and wanted to badly. But he was taut with tension. He looked down at her through hooded eyes like he was on the brink. Pride and lust swirled through her that she could do this to him.

Raking her nails over the skin above his waistband, she teased his flesh before popping the button open. He swiftly inhaled and pushed the hair from her face. Though his touch was gentle, need radiated from him in waves. She lowered his zipper and he snapped, grabbing her wrists.

"Gabby, I..." He huffed and shook his head, stiffening.

The desperation from when she'd first arrived flooded back into his eyes. And she understood. He'd been frantic with fear today, for her, for them both, and he needed control. Release. There would be time later for exploration. The past few weeks had been a buildup of insane desire. Couple that with stress, and she knew where his head was.

She urged him to let go of her wrists, and then reached behind her back to undo her bra, letting it slide off her arms. His heated gaze dropped to her breasts and his nostrils flared. Lying back, she slid her panties down her thighs and kicked them aside.

His chest rose and fell in quick successions as his gaze got his fill. Nerves swam in her belly and heated embarrassment filled her cheeks. Their history as friends collided with what line they were about to cross, and the reality that there was no going back slammed into her. Did he like what he saw? Was he disappointed in her? Because he wasn't moving and—

Down went his pants, his gaze never leaving her body as he chucked the last of his clothes. And holy cow. She'd had that beautiful body and erection pressed against her, but the sight of him was breathtaking. Wide shoulders, defined biceps, six-pack abs, bulging veins, and a goody trail of sandy blond hair that led right to the heart-stopper.

Long and thick with a wide head, his erection was hard steel covered in velvet flesh. Gaze on her, he stroked himself as if suddenly unsure of her reaction, too. He reached for a condom, ripped it open, and rolled it down his length.

"I'm at the end of my rope. I've never...been with someone when I'm like this." Bending over her, eyes locked on hers, he slipped an arm under her back and positioned her in the middle of the bed. Rising over her, knees straddling her hips, he swallowed hard, his gaze harder. "I'm trusting you to..." His jaw ticked. "To stop me if..."

"Shh." She cupped his face. "This is me, Flynn. Look at me. Do I look like I don't want to be here?"

"Gabby." He closed his eyes and dropped his forehead to hers.

Smoothing her hands down his back, she reveled at the shift in muscle, at the strength, and grabbed his firm ass. He sucked a haggard breath. Remembering how he went crazy when she'd kissed his neck the other night, she tempted his restraint and licked a path from his collarbone to his jaw. He panted, his arms on either side of her bulging with strain. She brushed her lips lightly over the tendon in his neck, flicked her tongue against his salty warm skin.

He cursed and sealed his lips to hers, licking to demand entrance. He stroked her tongue as if making love to her mouth, thrusting with firm caresses. He shifted, and she cradled his hips between her thighs. The weight of him pressed her into the mattress and she couldn't wait anymore.

She reached between their bodies and guided him toward her entrance. He broke away from the relentless kiss to stare down at her. His erratic breathing told her he was just as insane with lust. Tilting her hips, she took a few inches of him and set her hands on his shoulders, waiting for him to take the reins. To take her.

Ferocious, almost violent hazel eyes looked back at her. They widened as he hovered above her, suspending them on the edge. Untamed awe resonated in his gaze and his brows slammed together.

"Gabby," he groaned. "I promise, I'll make up for my lack of finesse the second time."

She didn't need finesse, didn't want it. She just wanted him, like this, raw and wild. But she didn't get the chance to tell him. With a swift jerk of his hips, he drove inside her. Throwing her head back, she gasped at the glorious stretch as he filled her. He pulsed inside her as he stilled.

"Look at me." He nudged her nose with his. "Need to see your eyes, Gabby."

With effort, she peered up at him. His pupils were blown, nearly muting the mesmerizing brown and green and gray in his irises. Tension wrinkled his forehead.

Watching her closely, he withdrew and pushed back inside, hard enough for their hips to slap and for her to slide up the sheets closer to the headboard. The slick, full glide of him against her walls was so good.

Panting, he stared at her another beat and seemed satisfied. Reaching up, he removed her hands from his shoulders, linked their fingers, and pressed them down on either side of her head. He adjusted to bear more weight on his knees and she trapped him with her thighs, tilting her hips to take more of him. His pubic bone rubbed her clit and sparks zipped through her bloodstream.

With their faces close, he pulled out and thrust. Again. Harder, faster. Rotating his hips, he came back to her, hitting her clit with every plunge.

Each time with shortened strokes until she was teetering on the brink of release and clawing her way there. Friction. Resistance. The push and pull was staggering.

His gaze burned into hers as he pounded with more force, desperation and blinding need creating a sense of urgency. He released her hands to place his palms on the bed by her shoulders, his muscles straining. Grunting, his speed increased, and the frenzied motion rocked her into shattering.

She grabbed his face and brought it to hers as she came undone. Forehead to forehead, their gazes locked, blurring in a swirl of color and light. Her walls gripped him and her back bowed as the orgasm ripped through her.

He shook his head as if to clear it, not ceasing the maddening rhythm. His mouth opened wide against hers as he followed her over, his body stiff. He barked a hoarse cry of pleasure as his spine arched. A full body shudder resonated through him and he collapsed.

Chapter 20

When he caught his breath, Flynn rolled off of Gabby, padded to the adjoining bathroom to dispose of the condom, and returned to her before the sated expression left her face. Throwing the covers over them, he pulled her on top of him and held her, spreading his legs to bring them closer. He was still quaking with leftover currents.

She pressed her cheek to his chest and he sighed. Utter contentment. Her finger drew lazy patterns on his pec, and even that was wonderful. Rubbing his hand up and down her spine, he breathed in her honey scent and smiled.

Through the years, he'd wondered what it would be like between them. It wasn't something he'd lingered over or spent too much time harboring since that path led to torment. But, yeah. He'd wondered. He hadn't been prepared for her in the slightest. Not with the way she simply just understood him better than anyone, nor the way their friendship carried across the line they'd drawn. It had ramped the connection, the experience, to holy shit levels.

Not prepared at all.

Being with Gabby had been about more than the finish line, about more than the end result. She'd made sex...enjoyable. Not an act, but an act of God. Perhaps he was exaggerating this a tad, but...no. Not for him. Sex had never been like that for him. Had it been as good for her or was he being a sap?

"Did I hurt you?" He didn't think so. She'd come, he was sure of it. If it hadn't been Gabby, if he didn't trust her implicitly, he never would've gone there in that kind of mood. He'd barely managed to watch her face during, having been so caught up in her and the assault of emotions. He tugged lightly on her hair to get her attention. "Did I?"

She lifted her head, a cat-like grin on her pouty lips and sleepy haze in her eyes. "No, you didn't hurt me. That was pretty amazing."

He agreed. Something akin to biblical. For years, he'd banked his desire for her in order to maintain the unit they'd been, but what they'd just done there were no adjectives to describe. Emotions and sensations he didn't recognize swirled around in his chest, making his throat restrict.

She traced his jaw with her fingers. "Is this...weird? I mean, after being friends, we..." She looked away. "Do you feel weird?"

Moved by her uncertainty, he tucked a finger under her chin and brought her attention back to him. "Do you feel weird?" She shook her head. "Me either." He was feeling a whole lot of things, but weird didn't make the cut.

"What do we do now?"

He suspected she meant in the figurative sense, but he went for literal to put the smile back in her eyes. "Give me twenty minutes and we can do that again. I could possibly feed you first, but it would have to be quick. We need to come right back here and make up for lost time." He wanted to explore her body, kiss every inch of skin and watch her come apart again. Take his time for round two.

"Lost time, huh?" Her pouty, swollen-from-his-kisses lips pressed into a line to hide her grin. Fail. He could stare at that mouth all day.

Nodding, he tucked her hair behind her ears. This was another first for him. Cuddling and after-sex conversation had never been a part of intimacy. Hell, she was the first woman to which he'd actually spoken. After the past few weeks, it hadn't even crossed his mind to just open his mouth in her presence.

She studied him. "Truth. What was all that about back in your living room? The displeasure thing?"

And...buzzkill. He rubbed his eyes, trying to figure out a way to answer. He'd always been honest with her, able to say just about anything. But there was honesty and then there was emasculation.

Sighing, he looked at her. "I'm deaf, which means I don't always know if the rumbles are moans of pleasure or requests to stop. If my sole attention isn't on my partner, I can't tell what they want."

Her gaze dissected, ripped him apart cell by cell. "But in other matters, you use your additional senses, your intuition. You could tell by body language if they were into it or wanted you to stop."

He fumbled with an explanation. "Sex is different. Physically being with someone and succumbing means I could miss signs."

"Because you're so wrapped up in the act?"

He nodded. Leave it to Gabby to get him on a molecular level.

She frowned. "Has that ever happened? You not seeing the signs?"

So badly, he wanted to talk about something else, but if they were going to make a run of this relationship, she had to understand this one tic of his because he'd never drop it. Even just a few moments ago, when he'd made love to Gabby and his emotions were whack, he'd held onto a thin tether.

Closing his eyes for a beat, he grappled with the right words before lifting his lids. "My first time was also the first time for the girl. Teenage hormones." He shook his head. "I hurt her."

She cupped his jaw. "A girl losing her virginity is always uncomfortable."

"I know, but at the time, it upset me, made me realize I couldn't ever lose focus again." He swallowed. "It sort of made me paranoid. Women tend to not like being watched for every nuance. I learned to hide my observations, but..."

"But you've never fully let go." Not a question, so he didn't respond. She offered a slight shake of her head, sympathy in her eyes. "I'm not them. You know me. With me, you can go with your gut, have confidence that your signals aren't crossed."

Christ. She was right, but that didn't mean he could unwind years of behavior, or even that he should. If he unintentionally did something to hurt her, he'd never forgive himself. He ran his fingers through her hair. "Gabby, please understand. There's just certain things I can't do."

A flash of irritation crossed her face. "Don't think for one second you're less of a man. You hear me?" Just like that, her anger subsided. "What do you mean there's things you can't do?"

This whole conversation was going to crap anyway, he might as well make it worse. "I need to see my partner's face. I've done missionary, sitting up, the woman on top and, a couple times, up against the wall. But I've never taken a lover from behind, for instance." He'd wanted to on many occasions, but such was life.

Her expression indicated she didn't know how to respond, and when she looked away, he wanted to punch something. They'd been together a couple of weeks, but he had no idea if she would be satisfied long-term. Sure, there were many positions they could get into, and he'd love to attempt every one, but he definitely had limitations. He'd never really been in a serious relationship either. Not one that had potential, anyway.

Leaning forward, she kissed him. Tenderness and understanding swept through her with every stroke of her tongue and brush of her lips. She dropped her hands on his chest, fingertips tracing the contours. Her hair fell in a curtain around them. Because she was on top and it was Gabby, he closed his eyes to savor the taste of her, relish the warmth of her skin.

Her fingers moved south and his shaft stirred. Down his sides and back up again, her touch sent his heart into overdrive. He held the back of her head to deepen the kiss and she rocked her hips between his thighs. His eyes flew open and he hissed.

She brushed her nose with his and lifted her head. "Do you trust me?"

"Yes." Sad truth was, she might be the only person he trusted explicitly. He banded his arms tighter. "Of course, I do."

Her gaze ran over his face, and he could all but see her brain clicking. She held up a finger telling him to hold on, and got out of bed. Missing the weight of her, he groaned. She walked to his closet and disappeared inside. What in the hell was she doing? She returned with one of his neckties and his heartbeat screeched to a halt.

"No," he said, suspecting where this was going and...no.

Climbing back in bed, she straddled his hips, setting the tie next to her. "You've never had anyone focus solely on your pleasure, have you?"

Didn't matter. He wouldn't let her be the first. "Not happening."

She framed his face with her hands and erased the distance as she leaned forward, kissing some of the anxiety away. But then she lifted her head, determination in her eyes. "Let me blindfold you."

"No." Even as his cock stirred at the thought, his heart was jackrabbiting around his chest cavity.

"I wouldn't do something I didn't want to, and I really want to do this, Flynn. Consider it a fantasy of mine."

He almost believed her. Though her heart was in the right place—because when wasn't it?—he couldn't give up the one sense he had that he'd depended on all these years. Swallowing hard, he shook his head.

One corner of her lips quirked like she knew she was wearing him down. She rocked her hips, coating his erection with her wet heat, earning another hiss from him. "You want it, too."

Hell, he kind of did. The selfish part of him wanted to take this chance. She was right. He'd never had anyone do something like this, make it all about him.

His brain filtered information at the speed of light. She was on top, thus no possibility of hurting her. He would still have his hands to touch, to make note of her response. And...this was Gabby. She'd never take advantage.

"Trust me." She traced his lower lip with her thumb.

With the breath stalled in his lungs, he nodded.

While he shook like a wounded animal, she knotted the tie around his forehead and looked at him. "Just feel, Flynn. I'll take care of you." Then—Christ, *then*—she slid the tie over his eyes and the world went black.

Panting, panicked, he grabbed for her, settling his hands on her waist. Her lips came down on his and he jerked in surprise.

She patiently waited, her mouth pressed to his, for him to respond. He gripped her waist tighter, letting the familiar softness of her skin and weight of her body orientate him. He breathed in her honey scent and a measure of calm settled over him.

"Gabby," he said against her lips.

Her palm cupped his cheek and he turned his face toward her touch. It was insane how potent her skin felt against his when he couldn't see what was happening. If he thought the contact before was intense, this put that to bed. As if he could pinpoint every red blood cell in his veins, follow the path of his nerve endings, his breathing grew erratic in anticipation.

Her hot tongue traced his lips and he parted for her, accepting what she offered. She could knock him from zero to all-systems-go with just her kiss. Like her personality, she kissed from the tender underbelly of her giving heart. Attentive and clever. Playful and sweet. A hint of naughty and a lot of gumption. His skin heated and a ball of need spread from his gut.

Kissing her way to his neck, she placed her hands over his on her waist. She licked the tendon near his pulse and he threw his head back. Combustion was imminent if she kept that up. Her warm breath caressed his flesh as she worked her unbelievable mouth to his ear. A nip of the lobe. A trace of her tongue around the shell.

He struggled to breathe as his body fired on all cylinders. "Fuck, Gabby. That's my weak spot." He felt her smile against him as if she knew that. She made her way to the other side of his neck and repeated the sweet torture. She was killing him. Killing. Him. "Want you."

She squeezed his hands in encouragement, a silent way to acknowledge him since she'd taken his visual away. Any residual doubt about this adventure fled and only need remained. White-hot burning desire, unlike anything he'd ever experienced, surged through him. His erection became almost painful.

A sharp tinge of pain hit his right nipple, and he realized she'd nipped him. The ache was soothed by her tongue before she did the same to his other one. He bucked under her, gliding his shaft against her slick folds to alleviate the throbbing. She was drenched, just as turned-on, which pulled a moan from deep in his chest.

Linking their fingers, she shifted lower, and he lost his anchor where he'd been holding her. She squeezed his hands, telling him she was right there, and kissed his abs. Belly button. Her nipples dragged across his skin while she moved, only amplifying the sensations she uprooted. Lower, she drifted. Anticipation clawed at him, sending goose bumps across his skin. Heaven help him if she—

Wrapped her lips around him.

His jaw unhinged with a short cry, his chest rumbling in the wake. "Gabby." His throat was raw, but hell if he cared when she was taking him deep. So, so deep into the cavern of her mouth. Pressure. Heat. His tip hit the back of her throat and he gritted his teeth.

He let go of one hand to reach for her, but left it suspended in air, unsure. His heart pounded, waiting. Her fingers wrapped around his wrist and guided it to the back of her head where he buried his hand in her soft strands. Releasing a slow breath, he gently thrust into her mouth and stilled. Her other hand squeezed his in approval.

Then she was using teeth and tongue, and his balls pulled in warning. "Gabby. I'm close." Vibrations shot up his shaft with what must've been a moan from her. Effing unbelievable as this was, he wanted to come with her. "I want inside you, sweetheart."

She released him, sending cool air along his erection, and crawled up his body. The bed shifted and then her fingers were around him, rolling a condom down his length. Taking his wrists, she guided his hands to her hips as she rose. His tip grazed her opening and the heaven/hell suspension when she paused stole the oxygen from the room.

Her knees caged him in, pressing firmly against his ribs as she lowered herself onto him. Christ. Nothing felt better than being inside her. The velvet heat of her walls gripped him and he was amazed by how well they fit. Like she was made just for him. When she was completely, entirely surrounding him, she placed his hands over her breasts. Her peaked nipples teased his palms.

She rocked her hips forward and the glide of stirring inside her had him even closer to release. Taking her cues, he ran one palm down her torso to where they were joined. He circled her clit with his thumb and grabbed her hip with his other hand. He pulled out and thrust up, bringing her down as he did.

On her hip, she covered his hand with her own and squeezed, telling him she liked that. She gripped his forearm and encouraged his fingers to keep working her body.

He paused a fraction of a beat, taking in this unbelievable moment. One he'd never thought he'd ever get to experience. His partner running the show and him—literally—blind to her needs. But that was just it... Two senses down, yet he knew exactly what Gabby, *his Gabby*, needed. Not just by her direction, but from knowing her. He could finally let himself go and just seek...pleasure.

Emotion wove around his heart as his throat tightened. The sensory overload had his body's visceral reaction kicking in hard. Easing out of her again, he bucked back inside, pulling her down on him and rubbing her tight little nub. Her nails dug into his forearm. She liked it.

They moved as a unit toward bliss, just like they were in sync outside of the bedroom, and that knowledge wasn't lost on him, despite how she was short-circuiting his brain cells. Her walls gripped him harder and he knew she was close. He circled faster, thrust harder. His spine tingled and he fought to hold on until she got there, too.

And, *yes.*

Have mercy, she shattered. Trembling over him, she stilled, body taut. She clenched him in a vise, drawing the orgasm right from him until he'd spilled. Pinpricks of light danced behind his closed lids. He bowed off the bed with the force of his release. She collapsed on him, and he reached around to grab her ass as he rocked through the last of the shudders.

His breaths soughed and her exhalations fanned his neck. Damn, that just happened. He ripped the tie off his head and tossed it aside, then cupped her cheeks to look in her eyes. He blinked at the light, his retinas readjusting.

Her pupils were still blown, nearly swallowing all that blue. Cheeks flushed, hairline damp with sweat, she smiled at him. Sucker punch to the heart.

She was...he had...there were just *no words.*

Shaking his head, he tried to get a grip and couldn't. He rained kisses over her brows, her lids, her cheeks, then took her mouth. He tried to pour how grateful he was into the kiss, telling her just how much she'd moved him before breaking away.

Nuzzling his palm, she closed her eyes. "Now you can feed me."

His head slammed onto the pillow and he laughed.

Chapter 21

With the bed sheet around her, Gabby stepped onto the back deck to let Fletch out, leaving the patio door open while Flynn scrounged up something for them to eat. The temperature had cooled, but it was relatively comfortable with the humidity lingering. Stars winked overhead and she smiled remembering the other night out here with Flynn. The things he'd said. The way he'd kissed her.

Not wanting to get her feet wet in the dewy grass, she stayed on the stairs while Fletch did his doggy business.

Flynn had a great yard. Unlike her postage stamp she'd tried to make cute with a perennial garden, he had raw wilderness. Off in the distance, a thick copse of trees sheltered the creek loping through the forest. Its trickle was faint over the call of an owl. There were at least five acres of clearing he'd done little with aside from the wildflower patches she'd planted when he'd first built the cabin. That, coupled with birdfeeders, was about it besides grass. Maybe she'd try talking him into an outdoor fireplace, something cozy to cuddle up in front of on cool nights.

Fletch made his way to her and ran in circles. She squatted to pet him, clutching the bed sheet with her other hand. The material smelled like Flynn's light woodsy cologne, and she buried her face in the white cotton to breathe him in. Fletch barked.

"I know. I'm being girly. I can't help it."

Head tilt. Tongue wag.

"He's just so...perfect. He's great in bed, he's nice, he's funny, and he's good with animals. I'm not seeing a flaw here." She rubbed the retriever's ears. "You live with him. Tell me something bad. He leaves his dirty underwear on the floor, doesn't he?"

Fletch barked.

She laughed. "I knew it. Give me all the dirt. I know he snores, but only when he's lying on his back and it's pretty quiet. Hardly disturbing. Does he leave the toilet seat up?"

Two barks.

Sigh. "Guess I'll just have to look before I sit, right?"

Feet shuffled behind her and she rose, looking at Flynn over her shoulder. He had his cell in hand raised to take a picture. She turned fully to face him and made a goofy face. He grinned and set the phone on the counter just inside the door, then leaned on the jamb, arms crossed over his bare chest.

She hadn't bothered with clothes, just the sheet, knowing they were going back to bed after they ate. He'd thrown on a pair of red boxers that made the natural strawberry highlights in his hair more pronounced. Wow. Such a great body, her best friend. Her gaze dipped to his feet and her cheeks heated. What was it about a man's bare feet that was so sexy?

Amusement in his eyes, he stared at her as if he wanted to do so all night. The light from the kitchen illuminated behind him, creating shadows in the dips of muscle. Heck, she could stare at him all night, too.

She dropped her gaze to Fletch and back to Flynn. "Your dog told me all your secrets."

That brought out his full watt grin, and...swoon. The guy smiled from his eyes, damn it. *"Did he, now? What did my dog say?"*

She rolled her eyes as if in thought and stepped closer. She wrapped her arms around his waist, holding the sheet to cocoon them. "He said you have terrible laundry habits."

He breathed a laugh, playing with the ends of her hair. "I wash my own clothes every week, thank you very much."

"And you leave the toilet seat up." She kissed his chin, loving the scratch from his whiskers.

He glanced over her shoulder in thought. "Not sure on that one. Mom reinforced with me and my brothers to keep it down. Plus, you're over a lot. I think I'm good on that bad habit."

"Damn," she said playfully. "Fletch lied to me. There must be a defect here. I'll find it."

He worried his brow, smile slipping as if not knowing whether to take her seriously. Tucking her hair behind her ear, he brushed his knuckles over her cheek, adamant affection warming his eyes. He studied her face, no aspect untouched by his gaze like he was memorizing her features or collecting a memory. He opened his mouth as if to speak, but then thought better and closed it again.

She brushed her thumb across his lower lip. She loved his mouth. Full, soft, warm. He could thin those lips with a frown when angry, twist them when nervous, or stop time with a smile. Even though he only used it to speak to her, his mouth was very expressive. And when he kissed her, it said a whole lot without words.

He cleared his throat. "I have lots of flaws, Gabby."

Ah, her joking had upset him. "I don't care."

Letting out an uneven breath, he shook his head as if in awe. "You don't, do you? I think you might be the only person who looks at me and sees me before the disability."

God. Just...God. Way to reach in her chest and root around. She swallowed the unexpected emotion. "You're right. Being a male is a terrible disability. Guys are inferior to women, of course. But I assure you, when I look at you, I notice you're a man first."

His chin dipped as he blinked those criminally long lashes and leveled her with a disbelieving look. Then he closed his eyes and threw his head back, laughing. He stared at the ceiling as if praying to a higher power and shook his head before looking at her again.

He shifted to serious the longer he stared at her, and her heart stuttered in response. "You level me, sweetheart. You really do. Two decades of friendship, and you can still surprise me."

She shrugged. "Like I said, women are the superior gender. We're just more clever."

His quiet laugh dug under her skin and took up space. "I think that's just you, Gabby," he said against her lips, then kissed her. He eased away. "You hungry?"

"Duh." Fletch tugged at the sheet, and she glanced down. He wagged his tail. "I think my other boyfriend is jealous."

Flynn rolled his eyes and stepped inside. "Heaven forbid."

She followed and picked up his phone on the counter. Unlocking the screen, she found his camera roll and grinned. He'd taken a few shots of her outside. One with the goofy face. Another with her back to the camera looking over her shoulder at him. The white sheet against the night sky and woods in the background made it sexy and mysterious. She texted it to herself. The first picture from tonight was of her crouched in front of Fletch, smiling.

Scrolling through a couple more, she came across quite a few of his brothers and Fletch. She stopped on one of herself from last summer. It had been taken at the park where they played softball in one of Redwood

Ridge's leagues. A close up of her face, head thrown back, sunlight filtering through her hair. He'd caught her mid-laugh.

Flynn stepped beside her. "That one's my favorite." He kissed her cheek. "Food's ready."

He should've been a photographer. He had a great eye.

She sat at the table where he'd deposited two plates with scrambled eggs and toast. They ate in comfortable silence, and her mind started clicking back to the things he'd said earlier. About all he hadn't experienced. Her former lovers had treated her like the good girl. Thus, sex had always been meh. It wasn't as if she'd had a lot of practice when it came to positions either.

Flynn had been hesitant at first, but he'd let her blindfold him and take control. After he'd admitted what it had been like for him with other partners, she'd wanted him to experience someone giving him pleasure for a change. She knew how hard that must've been for him, yet he'd trusted her. She wondered how far he'd let her go with that trust.

Truth was, no one had made her feel so alive, so hyperaware of her needs like he did. He didn't treat her like glass or like she was someone who couldn't handle a little rough. Not that she'd bust out handcuffs and floggers, but why not branch out? Their lovemaking thus far had proven they could still be them in the bedroom. He was a very attentive lover who knew how to pluck heightened responses from her body.

She took a sip of juice and found both Flynn and Fletch were staring at her. Flynn's plate was empty, his elbows on the table and fingers running across his lips. His eyes watched her every move. Fletch just appeared interested in her crust.

Tossing him a small piece, she stared the dog down. "Don't tell him I just fed you from the table."

Head tilt. Chops licked.

"Good boy. It's a rare trait, a guy who can keep a secret. Carry on that way and the poodle you've been eyeing at the park is sure to notice you."

Fletch barked. She laughed, rubbing his scruff.

"Did you just propose to my dog again? I'm bound to get a complex."

Covering her face with her hand, she laughed until her side ached. She glanced at Fletch and shook her head before focusing on Flynn. "I'll have you know, he proposes to me."

The pine green on his kitchen walls brought out the mossy color in his eyes. Or maybe that was his easy humor. *"Because you bribe him with bacon. Or toast, in this case."*

She gasped, pretending to be affronted. "He likes me for my intellect, too."

Up went his eyebrows. *"Duly noted."* His gaze skimmed over her and her girly parts got excited. *"It's late and we had an adventurous day."*

She dropped her elbow on the table and chin in her hand. "Some really hot veterinarian did wear me out with a couple rounds of great sex." His eyes heated. "And before that, there was this little brush with a mountain lion." She shuddered and his eyes narrowed. "You feeling a little calmer about that?" He'd been so worked up, she'd—

"Let's not discuss it." He slowly inhaled, gaze searching. "Are you tired, Gabby?"

Oh. *His voice.* Dangerously, deliciously low. It was as if the rough timbre had caressed her skin and touched her nerve endings. And by his expression, he knew it. Her lips curved. She shook her head to answer his question.

His Adam's apple bobbed with a swallow. "Care to watch a movie?"

Uhn. This playful banter and his tone had her wet all over again. She shook her head.

Leaning forward, he singed her with a carnal look. "What would you like to do?"

Game on. She rose from the chair and walked backward toward the hallway, batting her eyelashes at him. She paused dramatically to drop the sheet, leaving her naked.

He surged from his seat and she squealed. She took off running for his bedroom. He caught up with her just past the threshold, his arms wrapping around her from behind. Pulling her flush against the hard wall of his body, he trailed his lips down her neck and ground his erection against her backside. She tilted her head for better access but, quickly, he turned her around and kissed her. Desperate. With purpose.

I've never taken a lover from behind.

His words came back to her and she broke the kiss. His gaze darted over her shoulder to the nightstand. The condoms. When he refocused on her, she smiled.

"I'm on the pill and safe." Before him, she hadn't had a partner in two years.

His breath hitched. "I'm safe, too." He vibrated with interest, with need. He said everything with his eyes. "You sure?"

Not only was she sure, she had an idea. Slapping a hand to his chest, she urged him backward. Confusion in his eyes, he allowed it and complied. His calves hit the recliner in the corner and he plopped, gaze never leaving hers.

Kneeling in front of him, she dipped her fingers into the waistband of his boxers and tugged them down. His beautiful erection sprang free and he lifted his hips so she could remove them the rest of the way.

Rising, she leaned over the chair and his heated gaze scorched a path over her body. When it stopped at her eyes, she smiled. "Breathe." His brow wrinkled as if he didn't understand. "In five seconds, I want you to remember to breathe."

His lips parted to speak, but she lightly kissed his mouth and swiftly turned around to straddle his lap backwards. His erection wedged between her cheeks and his arms instinctually came around her middle. Yet, his chest didn't move with air exchange.

She turned her head, tilting it back to look in his eyes. "Breathe."

He exhaled. Hard. "Gabby, I can't. We—"

"Look at me. You can." It wasn't totally from behind, like he'd said, but it was a start. In this position, he could see her face if need be. She circled her hips and he hissed, his lids dropping to half-mast.

Grabbing the back of her head, he brought her mouth to his. Though he was still tense, he stroked her tongue with his as if he was completely lost in her. His hand drifted up from her belly to mold her breast while the other left her hair to cup her mound. She sucked air through her nose, not breaking their connection, and bore down to encourage more.

He slid his fingers between her folds and groaned. She swallowed the guttural vibrations, shifting her hips to bring his shaft to her opening. He stilled, mouth still fused to hers, but opened his eyes. She guided him inside her and took him slowly, every inch making his eyes dilate darker. When he was as deep as the position allowed, she paused and dropped the back of her head on his shoulder, severing their kiss and eye contact.

He didn't move for several heartbeats, but then gingerly thrust his hips as if testing things out. "Christ, you feel so good."

Shivering in delight at his words, she rocked her hips, and the arm he'd placed around her waist tightened. He throbbed inside her and dropped his lips to the crook of her neck when she did it again, mouth wide. Breaths rasping, he stroked her clit with his thumb.

Her back arched, pulling him deeper, and he thrust again. And again. She rocked with his movements, urging her hips down to take him. His rock-hard thighs shifted beneath her, his abs constricting as he moved. She was so close, she pinched her eyes closed, reveling in the tight fit of him inside her and the way his fingers stroked.

He whispered her name over and over against the skin below her ear, and she detonated. Sparks shot behind her closed lids and tingles zinged through her body. He pistoned his hips faster and emitted a hoarse groan, body rigid as he spilled inside her.

After several seconds, he pulled out and turned her in his arms so she lay sideways across his lap. Cupping her cheek, this thumb stroked her jaw as he stared down at her, eyes a riot of emotion. His jaw ticked, and she grew concerned.

She placed her palm on his chest where his heart pounded. "Are you okay?" Had she pushed him too hard? He'd come, but that was a basic response, right?

He shook his head, then closed his eyes and nodded.

She waited for his eyes to open. "Talk to me."

Glancing away, he swallowed. Just when she thought he wouldn't respond, he looked back at her and smiled. "I don't... I'm fine."

"I don't believe you. Something's bothering you."

He let out a frustrated breath. "I don't know how to express this and have it make sense." His eyes glazed over as his gaze skimmed her face. "Before tonight, I never realized how much I was holding back. With other women, I couldn't be myself. Half the time, I was left feeling emasculated."

His gaze bored into hers. Hard. Penetrating. "You have no idea how fucking embarrassing that is to admit. But, damn it, Gabby. You just... I'm leveled, to be honest."

Good God. Moving quickly, she straddled his hips and brought her arms around him, holding his head to her shoulder. They stayed like that a few moments, his arms banding her back like letting go would cause pain, and her struggling to find words.

He buried his face in her neck and sighed. "I love my family. I love my friends. All of them have been supportive. But I don't know what in the hell I'd do without you. Stupid as that sounds, pathetic as that makes me, you need to know. Because, Christ Almighty, you're the only person in my life who never made me feel weak, yet you render me powerless."

Tears burned behind her lids, her lip quivering. Unable to hold in the sob, she trembled in the aftershocks of his statement. Torn. Ravaged. She never realized he'd felt this way. He wasn't weak or pathetic. He was brave and funny and sweet. She suspected he'd put a lot of these issues on himself trying to live up to unrealistic expectations or inserting criticism where it wasn't implied. But to know he had doubts, to think he'd questioned himself, had her chest ripping apart.

Encouraging her to look at him by tugging her hair, he smoothed her strands and shook his head. "If you wouldn't mind, could you please decline my dog's proposal next time he asks. It just might be the nail in the coffin."

See? That right there. How many men could use self-depreciating humor after slicing a vein for the sake of brutal honesty? For that matter, how many guys would *be* that truthful? Unable to help it, she laughed through the tears and kissed him. She was sunk so deep she'd never crawl out, and she didn't ever want to try.

Chapter 22

Flynn stared at Gabby's hands while she translated the staff meeting. They didn't have routine meetings at Animal Instincts because they'd never been needed. But with all the crap he and Gabby had encountered on home visits as of late and his brother's upcoming wedding, Avery had thought it was a good idea to get everyone together.

They crammed around a table in the break room discussing on-call rotation for next week since Cade and Avery would be on their honeymoon. Well, not a honeymoon, per se. They were taking Avery's eight-year-old daughter, Hailey, with them and calling it a "familymoon."

Flynn twirled a pen around his fingers, zoning out. His mind kept replaying the best weekend of his life as if it had been a dream. They'd spent Saturday sleeping in and he'd made love to Gabby first thing, worshipping her body like he should've done the first time. They'd taken another hike at their favorite trail and watched a movie afterward. Sunday morning, he'd found her in the kitchen making breakfast and, unable to help himself, sank deep inside her after he'd set her on the counter. Breakfast forgotten, she'd set them in motion and they'd slow-danced in his kitchen with Fletch watching. Then they'd read out on his back deck and took a nap.

It was a little crazy, but absolutely nothing had changed between them except they were having sex. Knock-the-house-down, he-just-died-happy sex. Color him a narcissist, but when the hell was something going to go wrong? They didn't even argue.

Gabby snapped her fingers and waved, getting his attention. She jerked her chin toward Avery.

He focused on their office manager and hoped she wasn't about to sucker him into alphabetizing something. Woman was a hedonist when it came to organization. Thank Christ, but he'd rather run the other way. Let his baby brother deal. He was the one marrying her.

"Can you watch Hailey tonight for a couple hours?" Avery bit her lip. "We've got last-minute wedding stuff to do and I think she might get bored if we brought her along."

Hailey had autism. Avery didn't ask just anyone to babysit, and though Hailey was pretty high-functioning, she was nonverbal. She had a few quirks, too, which the people around this table knew. About the only ones Avery trusted with her daughter were in this room, barring a few exceptions. Flynn had loved the kid incredibly hard from the first second Avery stepped into the clinic this past winter. Kindred souls.

Avery kept going like he'd say no. "Zoe and Gabby need to go with for the last dress fitting. Mom has—"

He lifted his hand to cut her off. *"I'd be happy to."*

She whipped her head to Brent, but Flynn hadn't caught what their tech said. "Oh no. The last time my daughter was in your care you..."

Flynn missed the last part, something about Hailey's hair, and he looked to Gabby for clarification.

"B-E-D-A-Z-Z-L-E-D," she spelled out, but he was still confused. *"What's that?"*

Avery's shoulders shifted in a sigh. "It's a little handheld thingy that snaps fake rhinestones to stuff. It's meant for clothes," she jerked her head to Brent with a scowl, "but someone used it on Hailey's hair."

Brent waved his hand in dramatic fashion. "She loved it and you know it. Stop getting pissy, doll."

Avery deflated in her chair. "Yes, she did love it." She straightened. "It still took me two hours to get that stuff out of her hair, though. You're off babysitting detail and you'll be strip-searched before being allowed to come back."

Brent grinned. "Strip-searched by whom?"

Zoe dropped her head to the table, shoulders bouncing in a laugh before she looked up. Her hair was an interesting shade of purple this week. She'd been dyeing it outrageous colors for so long he couldn't remember her natural tone. "Watch out, Cade."

Cade shrugged. "I'm taken. I will not be doing any strip-searching unless gorgeous here is involved." He kissed Avery's hand.

Zoe rolled her eyes and gagged.

Gabby grinned. "Oh, stop it. They're so cute. We should all be so lucky."

Shaking her head, Zoe fixed Gabby with a deadpan expression. "Someday, a guy will sweep you off your feet and promise you the world. You just punch that lying bastard as hard as you can and run."

Brent did some kind of jive in his seat. "Preach it, girlfriend."

"I think I'm offended." Cade rubbed his neck with a lopsided grin.

Avery was too busy laughing to respond.

"All right." Drake rubbed a hand over his hair, his expression indicating he didn't know what to make of Zoe. "Recap. All patient charts are fully electronic now. The dog-fighting ring case has pleaded out. Cyprus got along with Moses this weekend, so it looks like I have another pet. Flynn's watching Hailey tonight and promises not to put sparkly shit in her hair. Rehearsal dinner is Friday at six. Don't be late for the wedding Saturday, which is at noon, or Avery will rain hell. And if Brent needs to be strip-searched, Avery will do it." He glanced around. "That about covers it." He looked at Avery with a fond smile curving his lips. "Anything else?"

Huh. That was the most Flynn had seen Drake spout in eons.

Avery dropped her chin in her hand and looked at Drake dreamily. "You *were* listening."

Drake grinned. "Meeting adjourned."

Everyone filed out of the break room.

Flynn took his time since his first patient wasn't for another thirty minutes. Laying his head against the chair, he closed his lids and scrubbed his hands over his face. When he opened his eyes, Drake was staring at him. *"Don't you have surgery?"*

"It'll hold for a few." His big brother's gaze was direct and probing. "You're distracted today. Everything okay with you and Gabby?"

He sighed. *"Yes, everything's perfect. Which is the problem."*

Drake frowned. "Did that sound as stupid in your head as it did mine?"

He pinched the bridge of his nose, unsure how to explain. *"We're great in bed. We're great out of bed. We don't fight."* He shrugged. *"I don't know. I just keep wondering how long it'll last."*

Leaning back in his chair, Drake crossed his fingers and set them behind his head. "Let me ask you something. Did you two fight in elementary school? What about high school? No," he answered. "Do you bicker while working together? How about all the times you hang out? No. You both want the same things out of life, have similar goals. Why would sharing a bed suddenly throw a wrench into your dynamic?"

Fine. When he put it that way, it did make Flynn's concerns sound stupid. And wasn't Big Brother awfully chatty today.

Drake rose. "Heather and I didn't argue much either. And up until the day she died, even now, I never questioned my love for her." His gaze drilled Flynn to his chair. "You keep looking for trouble where there isn't any and you're going to ruin the best thing to ever happen to you."

Yeah, okay. But Flynn kept circling back to what she was getting out of this relationship. In every area except dating, he had confidence, was assured in his skills and place. Maybe because Gabby was so entwined in every aspect of his life it was screwing with him.

As if psychic, Drake gave him a once-over. "I don't know why, but everyone tends to overlook her, see right past her as if she's not there. Except you. Have you really looked at her lately? The goofy grin and light in her eyes? That's all you. You did that. You make her happy."

After Drake walked out, Flynn banged his head on the table a few times and called it a successful morning. Of course, Drake was right. Kind of irritating, but when wasn't he? Flynn needed to get over his shit, and so he would. Somehow.

He stood and made his way to the front desk to check out his schedule, only to stop dead in his tracks. His mom and two aunts were here. Damn. The Battleaxes. They were engrossed in conversation with Gabby and Brent. Avery looked on from behind her computer as if trying to stay out of it.

Aunt Marie turned and grinned when she'd spotted Flynn. "We were just discussing Gabby's wedding date."

He was her wedding date. And hadn't they, just weeks ago, played Cupid to shove him and Gabby together? Ergo, what the hell? And why did Gabby look like a trapped animal?

Hand on her hip, Aunt Rosa gave him a roll of her eyes. "We think it's really cute you're her plus one. You guys always seem to fall back on that, but we have something else in mind. They hired a new doctor at the walk-in clinic—a recent transplant. We think he and Gabby will hit it off."

No way in hell. A growl rumbled his chest and he looked at Gabby. She'd wanted to keep their relationship under wraps for a while, but he was over that. *"No. She's going with me."*

The smile hit Gabby's baby blues before her mouth caught up. "That's what I told them."

Undeterred, Aunt Marie tilted her head. "But he's a doctor, Flynn."

Irritation pounded his temples and he'd had enough. *"So am I. She's going with me."*

Before they could argue, he stalked over to Gabby, pressed her back to the counter, and kissed the living shit right out of her. In front of everyone. Breathing hard, he pulled away. Her heavy lids lifted and she grinned.

"You're *my* date," he whispered.

Gabby glanced over his shoulder and he turned.

Brent high-fived Aunt Rosa.

Avery shook her head, her lips twisting. "You walked right into that one."

"Nicely done." Aunt Marie nodded.

He narrowed his eyes. *"You're the ones who tried playing matchmaker in the first place. This shouldn't surprise you."*

"Oh, it doesn't." Aunt Marie straightened her power suit, shifting back into mayor-mode. "You two were easier than we'd thought."

With that, Mom kissed his cheek and the three strolled out the front door to go torment some other soul.

Later that evening, he sat next to Hailey on the couch in Cade's house and shook his head. She'd beaten him three straight at tic-tac-toe. She'd already had her PB&J for dinner and had about twenty minutes before bedtime. Fletch, along with Cade's black lab, Freeman, and Avery's yellow lab, Seraph, were zonked out in front of the fireplace.

He glanced at Hailey. Kid was a spitting image of Avery with wavy brown hair and a button nose. "Great job, kiddo. You kicked my butt."

She shifted on the seat, but instead of flapping her hands and grinning at the compliment, she twisted her head away and twitched like her skin was on fire. Wondering what had upset her, he set the tablet aside.

Hailey stood, gaze darting around the room, her distress growing.

She didn't like touch, so Flynn knelt in front of her. *"What's wrong, favorite niece of mine?"*

Her gaze flittered to his hands long enough to read. Before Avery had moved to Redwood Ridge, one of Hailey's therapists had taught the girl sign language because she was nonverbal. He considered it a major blessing. He loved hanging out with this kid and he'd hate to not be able to communicate.

Though some of the tension left her frame, she was still jerking as if uncomfortable.

At a loss, he looked around. *"Can you show me what's wrong?"*

She darted past him and up the stairs.

He grabbed her tablet since it had a talking app on it for her to point out words, and followed. She was parked on her bed in her pretty pink room, rocking. Not wanting to set her off again, he sat on the edge of the mattress, giving her a wide berth.

"Are you tired? Do you want to go to sleep now?"

Hailey didn't offer much by way of eye contact, she rarely did, but her gaze locked with his for a few beats, then dropped to his mouth. She twitched and glanced at the ceiling.

Not understanding her mood and getting concerned, he swiped the tablet screen and brought up the app. *"Show me, pretty girl."*

Instead of taking the device, she opened her mouth. At first, he thought she was yawning, but she leaned forward almost as if she was going to be sick. Shoot. He hadn't given her any dairy—which her body didn't tolerate—so maybe she'd caught a flu bug at school.

As he was about to text Avery, Cade rushed into the room and squatted by the bed. Eyebrows furrowed, he looked at Flynn. "What's wrong with her?"

"I don't know. We were playing a game and then she started acting unusual. We just got upstairs."

"Hey, squirt. Did you have fun with Uncle Flynn?"

Hailey's gaze darted to Flynn's mouth, then away. The twitching started again. As she'd done a couple of moments ago, her mouth opened and she leaned forward.

Cade ran a hand through his hair. "She's making strange sounds. I've never heard her do that. Did she eat something funny? Has she vomited?"

Flynn shook his head. His heart pounded behind his ribs and concern clawed his gut. He hadn't known she was making noise. Had he done something wrong? Perhaps she'd accidentally gotten into something?

"I'm calling Avery." Cade whipped his phone from his pocket and paced the room, eyes on Hailey. He exchanged a few words on his cell and pocketed the phone. "She's already on her way home. We split up tonight so she could do the final dress fitting and I could pick up my tux. Had to stop by the bakery and pay for the cake." He ducked his face to look in Hailey's eyes. "You're scaring me, squirt. Mommy's on her way."

Hailey's mouth opened wider, and judging by the panicked way Cade's eyes rounded, the girl's noises were louder.

"I'm going to touch your head for just a minute." Cade pressed his palm to her forehead. Hailey batted it away. He looked at Flynn. "She's not warm. Were there any loud sounds to set her off?" Cade closed his eyes and winced. "I'm sorry. Of course, you wouldn't know that."

Flynn watched the girl, feeling so fucking useless he could scream. *"The dogs didn't move. I don't think it was a noise. We were just playing and—"*

Avery rushed into the room and threw her purse aside. Sitting on the opposite side of the bed from Flynn, she studied Hailey, who appeared somewhat calmer. "What happened?"

He shrugged and relayed what he'd told Cade. *"Whatever the issue, it just started maybe twenty minutes ago. We just got done with a game and—"*

Hailey opened her mouth, jaw wide, eyes round.

Avery, still as stone, watched her daughter. After several panic-filled moments, Avery's lip quivered.

Cade quit pacing. "What is it, Avery? What's wrong?"

Her watery gaze met his. "She's trying to talk. Back in California, one of her therapists was working on sounds with her. She never really took to it. I wonder why—"

Hailey flew to her knees and tapped Flynn's jaw, startling him. The bed shook as she sat back, then she repeated the process twice more.

Oh. *Oh shit.*

Flynn scrambled to remember exactly what they'd been doing when the episode began. He'd had the tablet in his hands and praised her for winning. He'd...spoken aloud. Damn. He hadn't even realized it.

Verbally communicating with Gabby the past few weeks had put him more at ease with talking but, thus far, she'd been the only one he'd done that with, solely because she was in his comfort zone.

Shit. He'd probably frightened the girl half to death. Guilt punched his gut. His voice was different than the average person. Just based off how the kids at school had reacted, he'd never doubted it. Damn it. He was an asshole.

"I spoke out loud."

Avery's gaze whipped to his. Cade turned toward him, confusion and surprise wrinkling his forehead.

"I'm sorry. I didn't mean to scare her." He looked at Hailey and tried to swallow. He hoped she still liked him after tonight because he loved this kid an awful lot. Christ. He'd screwed up bad.

"I thought you were mute." Avery's attention went from him to Hailey and back again.

He shook his head. *"I can talk. I choose not to. With Gabby, I..."* He sighed. *"It doesn't matter. It won't happen again."* He dipped his face so Hailey knew he was talking to her. *"You know Uncle Flynn is deaf. I sound funny when I speak. That's why I sign. I'm very, very sorry I upset you."*

Throat tight, he closed his eyes for a second and opened them. Cade still looked like he'd been smacked upside the head. With his arms crossed, jaw hanging open, and eyes round, he stared at Flynn.

"I'm sorry. I'll leave."

Hailey surged to her knees again and tapped his jaw, then sat back down, returning to her distracted gaze wandering.

Avery grabbed Flynn's arm before he could stand. "She's not angry or scared. She's frustrated. I think she wants you to talk."

Hailey bounced her bottom on the bed, sending her brown waves into chaos. She flapped her hands in excitement.

Looked as if Avery was right. His skin prickled. He clenched his fists, habit and training ingrained to sign. At war with himself, he sat rigid trying to figure out what to do.

Cade waved at him. "It's okay, man. Say something."

Refocusing on his niece, Flynn shook his head. Heat flared up his neck in embarrassment. Aside from Gabby, his family were the only people who'd heard his voice and that was a rare occasion. He resisted the urge to walk away and opened his mouth instead. "Hi, Hailey."

With her hands flapping, she got in his face. Her tiny mouth opened and her warm breath fanned his jaw, smelling faintly of peanut butter. He forced himself to stay still when he wanted to hug her. Aside from hand-holding, she barely tolerated touch.

Avery clapped a hand over her mouth and dropped it to her lap, eyes welling. "She's grunting a *hi* sound. Oh my God." She laced the girl's fingers with her own. "You're so smart, Hailey girl. We'll tell your teachers you want to start working on speech therapy. Do you want that?"

Cade and Flynn left the room a few minutes later to let Avery tuck her in for the night. At the bottom of the stairs, Cade said, "I'll be damned," upwards of five times.

Conflicting emotions churned inside his stomach, pounded his head. Flynn crossed his arms by the front door. Uncomfortable in his own skin, he wanted to leave. On one hand, this was a great breakthrough for Hailey and Avery seemed pleased. On the other, he was confused about why Hailey had chosen now to get interested in speech. He had the niggling sensation he'd overstepped somewhere. Honestly, he was no role model for this kind of thing.

Cade stood staring at him from across the room as if unsure what to say, but hell if his eyes didn't radiate pride and appreciation.

Avery came downstairs, and before Flynn knew what hit him, she launched herself at him. He barely caught her and took a step for balance so they wouldn't topple. Arms around his neck, legs tangled, she hugged him. Hard. Like squeezing the air out of his lungs hard.

She drew back, eyes wet. "Thank you. She must've connected with you since you don't talk either. Now she wants to try. She probably won't ever be able to speak normally, but maybe she'll learn a few words."

Hell. He nodded and forced a smile.

Chapter 23

In her parents' driveway, Gabby turned in the passenger seat and blinked, looking about as happy to be here as Flynn. "We don't have to go inside."

He offered a crooked grin and looked out the windshield at the Cosette's brick ranch lined with neatly trimmed bushes. He'd been to her folks' house a million times, but this was different. This time, he was dating their daughter.

After word had gotten out they were officially a couple—in Battleaxe record time of about thirty seconds—her mother had insisted they come over for dinner. With Cade and Avery's rehearsal tomorrow, coupled with what had happened with Hailey earlier in the week, plus the job stress he wasn't used to as of late, this dinner was just one more thing determined to drive him batshit.

He sighed and fidgeted behind the wheel.

Screw it. He was with Gabby now and wanted to keep it that way. He needed to grow a pair and just open the car door. Her parents were nice people, had always treated him kindly, but again...he hadn't been dating her those other instances. Not to mention, Gabby's evil sister would, no doubt, be inside. He wouldn't shed a tear if he never crossed paths with Rachel again. He could take the crap she dished out to him, but he would not tolerate the way she often treated Gabby.

She waved her hand to get his attention. "They already love you, you know."

Yep. As her best friend, they loved him just fine. Except he had the sinking suspicion that was about to veer way south.

Smiling when he felt like yakking, he kissed her forehead and attempted to shove the foreboding sense of dread back into its cage. *"Let's go."*

The scent of roasted chicken filled the house as they stepped inside. Her father was doing a crossword puzzle in front of the TV, but set it aside to hug his daughter. He smiled at Flynn and shook his hand. "How have things been with you?"

"Good, thank you."

Gabby translated and glanced around. "Mom in the kitchen?"

Her father nodded and gestured for Flynn to take a seat.

She headed out of the room and Flynn hesitantly eased into a recliner, staring at the dark brown shag carpet, then the flower-printed furniture. He never noticed they matched the drapes. Aside from the neutral beige walls, the room was raging femininity.

The Cosette house always looked like a crochet party had thrown up on every available surface. Gabby's mother had been a stay-at-home mom, and ever since the girls were old enough to move out, she'd filled in that time with knitting. Doilies. Afghans. Picture frames. Seat covers. A creepy-looking doll.

Craft hell.

Photos of the girls lined the mantel, and from his chair, he zeroed in on one in particular—him and Gabby from senior prom. Last time he'd been here, her cheerleader shot had been in that frame. He didn't know what to make of it, wondering if the change was some kind of silent support of their relationship or appeasing it.

Without Gabby around to translate, her father had gone back to the crossword puzzle. Unlike Flynn's family and friends, the Cosettes never showed interest in learning sign language. Maybe Hailey had been onto something with getting him to speak the other night. It wasn't like he was a clumsy five-year-old anymore. He might feel awkward talking, but it couldn't be more uncomfortable than sitting here twiddling his thumbs.

"You want me to change the channel?"

Flynn lifted his hand and shook his head with a smile that bordered on plastic. To prove it, he focused on the set and pretended the fishing program was interesting. The only thing that rated more tedious than going fishing was watching it. He subtly checked his watch. Christ. It had only been five minutes since they'd arrived.

Bless her sweet, perfect, gigantic heart, Gabby came back with a beer for him and sat on the arm of Flynn's chair.

"What's a seven letter word for fatigued?"

"Haggard."

Gabby translated, and her dad pointed at him. "You're a keeper."

Yay him. Flynn strummed his fingers on his thigh and got lost in thought. He stared at Gabby's profile while she watched TV. She was the spitting image of her mom with her fair skin and blond hair, but she'd inherited the curves from her dad. Flynn had no clue where the baby blues had come from as both her folks had brown eyes. She also had her mother's hospitality in spades and her father's calm, reserved presence.

It had him wondering where the hell Rachel had gone wrong.

Tick-tock.

After a hundred years, Mr. Cosette set the crossword aside. "So, I hear you two are an item."

Flynn deflected to Gabby, who smiled. "Yes, for a few weeks now."

"Kind of surprised it took you this long. You two have been joined at the hip since kindergarten."

"Flynn's a little slow on the uptake." She nudged Flynn's shoulder and winked at him, her smile the epitome of adorable.

He narrowed his eyes in good humor. *"Such a comedian."*

They talked about his brother's upcoming wedding and mundane crap like the weather until her mother poked her head through the doorway to announce dinner.

Flynn followed Gabby into the kitchen and paused when he found Rachel at the table. Since he hadn't spotted her before now, he'd been hoping she'd not been able to come. She squinted at him with a sneer, and he bit back a sigh.

At least dinner smelled good. Mrs. Cosette had always been a great cook. Roasted chicken, baby carrots, biscuits, and mashed potatoes lined the table. He took a seat next to Gabby and across from her wretch of a sister.

Dishes got passed. Conversation started. Stink eye from Rachel abounded. Great times.

Mrs. Cosette wiped her mouth with a napkin. "Flynn, are you going to give a toast at Cade's wedding?"

She was probably just issuing polite chat, but he got the sense he was being baited. *"I'm not sure. Probably."* He glanced at Gabby. She'd helped him get more comfortable with the idea of dancing, but a toast hadn't much crossed his mind. She'd have to translate if he did do one. Or maybe Drake. Cade never mentioned a speech preference.

Rachel rolled her eyes and whipped Gabby's mom an *I told you so* look. Pretty sure he didn't want to know what that was about, he focused on his plate.

He was a quarter-way through his meal when he noticed Gabby had barely made a dent. She'd been too busy translating everything to pick up her fork. By her mother's expression, she hadn't missed the fact either.

Flynn tapped Gabby's thigh. *"Just eat, sweetheart. I'm good. I'll follow fine."*

She gave him an *are you sure* look, and he nodded. When she started eating, he dug back in and did the same.

From what he could tell, none of the conversation involved him and they were all talking too fast for him to keep up very well. Something about Rachel and her apartment and her job or whatever. Tuning them out, he focused on his plate and forced himself to swallow food he didn't taste, even though his appetite had taken a hike.

This sort of felt like elementary school all over again. Him left out of the mix, only being included because of the pretty blonde next to him.

What the hell? Could he be a whinier bitch right now? She had a right to enjoy her meal, to spend time with her family.

After he finished, he sat back and draped an arm over the back of Gabby's chair, idly running his fingers through the ends of her hair to calm himself and adjust his mood. He glanced around the kitchen for something to do. Bare oak cabinets, white countertops, black appliances. Nothing much to see. They had an apple-print wallpaper design which he stared at hard enough to have the fruit blend together.

He suddenly got a glimpse into his future if he and Gabby stayed together, and it made his stomach burn. Holidays and birthday parties and family picnics. Her sitting on the floor, translating every word, trying her damnedest to make sure he was a part of things. Constantly looking his way to be sure he was okay.

She set her fork aside and smiled at him. His Gabby, the sweetest damn person on the planet. "Mom wants to know if you'd like dessert?"

He forced his gaze off her and onto her mom. *"No, thank you. I'm stuffed. Dinner was delicious."*

Mrs. Cosette stood, gathering plates. "I'll send some home with you. You can eat it later?"

"Thank you."

Rachel must've said something snotty because Gabby whipped her a steely glare. Then she rose to help her mom with dishes.

Before she could get too far, he kissed her cheek. *"I'll be in the living room with your dad. Need anything?"*

She wrapped her arms around his waist and pecked his mouth with a quick kiss. "We can take off soon."

There was a God. He nodded and occupied some time helping her dad with a crossword. Mr. Cosette would point at a hint he couldn't solve. Flynn would fill in the spaces. Thirty minutes passed, and Gabby hadn't returned. He made a stop at the bathroom and then hunted her down in the kitchen.

She stood in a circle with Rachel and her mom, her back to him. Her shoulders were tense and her hands fisted on her hips. He stopped in the doorway, wondering what was going on, his stomach twisting in concern.

Rachel flung her hand in the air, drawing his attention to her. "Do you really want to date a deaf guy?"

He froze, his muscles going rigid to the point of pain. They were discussing him? Rachel talked too fast to read her lips for the rest of her statement. Her mother seemed to be following up that declaration, anyway.

"Are you really happy, though?"

At that second, Rachel glanced up and a wicked gleam lit her evil incarnate eyes.

Gabby whirled, saw him, and closed her eyes. Regret pinched her brows. She rubbed her forehead before her apology-laden gaze met his. "Hey. Are you about ready to head home?"

With his stomach bottomed out and his throat in a vise, he scanned the faces and resettled on her. And here he thought things were going well. Too well, he'd told Drake. He should've known something was coming to ruin their happy. In fact, he'd been sure of it. Their relationship had been almost too good to be true.

Regardless, it didn't matter what her family thought of them together. Gabby was the only one who got a say in this, the only one who mattered.

Instead of making it easy on them, he confronted the issue. *"Is there a problem?"*

Gabby crossed her arms, refusing to sign, her head cast down. For all her sweet bravery, she gazed at the floor as if hoping it would swallow her whole. Embarrassment tinged her cheeks.

Fine. He repeated the question out loud.

Mrs. Cosette's head whipped back, her eyes round, obviously not expecting him to speak. She glanced at Gabby and back to him. Her shoulders dropped, posture deflating. "We like you, Flynn. You've always been a good friend to our girl. Yet..." She glanced up, seeming to collect herself. "It was one thing when you were young and she did things for you, but she's wasted her whole life making yours easier. Now, to have you start dating, is too much."

Gabby stepped forward, her hands flying in rapid sign, but he kept his gaze on her mother. The edges of his vision started to gray, spots dancing before his eyes. He was pretty certain he'd stopped breathing, but his thoughts were too jacked up to figure it out.

Mrs. Cosette addressed her daughter. "You could have been anything, done anything you wanted. Did you even have a desire to be a veterinarian technician or did you simply follow him?" She faced Flynn, stark pity in her eyes. "I know you care about her, but when does she start getting to live her life?"

He swiped a hand down his face and looked away, not needing to read any more. He got the picture. Worst part? She wasn't wrong. Not completely. Her words had hit a nerve because he'd had the same apprehension himself. More than once.

He fisted his shaking hands, trying to wrap his head around the facts, but it was a moot effort. Raw pain tore at his chest, stealing his breath. He couldn't latch onto a tangible thought to save his life.

Gabby stepped in front of him, signing so fast air whooshed between them.

Not reading any of it, he stilled her hands with his own. Now was not the time for this, here not the place. Later, when they were alone, they'd hash this out, find out if there was any validity to what her mother said. He'd like to know the answer to that himself.

He forced a swallow past the rock in his throat and dropped her hands. *"I think it's best I leave."*

"I'm coming with you—"

Shaking his head, he cupped her cheeks. With his heart hammering, he pressed a kiss to her forehead and stepped away. *"I'll see you tomorrow."* He left her standing in her mother's kitchen with wounded eyes and her lower lip quivering, feeling like an asshole.

How he got home was a mystery, as was how he wound up sitting on his back deck with his dog at his feet and stars winking overhead. A numb state of shock threatened, and it was all he could do to hold onto reality a little longer. Oblivion beckoned, but he couldn't give in.

Gulping air, he let the breeze wash over his chilled skin and wondered if he'd ever be warm again. Dropping his head in his hands, he fought the tears burning behind his lids and replayed the I-told-you-so rhetoric for good measure.

Because shit...he had known. He'd known in high school when he'd shut down his attraction to Gabby and he'd known a month ago when it flared back to life. Yeah, they had something great going. And yeah, there was a lot more than basic desire at play here. There were emotions. Strong, consuming emotions. The forever kind.

But what was at the root of them? Even with all the miles and years accumulated between him and Gabby, he knew his answer. Yet hers wasn't clear. And that was the gutting, eviscerating part. He'd trust Gabby with his life if it came down to that. But in this, when it came to his heart, if he wasn't one-hundred percent certain her feelings weren't misguided, they would be doing both themselves a great injustice by staying together.

The wooden deck planks vibrated and, without glancing up, he knew it was Gabby. Damn her, anyway. Fletch brushed by, scrambling to greet to her.

"I said I'd see you tomorrow," he mumbled without looking at her. Keeping his head buried in his hands, he prayed she'd go home.

Cool fingers closed around his wrists and pulled his arms down.

He sighed, meeting her gaze. He'd been looking into those blue eyes so long and so often he wasn't even sure they were two separate people anymore. Moonlight bathed her fair skin, illuminated the loose strands of her hair as if creating a halo. How fitting, since she *was* an angel. Cherubic face, huge eyes, long lashes, and curvy body. Ability to make anyone comfortable in her presence, give unconditionally, and empathize with any creature who emitted a heartbeat. Girl next door to the world, yet a seductive temptress in the bedroom.

"I'm sorry you overheard that conversation. Mom meant well, but she doesn't know what she's talking about." She gripped his forearms, squeezing. "She was wrong."

Leave it to her to ignore him.

He did not want to do this tonight. He felt too unguarded and raw to be civilized. Much needed to be hashed out and, since she was here, he started with the least invasive. "You need to think about what your mom said. If there had been no me in the picture, if we'd never been friends, would you have wanted to be a technician?"

A helpless gesture of her hands fluttered the space between them and she pinned him with a frustrated narrowing of her eyes. "I don't know, Flynn. I wanted to be Rock Star Barbie and an Olympic gymnast, too, but I can't sing and I'd kill myself on a balance beam."

He growled, rose from the chair, and stalked the length of the deck. Strain wrenched his muscles until he was brittle with irritation.

She rounded him and planted her feet, stopping him mid-pace. "The point is, you *do* exist and we *are* friends. The rest doesn't matter."

"Of course, it matters!"

"Why, Flynn? The people in our lives shape us. We grow with them. Taking you out of the equation is like removing a limb. It's impossible to know the result. The outcome is, I'm happy."

He rubbed the back of his neck. "And what about the rest of it? The years wasted in an attempt to make my life easier?" He never saw it that way, or maybe never considered the option, but did others? Like her family apparently had? Yeah, she made his life easier, but it wasn't as if he couldn't do things by himself. And she had a life of her own, her own interests outside of him.

Her typically affectionate eyes morphed to blue ice. "Are you kidding me right now? Not one minute of the time I spent with you was wasted." Tears brimmed her lashes and she shook her head like she didn't comprehend. "I love you."

There went all the air. Hell, this hurt. Like ripping apart organs kind of pain. "I may be deaf, but that big heart of yours might be blinding you."

She stared at him, gaze steady, tears trekking her cheeks. "I would love you if you weren't deaf. I'd love you if you were blind. I'd love you if you had all your senses or none at all."

She angrily wiped her tears with her palm, and he had to clench his fingers in order not to do it himself. "You were the first person to see me, a scared little girl in a classroom full of strangers. And all these years later, you're still the only man who does. You're funny and kind and courageous."

He believed her. She could tell him Elvis was living in sin with Little Orphan Annie on the island of Atlantis and he'd believe her. Trust wasn't the problem.

She wasn't alone in her feelings. He'd fallen so hard, he hadn't even realized he'd smacked pavement until he was in fragmented pieces. And he loved her too much not to let her go, just for a little while. Long enough to give her time. The only way to be certain she'd really dissected the grating issue was for him to not be right in front of her.

He'd never been an insecure person. Lonely on the outside looking in, often irritated by being disregarded, sad to be different from his peers, sometimes hurt to be laughed at behind his back...but not insecure. His family and friends were loving and encouraging. He had a great support system. But lately, ever since he'd gone all in with Gabby and succumbed, he'd been a twisted ball of self-doubting, unsure, confused chaos.

It wasn't like him and he hated it. Not that it was her fault, because it wasn't. Perhaps he just wasn't cut out for a long-term relationship, even though that's what he'd secretly desired. For too long, he'd craved that connection to another person. He had that with Gabby, but they weren't the only two people to consider. Her family meant a lot to her. And the last thing he wanted was for her to wake up one day and resent him. For settling. For not venturing out. For inadvertently trapping her.

Letting out a deliberate breath, he took in her features, his beautiful Gabby, and begged for strength from any higher power that would listen. "We've spent too many years knotted together to see the bigger picture. I'm not saying this is the end or that we're over, just that we need some space."

Slowly, her features slackened, her eyes pitting to a void of nothing. Like putting on a shell of armor to protect herself. And how ironic. The one person she never needed protection from was him. Her chest rose and fell in rapid succession and, eventually, she squared her shoulders.

She leveled him with a penetrating stare that obliterated anything in her path and shot right to his soul. "There's something you don't understand, that I fear you'll never understand. We all have our handicaps, Flynn. You're not mine."

Chapter 24

Coffee cup halfway to her mouth, Gabby eyed her reflection in the bathroom mirror and tried not to wince. She'd spent the better part of last night crying after she'd left Flynn's, and her puffy, red-rimmed eyes were a testimony. Dark shadows from lack of sleep only added to the wreckage.

At least the clinic was closed the next three days for Cade and Avery's wedding. Today, she and Zoe were heading to the botanical garden pavilion to set up for the big day tomorrow. She had to get her act together or she'd look like the floor of the New York subway in wedding pictures.

Damn it, though. It hurt so bad. Flynn had said this wasn't the end, but it sure felt like it when he'd looked at her last night as if he couldn't take the relationship anymore. And what did that say about her when even Flynn couldn't stick?

She didn't get it, didn't think she ever would. They were so great together and he'd never struck her as insecure. It was as if he didn't trust her to know her own feelings, didn't understand why in the hell she loved him in the first place.

And...he'd never said he loved her back.

Her stomach cramped and tears threatened again. She had no doubt Flynn loved her. As a friend. Through the years, he'd proven that time after time. A sickening swirl of pain filled her head, her chest. Perhaps that's what all his reservations were about. Not her feelings, but his. Sex didn't mean love, and maybe he realized his physical attraction and friendship had blurred the lines. That this wasn't something lasting, just...lust.

She blew out a ragged breath and closed her eyes. If Flynn couldn't fall in love with her, it was time to face reality. Twelve cats wouldn't look too bad in her cute little house, right? She'd go broke on litter alone, but hey. Company was company.

God. Her heart hurt. Regardless of his feelings, she'd fallen for him. All her life, she'd wished for this. For love. To have someone look adoringly into her eyes and tell her without words she was his everything. Stupid, stupid.

Setting the coffee cup on the vanity, she shook her head and splashed cold water on her face. Zoe would be here to pick her up in twenty minutes. She needed to get her act together. This weekend was about Cade and Avery, not her own drama. Forgoing a shower until after they'd set up the pavilion, she pulled her hair into a high ponytail and called herself presentable.

Popsicle jumped up on the vanity as she was debating whether to bother with foundation to hide her dark circles. The cat eyed her coffee cup, then her. She had a thing for knocking stuff over. Just for the hell of it.

"Don't even think about it."

She lifted her paw and lazily blinked. *I'm gonna do it.*

"Popsicle," she warned.

Blink. *Sounds like a dare to me.* Eyes on Gabby, the cat brought her paw within striking distance of the cup. *Look, I'm so close. Whatcha gonna do?*

Gabby sighed. "Can you not be a diva? Just for today? I had a really rough night and—"

Flink. The cat swiped her paw, sending the mug across the vanity.

Gabby grabbed it at the last second before it could crash to the floor. "Just for that, you don't get your treat. I was going to adopt you a dozen brothers and sisters."

Popsicle arched her back, fluffing her orangish fur, and jumped to the floor. *Your threats are beneath me, peon.* She stalked from the room with the air of a queen.

Rolling her eyes, Gabby headed to her bedroom to throw on a pair of jeans and a tee, then made it to the living room just as Zoe keyed her way inside the front door. Her hair was still bright purple. At least it matched the bridesmaids' dresses.

Popsicle pranced into the room, realized Zoe wasn't Flynn, sniffed, and strode back down the hall.

"Something I said?" Zoe shrugged at the cat's retreating back and gave Gabby a once-over. "Wow. I like the train wreck look. It's so in right now."

Gabby glanced down at herself, noting her shirt was inside out and her socks mismatched. Cute socks, though. One from her bright green shamrock set and the other a pink from her Easter egg...

She sighed. "Thanks. I've been perfecting it all night. I was going for desperate and pathetic, but train wreck works." She headed into the kitchen to turn off the coffeepot and set her mug in the sink.

Zoe followed. "What's up, Gabs?" She leaned against the counter and crossed her arms. She was a tiny person whose head barely reached the bottom of the upper cabinets. She seemed even more petite in Gabby's kitchen for some reason. Zoe had such a take-no-crap personality that she'd seemed bigger usually.

Pulling her tee over her head, Gabby righted it and put it back on. She rubbed her forehead to alleviate the tension. "Flynn broke up with me. Or I think he did. He said we need"—she made air quotes—"*some space.*"

Scratching the back of her head, Zoe frowned. "Twenty-five years of friendship where you two were inseparable and *now* he wants space? What did you do? Threaten his dog? Hijack a bank? Forget he liked ranch dressing over thousand island?"

Flynn liked French dressing best. A sob tore from Gabby's chest. A fresh wave of pain threatening to pull her under. God. She'd dehydrate at this rate.

"Hell." Zoe crossed the space and wrapped her arms around her, the top of her head barely reaching Gabby's nose, but her hug was mighty. "I was only kidding. You have the vagina in the relationship, so of course he was the one in the wrong."

She gave a watery laugh and stepped away, wiping her eyes. After a beat to calm herself, she told Zoe what happened. "I just don't get it, you know? The only thing I can think about is, what if he doesn't feel the same way about me?" She thought she'd known him and what he'd wanted, but everything was out of whack now.

Zoe eyed the ceiling. "I'm not as close with Flynn as I am to Drake or Cade, mostly because you two had that stronger bond, but this seems out of character for him."

"Yeah. Perhaps I just bring out the worst in him, or being together did. All it took was one misguided comment from my mother and he suddenly questioned everything. He's never lacked confidence or doubted us."

Seeming to absorb that, Zoe nodded. "First, it's impossible for you to draw out anyone's bad side. Seriously, look at you. The good girl, a great buddy, the town sweetheart. Annoying, really. You make the rest of us look like henchmen with leprosy." She waved her off when Gabby tried to comment. "I'm serious. Your heart's bigger than the damn state and if anyone knows that, it's Flynn. And I don't think this is about him not returning your feelings. I get the impression he thinks he's not good enough."

Gabby stilled. The thought never occurred to her, not long enough to gel, anyway. She shook her head. This was thought for later. "We better get going. We have a lot to do before the rehearsal dinner and I need to come back and shower first."

"Yep. I could smell you all the way outside."

Laughing, she grabbed her purse. "Shut up."

"I've bathed dogs who've rolled in skunk that smell better."

Gabby grabbed her side, laughing harder. "I mean it. Shut up. I'm fragile today."

Drake was standing inside the main hall at the botanical garden when they arrived, his back to the glass wall that led to the indoor atrium. At their questioning glance, he shrugged. "Avery enlisted my services." He turned to Gabby, his stare assessing. "What happened to you?"

She eyed the ceiling. Pouted. "Just lie and tell me I look pretty."

"You are pretty. No lying necessary."

Whipping her gaze to his, she had to swallow another threat of tears. "Aw." When he just kept his level gaze on hers, silently demanding she answer his original question, she rolled her shoulders.

"Gabby..."

Zoe scoffed. "Your brother happened, that's what. She's a weepy, gooey, white-hot mess because he's no better than any other male."

Drake flicked his glance at Zoe. "Go burn your bra over there. We'll be right along."

Zoe crossed her arms and set her feet. "Hilarious."

"I'm not a white-hot mess. More like tepid—"

He refocused on Gabby. "What did Flynn do?"

Curses. Was it too much to ask to get a distraction around here? "I don't want to talk about it."

His unmoving presence remained in front of her, hands in the pockets of his worn jeans, stance wide, telling her he wasn't going anywhere.

Out of nowhere, she was struck by how different the O'Grady brothers were in appearance. Drake's near-black hair was neatly trimmed just above his ears and his eyes were a rich cocoa, unlike Flynn's longish strawberry hair and hazel eyes or Cade's bedhead dishwater blond and blue eyes. They were all tall, though, averaging six feet, and had the high cheekbones from their mom and wide jaw from their dad. Lean, muscular builds. Their personalities were unique, too. Cade mischievous and charming. Flynn had dry humor and subtle wit. Drake was pensive and cautious.

But they shared one common trait that Gabby never took for granted and respected the hell out of their parents for teaching—they all loved hard.

Whether it was family, friends, or their pets, the O'Grady boys never shied away from feelings or thought it was beneath them to display affection. And when they fell in love, it was for life. Forever.

She and Drake hadn't been as cozy as her and Flynn, but Gabby never doubted Drake cared about her. And the conflicted look he was giving her said he wasn't comfortable with the drift between two people he loved.

After a tense beat, he nodded. "Just tell me if I need to kick his ass." Before she could respond with more than a grin, his gaze darted around the room. "Any idea what needs to get done?"

Zoe whipped a folded paper from her back pocket with a wry smile. "Avery made a detailed blueprint. It's color-coded."

Drake barked a laugh and took the paper from Zoe. "Sounds like our girl all right." He scanned the page. "I'll start pulling out tables."

Zoe followed him to the storage room.

Gabby glanced around. She hadn't been in here since the Valentine's dance. Light, open, and airy, the hall incorporated raw nature with subtle class. Long and rectangular, the room had the atrium on one side and a solid wall on the other. The public entrance was just off a small foyer and directly across the space was the built-in bar. Polished wood floors and rough-cut ceiling beams.

Ever since Drake and Heather's nuptials so many years before, Gabby had wanted her wedding right here. Like any other girl, she'd fantasized about the dress and the cake. How she'd wear her hair and what colors she'd incorporate.

A pang of longing filled her belly and she missed Flynn so badly she had to close her eyes to focus on breathing. It hadn't even been a day since she'd seen him, but this rift made it seem like an eternity. She wondered what he was thinking, how he was doing.

Honestly, everything between them, from their friendship to their romantic relationship, had always been smooth. Effortless. She didn't know what to do or if she should even do anything. Last night, he'd said she needed to think, but her heart wasn't conflicted. He was the one who'd pushed the pause button.

Zoe and Drake reemerged. Gabby shook her head and dug into the task at hand.

It had taken until midafternoon, but they got tables arranged and decorated with white linen. Votive candles were in pretty lavender dishes, adding ambiance. The florist would deliver flowers tomorrow. They'd strung twinkle lights along the beams and followed Avery's directions to the letter.

Zoe ran Gabby home, where she showered, then donned a light yellow sundress to uplift her mood. Strapless and snug on her torso, the skirt flared just above her knee. She finished off the look with white ballet flats and checked her hair, which she'd left in loose waves down her back.

She had Flynn in mind the whole time she'd prepped. They hadn't spoken since last night, and it wasn't as if her outfit would suddenly smack some sense into him, but she wanted to look nice for him.

Grabbing the vanity, she sucked air and tried to quiet the nerves fluttering. It was no use. The only thing that would make her mood better, that would stop the rampant panic and unease, was Flynn.

She was the last to arrive at the hall. Avery and her mom, Justine, along with Gayle, stood by the pastor up front. The O'Grady boys' mother was beaming bright enough to illuminate the room. Gabby figured it was because she never thought she'd see Cade settle down, and yet here they were. Brent, Zoe, and Drake were chatting nearby. Flynn was kneeling in front of Hailey, but his back was turned so she couldn't read what he was signing to the little girl.

As if sensing her, he stood and slowly turned. The air crackled between them and, for a second, she took him in, surprised by the hum of energy. He wore gray dress slacks and a white button-down that did little to hide the powerful display of lean muscle underneath. His hair was casually brushed off his forehead, more finger-combed than neat.

His gaze traveled the length of her, heating as it descended, and the burn singed her from across the room. Lips parting, his brows furrowed. His jaw ticked as if he were trying to grab a hold of a logical response, but his expression belied control. One glance said he thought her dress would look better on the floor. And he wanted to put it there.

She sucked in a rapid breath as his eyes met hers, shrinking the distance to inches without either moving. Her heart pounded. Abject longing and barely restrained lust stared back at her, unblinking. Hopeful, she smiled.

But...he flinched and turned away, his back rigid.

Her stomach plummeted in dread. She wrung her trembling hands, hurt pummeling her heart. He'd...dismissed her. The one person who'd never skimmed right past her as if not noticing her presence. The only man who'd ever bothered to truly look.

She was just another face in the crowd.

Unable to pull in oxygen, she teetered. With her throat tight and the hot sting of tears in her eyes, she focused on the floor until she could get her bearings. She would not cry and ruin this night for her friends. Her lip quivered and she cursed, pressing her mouth into a thin line.

Flynn, kneeling in front of Hailey, signed something. The girl tapped Flynn's mouth and darted her distracted gaze around the room. Unsure what that was about, Gabby watched with her head tilted. Hailey repeated the gesture twice more.

"He spoke to her the other night." Cade stepped beside Gabby. He took a sip from his water bottle and recapped it, attention on his brother and soon-to-be daughter. "As in, he opened his mouth and talked."

"Really?" she whispered and looked at Flynn. Hailey loved him. They had their own special bond Gabby had witnessed from the first time he'd met the girl.

"Yeah. It was the damnedest thing. He said it was a slip-up." The plastic crinkled as he fisted the bottle. "I can't tell you the last time I heard his voice. Hailey's been trying to get him to do it again ever since."

Flynn hadn't mentioned it. That was exactly the kind of thing he would've told her, too. It made her wonder what else he'd been keeping and why he suddenly felt the need to keep her in the dark.

The longer she stared, the more she ached. She brushed a strand of hair away from her face and forced herself to look at Cade instead. He was handsome in black slacks and a blue dress shirt. "It embarrasses him, his voice. Based on how others have responded, he knows his dialect and tone are unusual."

Cade shifted his eyes to her with one corner of his mouth quirked. "He talks to you, though. Imagine my surprise when he mentioned that."

She shrugged. "At work, sometimes his hands are occupied. And when we're, you know, it's not always ideal to sign."

He was shaking his head before she'd finished. "No, Gabs." After a pointed, pronounced glare, he studied his brother. "When Flynn spoke to her, Hailey started making sounds like she wanted to also."

Her hand flew to her chest. "God. Are you serious? That's amazing."

"It is amazing. Her teachers are going to start speech therapy after we get back from our familymoon." Cade nodded and breathed a laugh. "Christ, Gabby. I about cried like a baby, I was so fucking proud."

She grinned for the first time all day, warmth filling her. "You're going to be the best dad."

He faced her, crossing his arms, his eyes suspiciously misty. "Because you gave my brother the confidence to be himself, it started a chain reaction. There's no telling if Hailey might've started to do this on her own, but I doubt it. She's got a soft spot for Flynn, I think because he was silent, like her, and it gave her the boost to try."

He shook his head as if in awe. "I love that kid, Gabs. She's not mine by blood, but damn if every one of her milestones isn't mine, too. So, thanks for that."

"Cade." She pressed her lips together to keep from spilling tears. "This mascara isn't waterproof, you ass."

He threw his head back and laughed, then pulled her in for a hug. His heavy sigh stirred her hair. "Flynn will get his head out of the sand, I promise. It'll be okay. You'll see."

For a moment, she actually believed him.

Chapter 25

Unable to take any more emotional abuse, Gabby walked across the parking lot to her car and sank behind the steering wheel.

Back at the rehearsal in the pavilion, when they'd gone over placement and timing and what everyone was supposed to do at the wedding, Gabby had signed for Flynn. She was concerned he might miss a direction and, knowing him, if he did something wrong tomorrow, he'd be upset.

But he'd...completely ignored her. Just outright acted as if she wasn't there. A couple times, Avery had smiled at him and signed for his benefit. He'd smiled and nodded an acknowledgement. Yet, Gabby? If she didn't know any better, she'd swear it hurt him to look at her.

From there, they'd headed to a private room in Le Italy for dinner where she'd been even more invisible. The group chatted and laughed while she'd done everything in her power not to get sick.

At one point, she'd caught Flynn at the bar and walked over, asking if he needed a drink. He'd lifted his pint of ale with a look she interpreted to mean, *I got it. I'm not an idiot.* And God. If she'd been hit by a Mack truck, it would've hurt less.

Conversation. Dinner. Dessert. Drinks. Laughter.

She'd stayed quiet, idly fiddling with her silverware, hoping not to upset anyone. Avery's first husband was a jackass who'd pretended Hailey didn't exist. Her friend deserved this happy day, and so did Cade. Gabby had a hard time keeping it together, which only added more guilt to the bombardment already present.

Flynn never looked at her. Not once.

Closing her eyes, she laid her head against the driver's seat to give herself a moment of peace. Flynn wanted space, wanted her to think. There was space and then there was the Grand Canyon. And this couldn't have come at a worse time. Though the clinic was closed, they'd be together the next three days anyway because of the wedding.

What would happen on Monday when they went back to work? Would this cold shoulder continue? They were going to be insanely busy with Cade and Avery gone. For Flynn and Gabby to be out of sync would be like the sixth realm of hell.

She couldn't do it. She couldn't have another day like today with him and not require a padded cell, complete with basket weaving on Tuesdays.

Sighing, she started the car and headed for home. Though past sundown, it was still early yet. She could pop a sleeping pill, shove all this aside for eight blessed hours, and hope she looked a step above crazy cat lady for the wedding tomorrow.

Most of the town had rolled their sidewalks up for the night. Only the restaurants and a couple bars were open. The quaint storefronts were dark, quiet. Lampposts created shadows on the pavement, their yellow glows lighting the way.

Paused at the only traffic signal on Main Street, she glanced to her left where the clinic was located. When the light changed, she pulled into the parking lot and cut the engine. She had no idea why she'd come here instead of going home, but she got out and sat on the hood of her car, staring at the building.

The exterior was regional stone with shutters. The place looked more like a spacious ranch house than a commercial clinic. Inside, it was much larger than it appeared from the outside. The building was dark, of course, since they were closed.

Shutting her eyes, she breathed in pine, and a trace of brine from the ocean mingled with rain from this morning. It was warm tonight, comfortable, and a heavy fog had settled over the area. Not unusual for Oregon, especially Redwood Ridge since it was pocketed between the mountains and the Pacific. Still, the density was thick and blanketed the surrounding forest behind the shops on this side of the street, reducing the trees to a mirage.

Headlights cut through the night, tires crunched over asphalt, and she turned her head. Drake pulled his truck beside hers and climbed out.

She offered a smile, but it fell flat. "Are you following me?"

"Saw your car when I passed by." After giving her a once-over, he sat beside her on the hood, his expression guarded. "This goes above job dedication, for the record."

She laughed and tucked her hair behind her ear. "I don't know why I came here. I guess what my mother said is still bothering me. Or, rather, how it affected Flynn."

He grunted, his gaze on the clinic before them. "Cade told me what happened. He had to pry the story out of Flynn."

"I hate this. I don't know what to do." She cleared her throat. "Do you think I...treated him like he was helpless? That wasn't my intention. I—"

"Stop." He watched her profile, gaze heavy. "Do you feel sorry for him? Is this a pity situation?"

"What? No." She turned her head, studied him. His chocolate eyes appeared black in the darkness surrounding them and the tenderness staring back at her was unexpected. "You were baiting me."

His lips curved. "Your family might question your motives, but I don't. Never did. You didn't do those things because you thought he was incapable. You didn't do stuff *for* him, you did them *with* him. Included my brother in your life because you liked him, stayed because you love him." His brows rose. "Every guy should be so blessed."

"Drake." God, of all the O'Grady boys, he was the old-fashioned romantic. He felt things so immeasurably that he loved with his whole self. He didn't seem to know any other way. She'd witnessed it with Heather, his brothers, even Brent and Zoe. "Heather was a lucky woman. You're an old soul, Drake."

He grunted again like he was the lucky one. "You're as far from an old soul as they get."

She smiled. "I think I'm insulted."

His amusement notched to a grin. "Fresh and brand new. That's you. A clean slate uninhabited by ghosts and prejudice. Stay that way, kid."

Blinking the endless waterworks away, she looked at the clinic to collect herself and swallowed hard.

After Mr. O'Grady died, when the boys took over, they'd remodeled both the interior and some of the exterior of Animal Instincts. A memory niggled to mind, rough around the edges.

She tilted her head. "You know, when I was little, my dad and I found this stray puppy in the street. It almost got hit by a car. I must've been nine or ten." She remembered the smell of his dirty fur—soil and refuse—as her dad drove them here to get the little guy checked out.

Sensing his gaze, she looked at Drake. "Your dad called him a mutt and I was really mad. I thought he'd insulted the thing." She laughed and Drake grinned, encouraging more. "But he did the exam, his hands so gentle, and he talked to the puppy the whole time. He was a great man, a wonderful vet, your dad."

Drake nodded his agreement.

Her gaze drifted back to the building as if she were still ten-years-old and inside with his father. "His technician took the dog in back when your dad was done. She gave him a bath and cut his nails. She didn't know I followed her. I almost freaked out when she gave him his shots, but the little guy never noticed the poke. She cooed and smiled and the puppy ate it up."

She stilled, her eyes narrowing as a thought dawned on her. "I remember watching from the doorway and thinking, that's what I wanna be when I grow up. I want to take care of helpless puppies, animals no one loved." A laugh skated past her lips. "I forgot all about that until now. Mom's allergic to most pet dander, so we never got to have pets. This place was like heaven to me when Flynn and I would stop by after school."

Shaking her head, she sighed. She glanced at Drake and did a double-take, finding his intent eyes on her and a wisp of a smile. "What?" God, she'd babbled, hadn't she?

His eyebrows pinged, his expression telling her to think hard.

Oh. *Ohh.* "I guess I can tell Flynn not to feel guilty Rock Star Barbie didn't pan out."

"Please don't explain what that means. I'm sure I don't want to know." He laughed, shaking his head in confusion.

"It's nothing." She nodded, though. Flynn had been right to give them some space. It forced her to think about them together and evaluate what she wanted. With or without him, she had a feeling she would've wound up right here. And she loved her job, her life. "Drake, do me a favor tomorrow, would you?"

"What's that?"

She chewed her lip. "If Flynn wants to give a toast at the wedding, could you interpret?" His gaze sobered. "I'm sure he was planning on doing a speech and I'd feel terrible if he had to miss out because we're...you know."

He stared at her lengthy minutes, making her want to squirm, his expression unreadable. "I understand why my brother fell ass over elbow in love with you." He grinned. "Sure, kid. I'll help him out."

* * * *

In the living room of Cade's house, Flynn stared at his reflection in the mirror and fiddled with his tie. Avery and Cade had decided to go with three-piece charcoal gray suits instead of tuxes for the groomsmen, and it had been eons since he'd tied one. He got the knot done, but it didn't look right. Undoing it, he sighed and let the tie hang loose around his neck. Drake would be here shortly and could fix it.

Normally, Gabby would do this crap, but the girls were over at Avery's mother's house getting ready in order for the groom not to see the bride. Stupid tradition, if you asked him.

Cade was texting with a huge grin on his face when Flynn turned. *"You don't seem nervous."*

Cade pocketed the phone. "Because I'm not. Can't wait to see her in a white dress walking toward me." He wrinkled his nose, still grinning like a fool. "I don't care how idiotic that sounds. In a couple hours, Avery will be my wife."

Throat tight, Flynn shook his head, unable to hide his own smile. *"Not stupid at all. I'm really happy for you."* And he was, damn it. Flynn couldn't have picked a better woman for his brother if he'd scoured the planet himself.

Which only made his errant thoughts drift back to Gabby. And to think, he'd been proud of himself having gone a whole five minutes without thinking about her. He hadn't slept more than a handful of hours since she'd left his house the other night, and seeing her at the rehearsal hadn't helped the discontented, holy-shit sensation her absence created.

Like a giant gaping wound.

She'd looked so goddamn beautiful last night with that yellow dress and her caramel hair loose around her shoulders. Staring at her had stolen his breath and caused a searing pain to riddle his organs. As a result, he'd spent the better part of the night pretending she wasn't there or he would've caved, taken her right there in the pavilion, and begged her to forget the things he'd said.

Regardless of his recent blinding insight, their time apart hadn't been a bad thing. Without it, he might've kept seesawing with doubt, and she deserved better than that. As did he.

But he'd hurt her and that was unforgivable. His sweet Gabby, heart for miles. Last night was the first time in his memory her light had been... vanquished. He'd lay awake trying to conjure ways to fix it. Because when she'd walked out of the restaurant, he knew her love had nothing to do with guilt or obligation or familiarity. Had he been thinking more clearly, he would've known that all along.

Instead, he'd let her family's misgivings and his own damn suspicion cloud what he'd always relied on—her actions. Not because he couldn't hack it on his own, but because he didn't have to. And she was no pushover. Gabby might be kind and giving to a fault, but she was no doormat incapable of saying no. Nor was she gullible. If she'd wanted out of his life, if she didn't love him, she wouldn't have remained by his side all these years.

Gabby wasn't the only one who'd been there for him. His family and close friends had learned to sign, and in his presence, did so while simultaneously speaking in order to include him. That was only one of several examples, and it wasn't as if he didn't add value to his loved ones lives, too. Somehow, he'd forgotten that. He may be a little different, but he wasn't a charity case.

For whatever reason, he'd just let Gabby in deeper than the others. Perhaps part of him had always known she was it for him, had recognized her as the only woman he'd ever love.

He still didn't know how to fix the damage he'd done, though. Falling on his knees and begging her to forgive his idiocy didn't seem like enough.

Drake strode in the front door, already dressed in his suit. He kicked the door shut and headed straight for Flynn without stopping. Before he knew Drake's intention, his big brother slapped him upside the head.

"What the hell?"

"Exactly. What the hell?" Drake's pissed-off gaze swept Flynn from head to toe. "Did you happen to pay attention to Gabby last night? You broke her. You made her cry. Gabby who burps sunshine and farts rainbows. You tell me, what the hell."

Flynn's shoulders sagged and he narrowed his eyes at a laughing Cade before swiping a hand down his face. *"I know."*

"You know? What, exactly, do you know?" Drake's brows mockingly lifted. "That you've loved each other so long you called it friendship and that screwed with your head? That she'd move heaven and earth to make you happy because she loves you, not because she pities your sorry ass? That—"

"I know!" Shit. Flynn closed his eyes and sucked air, but there wasn't any to be had. She'd taken all the damn oxygen two nights ago when she'd walked off his deck in tears. "I know," he said, hopefully more calmly.

Cade's grin made him want to punch it off his face. He slapped Flynn's arm. "Welcome to the poor sap's club. It's a nice place to exist."

Drake was still radiating murderous vibes. "Mom and Dad taught you better than this. *We,*" he swiped a hand between him and Cade, "taught you better than this."

Letting out a gale-force wind from his lungs, Flynn eyed the ceiling for a moment. "I screwed up. I know that. She's just... I didn't think I was good enough."

There. Hell, the root of the problem right there.

Cade shrugged as if this wasn't news. "That's how you know, yeah? I'm not good enough for Avery and Hailey, but here I am in a monkey suit ready to try."

Drake smacked Cade upside the head. "You're good enough. And so is he." He jerked a thumb at Flynn. "Avery picked you." He looked at Flynn. "And Gabby picked you. That makes you both above good enough."

With a pout, Cade rubbed his head. "I'm telling Avery you did that."

"She can thank me later." Drake eyed Flynn. "What are you going to do to get her back?"

"I don't know." Flynn dropped his arms to his sides. "You're the fucking Jedi Master all of a sudden. Got any bright ideas?"

"You're talking."

"So?"

"You've been talking the past five minutes."

"So damn what?" Flynn ground his jaw. "What does—" He straightened suddenly and...son of a bitch.

He just might stroke out, his heart pounded that hard. His palms sweated and the room got a little tipsy. He wished he could blame it on whiskey, which he might need an entire bottle of if he were to go through with the plan that just slammed into his head.

Drake laughed, the asshole. "Now you got it." He knotted Flynn's tie, straightened it, and patted his shoulder. "Go get 'em."

Chapter 26

After the cake had been served, and while Avery and Cade shared their first dance as a married couple, Gabby sat back in her chair at the bridal party table near the front of the pavilion and sighed in utter contentment.

The day was perfect. Just perfect. The weather held out and the ceremony had taken place outside under a sunny, cloudless sky. The only thing cuter than Brent walking Hailey down the aisle was Hailey getting to Cade at the makeshift altar and launching into his arms. The whole group in attendance *awed*. Gabby had cried buckets when Avery made her way toward Cade, given away by her mother, and he'd pressed his hand to his heart with misty eyes.

God. Just...God. Was there anything more romantic than that?

They'd said their vows under a white lattice arch teeming with spring honeysuckle just starting to bloom. Hailey had spent most of the time in Cade's arms, but she'd eventually climbed down and run around the lattice. Guests found that adorable, too.

Gabby, more than once, had flicked her gaze over to Flynn, wanting to see his reaction to parts of the ceremony. She'd always found his eyes right on her, an endearing half-smile curving his lips and utter adoration in his gaze. When tears had threatened again, he'd subtly signed, *"Check your bouquet."*

And what he'd done was almost as sweet as all the love around them. Flynn had hidden tissues among her lilacs and white roses, knowing she'd get weepy. Sigh. They hadn't had a chance to talk, but he'd watched her as though he had no other choice.

Once the bridal party did their dance in a few minutes, she'd pull him aside and they could set things right. Talk, like always. Unlike last night, he'd trekked her every move today from walking down the aisle to the photos afterward. His eyes told her everything, his soul wide open for her viewing. Whatever the reason, something had changed his mind about their relationship overnight. He no longer seemed concerned and doubtful, just anxious and optimistic.

They'd be okay. She was sure of it. There were too many years, emotions, and love between them for them not to last.

Even her bridesmaid dress was pretty comfortable, all things considered. Lavender and strapless, it was fitted around the bodice with a loose skirt that stopped mid-calf. Simple and chic. The white heels? Not so comfortable, but she'd kicked them off as dinner started and her feet had cried a thank you.

Cade spun Avery around the floor, gazing into her eyes. Avery grinned, wearing an elegant thirties-style slip dress. She'd opted for no veil, and her wavy brown hair was pinned in a pretty updo. Lilies and freesia were centered on the guests' round tables with lavender votives flickering. Twinkle lights rained down from the rafters, setting a romantic ambiance of low illumination.

Zoe nudged Gabby's shoulder from the next chair. "When you and Flynn tie the knot—and make no mistake, you will—please just elope."

Gabby laughed. "No way. I'm going all out with all the frills. And stop acting badass or I'll make my bridesmaids' dresses pink tulle. You're just as moved by all this adoring love as me."

"Maybe. Just a little. Tell anyone and I'll murder you."

Slinging an arm around her friend's shoulders, Gabby smiled. "Admit it. You have a gooey caramel center under your hard chocolate shell."

"Take that back." Zoe's lips pouted. "And now I'm hungry again."

She could go for another piece of cake herself. Marble with whipped frosting. *So good.* "I like your hair, by the way."

Zoe had gone natural today. For the sake of wedding pictures, she'd said. Her light brown hair had chestnut accents and, like Gabby's, was curled in a twist with loose strands. Zoe's outrageous use of hair dye had been on a one-year streak, so the change was more jarring than if she'd used polka dots.

Gabby wasn't the only one who'd noticed either. When Zoe had walked down the aisle earlier, Drake had stilled from his place at Cade's side and looked like he'd forgotten how to breathe. Interesting.

Zoe shrugged. "Don't get used to it. I'm thinking fuchsia tomorrow."

The guests cheered as the first dance came to an end with Avery and Cade grinning through a kiss.

A DJ was set up in the corner at the front of the room on a small stage. Drake and Flynn stepped next to him. They'd loosened their ties and shed their coats, keeping the vest underneath. The sleeves of their white shirts were rolled to their elbows. Both were incredibly handsome all decked out.

Microphone in hand, the DJ addressed the crowd. "Could we get the bridal party on the floor?"

Brent held Hailey's hand and swung it gaily on the dance floor. He watched Gabby and Zoe make their way over to join Cade and Avery. Gabby eyed Brent suspiciously, wondering what he was up to with that wicked, naughty look he was giving her.

"All righty," the DJ said. "The groomsmen would like to do their toasts before the bridal party dance. Round of applause, please."

Drake took the mic from him with a smirk. The room grew eerily quiet waiting for what he'd say. Drake hadn't been a hermit, but he hadn't attended a lot of functions since Heather had died. Not until recently, anyway, and he wasn't a man of many words on the best of days.

Focusing on Avery, Drake cleared his throat. "I knew it would take a special woman to finally snag Cade's attention. I just didn't realize how special until you came into our lives. We all fell a little in love with you." The room *awe*d. "And though you alphabetized our office into order and I still can't find my favorite scalpel—"

"Top cabinet in the surgery room," Avery shouted, and the crowd laughed.

Drake lifted his hand as if to say, *now you tell me,* and the guests laughed again. "You stole all our hearts, Avery." More *aw*s. He turned to Cade. "I wish Dad was here to see this. He'd be damn proud of you. Many blessings, and I want more nieces. Hailey and Avery, welcome to the family."

Zoe passed Gabby a tissue when her chest hitched in a sob. "Honestly, how are you not a prune from all this crying?"

Drake hopped off the low stage and hugged Cade, kissed Avery's cheek, and fist-pumped Hailey. But instead of heading back up to help Flynn, Drake left him standing there, alone, mic in hand. The guests didn't seem to notice at first as they were focused on Drake.

Gabby's heart stopped as the room quieted and Drake stepped beside her. He was going to leave Flynn up there? With no translator? He'd be humiliated. His worst nightmare. Prickles of awareness skated up her arms. Flynn's gaze was focused on his feet, a blush creeping up his neck. His hand shook.

She stepped forward to help him, but Drake stilled her with gentle fingers around her arm and shook his head. "Just listen, kid."

What? Oh God. He was going to...talk? Why now? And for the first time in years, in front of all these people? Her gaze jerked to Flynn's.

He offered her a small smile, letting her know he was okay before swallowing and looking at Cade. "I know this comes as a shock."

Several gasps erupted behind them, and shock didn't cover it. Pride warred with awe in her chest as guests murmured from their tables. Her jaw trembled open. She pressed her fingers to her lips while her limbs locked in stunned surprise.

"Cade getting married is quite a shock. I know the single ladies are weeping in their champagne." The crowd laughed at his joke and Flynn looked down, probably not noticing as he collected himself. His eyebrows pinched together.

Though his tone had been a little higher than she was used to and his dialect slower, he was doing it. She didn't care if he never spoke a word to anyone the rest of his life. She loved him just the way he was, quirks and all. He was perfect just as himself. But he set his jaw, seemingly needing to do this. And all she could do was tremble, feeling every nervous hum she knew he was exhibiting.

Hailey squealed and flapped her hands. She dropped Brent's hand and ran to the stage. Flynn knelt to lift her, setting her beside him. She tapped his jaw like Gabby had seen her do last night. He held the mic to her mouth, and her squeal reverberated through the room.

Avery choked a sob from a couple feet away.

"Hailey says she's excited to be here." Flynn winked.

The guests, obviously touched, cooed. Gabby darted her attention to Avery and Cade, who watched, enraptured. Cade closed his eyes and kissed Avery's temple, seeming to fight off emotion. Gabby was having a hard time herself. Throat tight and eyes wet, she slowly exhaled the breath she'd been holding.

While Hailey's distracted gaze wandered the room, pinging everywhere at once, Flynn held the girl's hand. "Unlike my little brother, I've known the love of my life for a long time." Flynn's gaze shifted to hers and held. "Gabby Cosette walked into my kindergarten classroom and I was smitten with one glance."

"Holy shit," Zoe breathed, waving her hand in front of her face.

Gabby passed her the tissue she hadn't used yet, keeping her eyes on Flynn. Her heart tripped and her lungs stalled.

"For reasons I can't fathom, she loves me back. And that makes me the luckiest man in existence."

Aws from the guests caused a watery laugh to escape Gabby's lips.

Flynn mouthed, *"I love you,"* as if just for her.

Oh God, oh God, oh God. He was killing her. She pressed her lips together, repeating the sentiment in sign language.

Flynn directed his attention to Cade. "Watching my brother fall in love for the first time was quite entertaining." He smiled at Avery. "You can't get much better than him, even if he's more like a kid than Hailey." More laughter. "I wish you all the happiness I've found."

The guests cheered as Flynn handed the mic back to the DJ, who cued the bridal party's song. Flynn hopped down and passed Hailey off to Brent, then hugged Cade. Drake pulled Zoe in for their dance, Cade with Avery, and Brent with Hailey nearby.

Gabby hiccupped as she waited for Flynn, more tears spilling down her cheeks. That man, that beautiful damn man, was hers. Her lungs wouldn't work with the band clamping around her chest.

Flynn turned to her and the room spun. His forehead wrinkled, fierce devotion hungry in his eyes. He stood rigid for a beat as if he couldn't believe his luck, couldn't believe she loved him.

Then he stalked over and wrapped his arms around her, hauling her against his chest and off the ground. With her toes hovering above the floor, he crushed his mouth to hers, and she finally stopped trembling. Threading her hands in his soft, thick hair, she moaned while the song played an endearing melody in the fading background.

God, she didn't think it was humanly possible to be this happy.

Tilting his head, he urged the kiss deeper, cupping the back of her head with one hand to hold her to him as if his emotions could no longer be reined. His deep groan reverberated through her chest. The kiss grew desperate as he stroked his tongue against hers, saying a thousand things without words. He loved her...missed her...would do anything for her... never would he let her go.

As if her kiss had calmed him, the nervous tension in his arms relaxed and he let her slide down his body. He pulled back to look at her, exhaling hard, lids heavy with desire. "I love you, Gabby. I love you so much I can't think if you're not in my vicinity."

God. Swoon. She traced his lower lip with her thumb, her chest full to capacity. "I love you, too."

He carefully set them in motion, barely moving in a slow circle for their dance. "I see you wore the waterproof mascara today. Good choice, my weepy sweetheart." He swiped his thumbs under her eyes to catch the residual remnants of wetness, humor in his tender gaze.

"I'm a crybaby. Can't help it."

"*My* crybaby. I wouldn't want you any other way. You carry your heart on your sleeve, in your eyes. Your emotions run deep and I love that about you." He sighed. "I'm sorry about earlier. For doubting you, doubting us. It was stupid." His arms squeezed around her back like an exclamation point to his statement.

Her heart was so heavy it ached. "I understand. You weren't completely wrong in questioning things. The time apart made me really trust we are exactly where we should be."

He offered a slight shake of his head. "I should've known, though. You never once gave me reason to doubt myself or us."

She smiled, brushing her fingers over his smooth jaw. "You can make it up to me later. I'll keep you in suspense on which panties I'm wearing."

His laugh ended in a groan. "It's the red pair, right? Please, Christ." He sobered quickly, brows furrowed. "Was my speech okay? Did it sound all right?"

Framing his face, she stared into his eyes, willing him to see the emphasis she tried to project. "It was perfect. You were amazing. I know how hard that must've been, but you had nothing to worry about. I think I was more nervous than you."

He grinned and kissed her forehead. "Do me a favor. Tell me when the song's almost done."

She offered him a confused smile, but nodded. Resting her cheek on his chest, she closed her eyes and breathed in his familiar scent, cozied into his strong, welcoming arms, and had everything her little fairy tale wishes desired. He kissed her ear and dropped his chin on the top of her head as they swayed.

Glancing around at the guests, she found her parents' table near the front and locked gazes with her mom. Dad grinned from ear to ear. Rachel looked bored or irritated out of her skull, eyes rolled back in her head and fingers drumming the table. Mom gave Gabby a thumbs-up and, not that she needed her mother's approval, a surge of happy filled her chest, anyway.

The lyrics of the song drifted through her head and she pulled away to look at Flynn. "Song's about done."

"How long?"

"Three, two, one..."

A squeak passed her lips as he bent her over his arm in a dip. Keeping her there, he leaned his face close to hers. "Always wanted to do that."

Laughing, she stared into those gorgeous hazel eyes. "I didn't teach you that move. You've been holding out on me."

"You have no idea." His nose brushed hers before he offered a quick kiss and brought her upright. "You look beautiful, by the way."

Aw. "Thank you."

The song changed, but they stayed where they were as other guests filled the floor. One track bled into the next, but he didn't let her go and she had no interest in letting him.

"Hey, Gabby?" He swallowed and looked down at her. "About that pact you mentioned a while ago. The one where if neither of us is with someone by a certain age we marry each other."

She totally forgot about that. Besides, it had only been a joke. "What about it?"

"There's no need to rush if you prefer, but...if I were to ask you to marry me someday—and by someday, I mean soon—and I promised to say my vows aloud for the world to hear, would you say yes?"

Her chest pinched. God, this man. "No."

He frowned, lips parting in disappointment.

"I wouldn't marry you for a pact. I'd do it because I love you. And I wouldn't say yes. I'd say, I do." She smiled once he let out a relieved breath. "Flynn, I don't care if you speak your vows or sign them. I don't care if no one hears them but me."

Pressing his forehead to hers, he drew a ragged inhalation and closed his eyes. "Love you, love you, love you."

She waited for his eyes to open. "Love you, too. I think Fletch will be jealous, though." She shrugged. "Just sayin'."

Shaking his head, he laughed, eyes softening in affection. "He can be the best man. You're mine."

"Always have been."

Check out a sneak peek from the next Redwood Ridge book,

New Tricks

Chapter 1

"I'm going to kill you."

Drake O'Grady stopped dead in his tracks and pulled his cell away from his ear to glance at the screen.

Yep. It was definitely Zoe Hornsby who had called him, but that wasn't her voice. Not that she hadn't threatened to kill him before. She was usually more subtle about it than coming right out with it, though. Feisty, opinionated, and with a spine of steel, she was just attractive and smart enough to be a pain in his ass.

Wiping sweat from his brow with his forearm, he put the phone back to his ear and called her name. When she didn't respond, he sighed and glanced around, flustered. Always—*always*—she flustered him. Her favorite hobby.

Deep in a pocket of dense woods, he stood outside his cabin and caught his breath after a three-mile run. All he wanted was a shower, a beer, and two hours of ESPN. He inhaled brine from the Pacific a few miles away that mingled with pine and moss from the forest. Dusk had come and gone, and the residual humidity made oxygen exchange near impossible.

Or maybe that was worry. His heart tripped behind his ribs in the off-chance Zoe didn't have things under control. It sounded like he was on speakerphone. Crashes and screams and glass shattering emitted through the earpiece. Which meant Zoe's mom was having a rough night. And judging by Zoe's lack of response, she'd...

"Pocket-dialed me again." Drake glanced at his faithful German Shepherd, Moses, sitting by his feet, tongue lagging from their nightly run. If dogs could shrug, his just did.

Though he and Zoe had been friendly since they were both in diapers, and they worked together at the animal clinic where she was a groomer and he a veterinarian, he hated to get involved. Zoe was fiercely independent and she'd been handling her mother's early-onset dementia diagnosis the past few years better than a saint.

"Mama, please."

Drake's gut clenched at the weary tone in Zoe's voice. Heart pounding, he teetered in the decision to butt in or not. She'd probably maim him for the effort. Damn it, anyway. Unable to stand it, he whistled for Moses and opened the front door to let the dog inside.

"I'll be right back. Don't drink all the beer while I'm gone."

Bark.

"I heard that."

T-shirt soaked with sweat and muscles protesting the lack of cooldown stretches, he climbed behind the wheel of his truck. Disconnecting the call, he stared out his windshield, ground his molars, and shoved the vehicle in gear. He'd be in and out of her place in ten minutes. Then he could continue his fun-filled Friday night. Alone.

He drove the long, winding private road past his brothers' houses, then his mother's, and continued to the main strip in their small town of Redwood Ridge. Folks were out enjoying the Oregon summer, eating ice cream and walking the cobblestone sidewalks. Old-world lampposts lit the way, emitting a yellowish glow against the stars.

Truck at a crawling speed, he strummed his fingers on the wheel, avoiding eye contact with passersby. Eye contact meant encouragement to...chat. He shuddered.

After a few blocks and a handful of quick turns, he was in Zoe's subdivision. This older part of town consisted of gingerbread houses and postage-stamp yards teeming with flower boxes. Fireflies blinked over the neatly trimmed lawns. He pulled into her driveway, cut the engine, and strode up the porch steps.

In and out.

Screeching came from the other side of the door, and he rubbed the back of his neck while he waited for her to answer his knock. As he was about to pound again, the door swung wide.

All five-foot-four of her stood framed in the doorway. She was a bitty thing, though one would never recognize that fact with all her attitude. Wearing a pair of jean cut-offs and a white tank top, she cocked her hip.

And Jesus. Was a bra too much to ask? Avoiding the nipples poking out to bid him hello, he kept his gaze trained on her hazel eyes. Sometimes green, sometimes gray or blue, they were outlined by dark lashes and too big for her narrow face. Her once light brown, shoulder-length hair was pinned up in a messy knot, and was now a ridiculous shade of pink. For a year, she'd been dyeing it unnatural colors. Why, he hadn't a clue.

"It's not a good time, Drake."

To emphasize her point, something crashed inside the house.

"No kidding."

"Zoe? Zoe, honey." From the house beside Zoe's, her neighbor stepped out the front door, leaned over the porch rail, and wrung a towel in her hands. Distressed guilt was fraught all over her young face. "I just got the kids to sleep. Is there any hope your mom will calm down soon?"

Crash.

Closing her eyes, Zoe sighed. Shoulders deflating, she poked her head out her own front door. "I'm sorry, Mary. I'm trying."

"I know. I know you are, honey." She bit her lip. "Can I do anything?"

Drake would give her neighbors this, at least. They were good people who helped as much as they could. Except the deep caverns under Zoe's eyes and the fact she seemed thinner than ever could attest that no amount of aid was enough. Her mother had been declining at a rapid rate this past year, and Zoe was doing everything in her power to keep her at home. And killing herself in the process.

"Thank you. I'm okay." She crossed her arms and waited to speak until the other woman had gone back inside. "The pharmacy screwed up our refill request and I had to wait an hour. Thus, she's getting the sedative later than usual. With her sundowning as bad as it is, she's past confused and irate. I can't get her to take the pills."

He nodded. Sundowning—a common term for people with Alzheimer's and dementia—had been Zoe's worst enemy. Confusion tended to increase later in the day, ergo the term. Stepping around her, he walked inside, taking in a tossed coffee table and lamp on the bare wood floor. Around the divider island, her kitchen floor was littered with...spaghetti.

She followed his gaze. "That's what kicked off the festivities. She claimed I was trying to poison her. Feng shui via pasta. Has a nice look."

At least she still had her sense of humor.

She scrubbed a hand over her tired face. "What are you doing here, anyway?"

"You called me."

Her brow wrinkled in that adorable, defiant way it used to as a child. "I did not."

"Pretty sure you did." Since they were about to get into a he said/she said battle of kindergarten wits, he grabbed her shoulders, spun her around, and fished her cell out of her back pocket. He held up her phone and raised his brows.

"I pocket-dialed you again. Sorry." She took the phone back and set it down. A blush crept up her neck, and he felt like a dickhead for embarrassing her. It was a rare sight, indeed. She squared her shoulders as if channeling her last diva reserve. "Unless it was an excuse for you to touch my ass."

And there was the Zoe who made his temples throb and his left eye twitch. He narrowed his eyes in warning, even though she was only baiting him. "I have never touched your ass."

"You just did."

"To get your..." He drew a slow, deep inhale for patience. "Why do I bother?"

An eye roll, and she waved off the argument. "Relax. It's the most action I've seen in awhile. I should thank you."

He snapped his jaw shut to avoid putting his foot in his mouth. Four years, for four years he'd been living in an almost near state of numb autopilot. A ghost among the living. His wife Heather's death from ovarian cancer had left a gaping hole where love used to be, had killed hope. And in all that time since, the woman before him had been the only one to arouse any kind of emotion.

Irritation mostly, but emotion just the same.

Catherine came into view from down the short hallway. A wrinkled nightgown was all she wore and it slipped off one shoulder. Her hair was the same shade of Zoe's natural color and they shared similar waifish body types. Before the disease had taken her mind, Catherine had raised Zoe alone, making her the independent, self-assured woman she was today. Add to that, they'd been more friends than mother-daughter.

Hollow bewilderment and a trace of fear were all that radiated in Cat's eyes now. His stomach bottomed out at the shell she'd become. If he was this wrecked after five seconds in the same room, he could only imagine how it was affecting Zoe. He'd watched Heather slowly fade, get sicker, and it was the hardest damn thing he'd ever done.

"Oh crap." Zoe grabbed his arms, startling him. She stepped in front of him and blocked his route to her mother.

Catherine raised her arm.

"Duck—" A book flew across the room and into Zoe's back. She sucked in a harsh breath and pinched her eyes closed, then dropped her forehead to his chest. "Damn, that hurt. She's been throwing things all night."

He froze, shocked out of his shoes that Catherine had shown any signs of violence. She'd yelled and rearranged a room burglary-style, but he'd never witnessed aggression like this directed at her daughter. He stared at the paperback that landed at his feet.

Zoe's light scent of lavender filled his nose, swirled around them, and reminded him of their position. He held his hands up in surrender at her unexpected touch. It had been a long time since he'd had even accidental contact. He tried to regulate his breathing, get a grip on just *what* his reaction was, then he snapped out of it.

Anger sent his pulse hammering. Holding her at arm's length, he ground his jaw. "Did you just shield me? What the hell, Zoe?" He raked his gaze over her pained expression. "Are you all right?" The way her fingers dug into his forearms said no.

"I'm fine." Slowly, she straightened with a wince. "Mama, look who came for a visit."

Knowing his role, he offered a smile and took a step away. "Hey, Cat. I'm home." For whatever reason, she was more comfortable with men than women. The past year especially, she'd regressed to a time in her memory before Zoe and often thought Drake—or any other male she came in contact with— was her uncle.

Cat's confused gaze leveled on him and softened. "Jimmy?"

He eyed Zoe and spoke out of the corner of his mouth. "Who's that?" Cat's brother's name was Ed.

"I think it's my dad," she whispered.

He faced her fully, not liking the mask she'd donned to hide her true feelings. "I thought you never met your father." Far as he knew, Zoe didn't even know the guy's name.

"I haven't. He took off while she was pregnant and didn't come back. But by the way she brings up his name and the things she says, it's a logical leap."

He nodded, wondering what to do now. "Where are her meds?"

"On the kitchen table in a cup."

"Jimmy? Is that you?"

Smiling, he stepped over to Cat and cupped her shoulders. "It's me. It's very late. How about I tuck you in and we can talk tomorrow?"

She appeared to be thinking it over, her gaze darting around. "I guess that would be okay." She glared at Zoe through hell-hath-no-fury eyes. "Who's this tramp?"

The moment the words must've sunk in, Zoe swallowed hard and hung her head. "I'm your new neighbor. I just dropped off a plate of cookies." Her voice broke near the end and she cleared her throat. "I'll leave you alone."

With dejection radiating off her in waves, she shuffled into the kitchen. It took everything inside him to keep up the charade and not follow. Everyday. She did this day in and day out.

He took the cup of pills off the kitchen table and, with a hand at Cat's elbow, walked her to the bedroom. She'd torn the place apart. Dresser drawers were pulled out, clothing everywhere. The bedding was in a pile in the corner.

Quickly, he righted what he could and convinced her to swallow the meds. After he got her tucked in, he sat at her hip for a moment to ensure she stayed there. Zoe needed a few damn minutes of peace.

"I can't believe you're here, Jimmy. I missed you."

The only thing harder than watching someone in this state had to be living in it. His throat tight, he smiled. "Me, too. You should get some rest."

Her lids drooped. "I think we should name the baby Diane. Or maybe Zoe." She yawned, eyes shut.

Guess that meant this Jimmy guy was Zoe's dad. It took a special breed of asshole to leave a pregnant woman and never look back. No child support. No birthday cards. And now she was stuck, alone, taking care of her mother.

"Zoe's a wonderful name." She was a hell of a person as well, much as they got under one another's skin.

Once he made his way back down the hall, he noted Zoe had the spaghetti mess cleaned up and the coffee table righted. It was a cute little house. She'd grown up here and moved back in after her mother's diagnosis. But the place didn't fit Zoe's personality, not like her old apartment. Blue and pink striped drapes, floral-print couches, scarred pine tables.

He found her at the kitchen table, picking at a bowl of pasta. "She's asleep."

"Thank you." Refusing to look at him, she stared at the food. Silence stretched. "Are you hungry?"

"No." He pulled a chair out and sat next to her.

"The spaghetti is from the pot, not the floor." A dare lit her eyes.

He shook his head, his attempt at a smile failing miserably.

How many times had she been there for him, and he couldn't think of a proper thing to say. She'd been Heather's best friend and a damn good one to him. He wasn't a guy of many words, but Zoe was the only person who rendered him speechless. Always had, in fact. Not quite nerves, per se, but something uncanny, anyway.

Lacing his fingers, he stacked his hands on top of his head. "I believe you're right about Jimmy being your father." He paused. "Have you ever tried looking for him?"

A noise resembling a dry laugh burst from her lips. "I have no interest. He couldn't bother to stick. I don't need him."

Drake wholeheartedly agreed.

Her cat bumped his leg and, happy to have something to focus on, he picked up the white ball of fur to set in his lap. Cotton, she'd named the thing. Poor guy had probably been hiding out in all the commotion. "He's due for a distemper vaccination soon, isn't he?"

"Probably. I'll have Avery put him on Cade's schedule."

Avery was their office manager and his youngest brother's wife. Cade did most of the in-house clients at their veterinarian clinic. Flynn, his other brother, made house calls and traveled. Drake was the surgery vet, though he saw patients two days a week for appointments, like Flynn.

"I'll bring a vaccination over next week." She had enough on her plate. "Do an exam, too."

Her gaze whipped to his. Held.

He didn't know what to make of her expression or the way it made his stomach shift, so he eyed the cat. Cotton batted his arm in a silent demand for attention. Complying, Drake stroked the cat, letting the rumble of his purr settle him.

Zoe pushed her bowl away, not eating a bite. "I'm going to need to soundproof the house at this rate. Mama's getting louder. And worse. I'm lucky the neighbors haven't called the cops yet."

Jesus. "Zoe—"

"Don't." Her full lips thinned into a line. "Not you, too. I promised her I'd keep her at home. You did for Heather."

They hadn't outright said her name in so long it jarred him for a beat. "Heather had terminal cancer. Your mom's body is fine. It's her mind that's gone. One of these days, she could really..."

"What? Hurt me? She'd never—"

"She threw a book at you tonight." He closed his eyes to calm his temper, cool his tone. This situation wasn't Zoe's fault any more than it was Cat's. Fifty-five years old, and her life was gone. "She's not the same woman who raised you. This person doesn't know you. She's confused, scared. Not even she could've known how bad it would get."

Abruptly standing, she sent the chair across the floor. Her back to him, she walked her bowl to the sink. "I can't put her away, Drake."

No, she wouldn't. Not even at the risk to herself. Loyal to a fault. He couldn't blame her. If it were his mother, he'd do the same thing. He hated seeing her like this, though. Tough as nails Zoe Hornsby, reduced to a wilted balloon.

"I should go." He rose and set the cat on the floor, surprised he didn't really want to leave. "I'll see you at the game tomorrow." Their clinic had teamed up years ago with some of the doctors and nurses from urgent care to start a softball league every summer. Tomorrow, they played the firefighters and police officers.

Her gaze skimmed over him as if seeing him for the first time all evening. "Why are you all wet and sweaty?"

"Your call interrupted my nightly run."

"Oh. You're welcome, then."

Smartass. "You know, some exercise might do you some good."

Her hands fisted on her hips. "Are you calling me fat?"

Considering he could bench press her with one arm...no. She had a great body, if not on the slim side. Olive skin tone, compliments of her gypsy heritage. A few freckles on her pert nose. Long legs, slight hourglass curve to her waist, breasts that would fit perfectly—

What the hell?

He shook his head. "I meant that exercise raises endorphins and improves your mood." Pausing, he wondered what in Almighty's name he was doing. "You could come jogging with me in the evenings."

Indignation infused every inch of her expression. "And you call yourself my friend. Get out of my house. And don't come back without cupcakes or tequila."

Ah, yes. There was the real Zoe. Much better. It was awfully damn hard to fight a grin. Regardless, he managed and went home.

Meet the Author

Bestselling author Kelly Moran gets her ideas from everyone and everything around her and there's always a book playing out in her head. No one who knows her bats an eyelash when she talks to herself, and no one is safe from becoming her next fictional character. She is a Catherine Award Winner, Readers Choice Finalist, Holt Medallion Finalist, and earned one of the 10 Best Reads by USA Today's HEA. She is also a Romance Writers of America member. Her interests include: sappy movies, MLB, NFL, driving others insane, and sleeping when she can. She is a closet caffeine junkie and chocoholic, but don't tell anyone. She resides in Wisconsin with her husband, three sons, and two dogs. Most of her family lives in the Carolinas, so she spends a lot of time there as well. She loves hearing from her readers. Please visit her at authorkellymoran. com, twitter.com/authorkmoran, or facebook.com/authorkellymoran.

CPSIA information can be obtained
at www.ICGtesting.com
Printed in the USA
LVOW11s1827260617

539413LV00001B/172/P